HIDING
IN
ALASKA

HIDING
IN
ALASKA

By D. Anthony

Xulon Press

Xulon Press
2301 Lucien Way #415
Maitland, FL 32751
407.339.4217
www.xulonpress.com

xulon
PRESS

Unless otherwise indicated, Scripture quotations taken from the King James Version (KJV) – public domain.

Printed in the United States of America.

ISBN-13: 9781545624654

PREFACE

My wife, Carolyn and I go to church on Wednesday night. We were having a special program at church for the young people so Carolyn and I invited some neighbor kids to go with us to the program.

It is seventeen miles from our house to the church and it takes thirty minutes to drive it. Three kids in the back of a car for thirty minutes can get very rowdy. So, I started telling them a story that I made up as we drove to keep them quiet. And, to keep them from killing each other, and destroying the car.

I have always had an obsession with Grizzly Bears so I made up a story about a man and his pet Grizzly in Alaska.

After almost a year of this story, the kids wanted a written copy of the story and wanted me to write it down. This crazy story has turned into a book.

CHAPTER ONE

THE BEGINNING OF SORROW

I t was a beautiful spring day. The sun was glistening through the tree tops with a slight breeze tempting the tree tops to sway gently. John had just gotten a fresh cup of coffee and set back down at the table when he heard the sound of an automobile approaching.

"I believe we have company," John said to his wife Leigh.

When he got up from the kitchen table and went to answer the knock at the door he could see it was the county sheriff.

John opened the door and said "good morning, Bill. To what do I owe my good fortune to having such an honored guest this fine morning?"

"John, I have come to arrest you," Bill said.

Bill was a highly respected county sheriff that John had known from the time he was a child. John had actually recommended Bill for the office of sheriff and helped him get elected. In fact, they were very good friends.

John thought Bill was kidding about arresting him and he grabbed Bill around the neck and told him, "If you are going to drag me away in chains you will have to wrestle me first."

Bill gently pushed John away and said, "I am serious John; I have a warrant for your arrest for statutory rape." There was a silence that seemed to last forever. Leigh gasped, and John very solemnly asked Bill to repeat what he had just said.

"I have a warrant for your arrest for statutory rape," Bill replied.

John was a retired Professional Engineer who was highly respected for his engineering work in the community and in his work in the church with teenagers. He was especially active in helping troubled teens. He had organized several fund raisers and raised thousands of dollars for uniforms and equipment for the school band, football, and wrestling teams. With the support of the local church, he had built a large recreation building where the local teens could gather in a Christian atmosphere and play basketball, volleyball, table tennis, and just gather and have fellowship. There was an office in this building dedicated for the purpose of counseling and helping troubled teens. John was one of the counselors.

Fourteen years' prior, a thirteen-year-old girl had run away from the church and her grandmother, Mandy, (who was raising her) and had become pregnant. Her daughter Shelia—now eleven—was one of the troubled teens John was counseling. Shelia bragged to a friend that she had sex with John in his office. The friend told her parents, who told the Sheriff, and that started the investigation.

Bill went to Mandy's house and relayed to her what had been told to him about John and her great granddaughter Shelia. Mandy, who attended church with John and Leigh, was skeptical of the story, but Bill convinced her to allow him to question Sheila.

After two hours of questioning, Sheriff Bill was perplexed. Had his good friend actually done this? Sheila had recounted the event in such precise detail that Bill had to believe it was too detailed for an eleven-year-old child to invent.

Bill did not know what to do. After hours of deliberation, Bill had no choice: as an officer of the court, he had to report the potential crime to the grand jury and let them decide if there was enough evidence to bring it to trial.

The grand jury wasted no time. They read the report that Bill filed and voted unanimously to send it to trial. Within hours, the judge had issued a warrant for John's arrest.

Bill and John stood just inside the door at John's house as Bill told John about the report that he had filed based on the testimony that Sheila had given him.

John asked, "Bill do you really believe I did this?"

Bill replied, "John that is not my call. I am just the Sheriff. My job is not to judge, but to report the evidence to the grand jury and carry out the order of the judge. So here I am."

There was a long period of silence in the room. John spoke up and said, "Ok old friend, if this is the way it has to be, let's get it done." He put his wrist together in front of him, allowing Bill to put him in handcuffs.

Bill said, "That won't be necessary, just get in the car."

As they were going out the door, John turned to Leigh and told her to call Jerry, their friend and attorney, and have him to meet them at the jail.

Bad news always travels fast and there was no exception to the rule this time. When Bill and John arrived at the city hall, where John was to be arraigned, six news reporters with their cameras running tried to interview them. Bill opened the door for John to let him out of the car, but the reporters closed in so close that John could not exit the car. Bill had to get deputies to control the crowd and make a path for him and John to get into the city hall. Neither John nor Bill had any comments for the reporters but they formed their own opinions and Bill's and John's pictures were on the local evening TV news and the front page of all the local newspapers the next day.

John could do nothing but sit in the jail cell in disbelief. It all seemed like such a horrible bad dream. How could a person who had dedicated his life to helping young people have his entire life destroyed in such a single moment? The news on TV and in the papers was just absolutely vicious and cruel. John was described as a sexual predator that had used his position in the community to molest young girls. The news media suggested that he had molested other girls but just had not been caught.

It took three days to get through the arraignment and get bail set so John could get out of jail and get home to Leigh and await the trial.

The ordeal was extremely hard on Leigh. She had been sick as a child with a Rheumatic fever which left her with a weak heart. The stress of all that was happening to her and John was taking its toll on her. She became weaker and weaker as the ordeal dragged on. She and John were shunned in Church. Their longtime friends quit calling and quit coming around. John and Leigh became strangers in their own hometown. By the time the trial started, no one in town would speak to either of them.

The trial was very short considering what was at stake—John's reputation and life as he knew it was about to be destroyed. The only evidence against him was Shelia's testimony to which John had no defense. His reputation was all he had and that had been destroyed in the media so the jury was quick to convict him.

After the trial ended Friday evening, John was taken to the local jail to wait to be transported to prison. The only visitor that John had all weekend was Jerry, John's lawyer. Jerry attempted to comfort John by telling him that he had started the appeal process and that he would peruse it with all of his resources; it did not help. John was totally crushed by all that had happened and sat in the cell in total despair waiting to be transported to prison. Where was Leigh? Why had she not come to see him? While he wondered about his life's partner, all his thoughts were shattered by the arrival of the transport bus. John was shackled hand and foot and was dragged by the shackle chains to the bus by the bus guard and pushed into a seat. The chains on his wrist were locked to a steel bar on the seat in front of him. The guard ordered him not to talk or make any disturbances or it would not go well for him. There were twelve other prisoners on the bus, but talking was the last thing John was interested in. All of his life, John had earned the respect of his colleagues and had never experienced such humiliation. The life of respect that he had worked so hard all his life to earn had been stripped from him. There he sat in total disgrace and humiliation reduced to nothing but a number.

On the four-hour bus ride, all that John could think of was the sound the bus tires made as they struck the expansion joints in the pavement thump, thump, thump, click, click, click. John was all too familiar with this sound; he had designed many highways. He knew the importance of the expansion joints that caused the sound when an automobile tire struck the joints. One of his passions was to make the joint silent to the contact of an automobile tire. But, today none of this mattered. The sound taunted him. There was no thump, thump. The road was saying life is over, life is over. All the way to the prison, the road said to John: "life is over; life is over, life is over."

By the time the bus reached the prison, John was numb. What he was going through was not life not even an imitation of life it was a nightmare. He had been reduced to a number. Guards screamed at him, pushed him and when he did not respond fast enough, he was struck with a riot stick. Nothing mattered.

Three months into his incarceration, one of the inmates provoked him in the lunch room and John flew into a rage. He slammed the inmate's face into an iron pole, threw him on the concrete floor, stomped his face and kicked three of the man's front teeth out. The incident landed John in solitary confinement for six months.

Solitary was designed to break the spirit of the toughest inmate. It was a concrete box six feet by six feet with no windows and one door. It had a twenty-watt bulb for light and cotton matrices on the floor. In the center of the floor was a three-inch drain. Inmates were denied any comforts: no shower, no change of cloth, no toothbrush, no razor, and no toilet paper. Meals consisted of a stick of celery, a carrot, half an apple, a piece of bread, and a glass of water.

Solitary was a blessing for John. He did not want to be around other inmates or anyone else for that matter. In solitary confinement, he didn't have to work, move, or talk; he didn't even have to think.

Shortly after John was taken to prison, Leigh had a massive heart attack and died. John was not allowed to attend to her funeral and Leigh's sister had to come in from Tennessee to make the arrangements. All of John's and Leah's friends had abandoned them so no one attended the funeral.

CHAPTER TWO

NEW EVIDENCE IS DISCOVERED

S ix mounts after John's incarceration, Shelia started having severe abdominal cramps and had to be rushed to the emergency room at the local hospital. After the ER Doctor examined Shelia, he told Mandy that everything was ok. Sheila had just become a woman, but that she had a physical obstruction that stopped her from having a normal cycle. The ER doctor told Mandy he had removed the obstruction and everything should be ok.

Mandy ask the ER doctor, "Wouldn't the obstruction have been removed if she were with a man?"

The ER doctor said, "Of course. But this child has never been with a man. It was physically impossible before now."

Mandy said, "Doctor, will you put that in writing?"

The doctor said, "Everything will be in my report."

Mandy said, "Doctor, will you give me a sworn statement that Shelia has never been with a man?"

The doctor said, "Why do you want such a report"?

Mandy said, "A man is sitting in prison because Shelia testified in court that she had had intercourse with him in the man's office while he was supposed to be counseling her. I was skeptical of her accusations at the time but I did not have any proof."

The doctor asks, "Is this the girl that testified against John Henson over in Western County"?

Mandy said, "Yes, she is".

The doctor said, "I believe I understand why you want such a statement now. You are going to get John out of prison aren't you"?

"I am going to try," Mandy said.

Mandy took the doctor's report to the judge who had presided over John's rape trial. The judge called the ER doctor into his chambers for a personal discussion about the report. The ER doctor assured Judge Carter that it would have been impossible for Shelia to have had intercourse with John or anyone because of her physical condition. Judge Carter told Mandy he wanted to speak to Sheila in his chambers immediately. The judge demanded that Mandy and the ER doctor be present when he questioned Shelia. The meeting started with Judge Carter stating that the meeting was an official inquiry into the facts of the former trial and that all who were to give statements would be held to all the laws of any trial. They were all under oath to tell the truth. The judge then had the court recorder to read the court transcript of Shelia's testimony given during the trial.

The judge then turned to Shelia and said, "Is it still, your sworn testimony that you had sexual intercourse with John Henson in his office on the evening of October 4, 1999? Before you speak let me remind you, it is a serious offense to lie to this court young lady."

Sheila paused for a moment and noted that Mandy was staring at her with that look that only a parent has when they have caught you doing wrong. The doctor was staring and so was the judge. It was just too much for a twelve-year-old child and Shelia broke down into tears.

Judge Carter said, "Young lady, stop all of your squalling and answer the question. Did you have intercourse with John Henson on the date in question?"

Shelia said, "No. I didn't."

Mandy screamed at Sheila, "Why did you tell such a horrible lie?"

Judge Carter said, "Mandy set down. I will ask the questions." Judge Carter turned to Sheila and asks, "Why did you lie in court about having sex with Mr. Henson?"

Sheila replied, "My momma told me if I said I did, that Mr. Henson would give us lots of money, but he didn't give us any."

The Judge said, "You mean to tell me that your mother told you if you accused Mr. Henson of having sex with you that Mr. Henson would give you money to get you to stop saying that?"

"Yes," said Sheila.

"What is your mother's name?" the judge demanded.

"Dory," Said Sheila.

"Dory who?" demanded the judge.

"Dory Smith answered Sheila."

Judge Carter picked up his phone and called Sheriff Bill and asked,

"How long will it take you to get Dory Smith to my chambers?"

"It won't take very long sir. She and her boyfriend were arrested last night on drug charges and they are in jail."

"Get her in here now!" stated the judge sternly.

Fifteen minutes later Dory was brought to the judge's chambers still in handcuffs. She was instructed to set down because the judge had some questions he wanted to ask her. Judge Carter asks Dory if she was the mother of Sheila.

Dory hesitated to answer the judge and Judge Carter demanded, "Dory Smith, are you the mother of Sheila?" Before she could answer, Judge Carter reminded her she was under oath and if she lied, she would be held in contempt.

Dory replied, "Yes I am her mother."

"Did you tell Sheila to accuse Mr. Henson of having sex with her to extort money from him?" The judge asks.

"I didn't tell her to do nothing like that," said Dory.

"Momma you did. You told me to say that." Sheila added.

"Shut up you little witch. Are you trying to get me in trouble?"

Judge Carter said, "Quite everyone! Sheriff, take this woman, referring to Dory, back to her cell. I am charging her with conspiracy to commit fraud and extortion." He then turned to Sheila and said, "Young lady you are in a great deal of trouble. For now, I am releasing you into your great grandmother's charge. Mandy have her in juvenile court next Tuesday at 10:00 A.M."

Mandy responded, "Yes your honor," and they left the judge's chambers.

Judge Carter wrote an order overturning John's conviction and wrote an ordered of release to get John out prison. He told Sheriff Bill to take the order of release and personally escort John home.

CHAPTER THREE:

JOHN IS RELEASED FROM PRISON

B ill went to his office and left instructions to his staff about their duties while he was going to be away. The trip to and from the state prison would take four hours each way so Sheriff Bill made plans to leave early in the morning on Thursday. He would spend the night if necessary and do what it took to get John released and return Friday afternoon.

Bill called the warden at the prison and told him about the order from Judge Carter and told the Warden of his plans to come to the prison and get John.

Warden Lacy had been in charge of the prison for thirty years and did not let anyone tell him how to run it. When Bill told him that he had a release order from Judge Carter, the Warden told bill that no stinking county judge was going to tell him who he was going to release or not release. If Bill wanted inmate JH294763 released, he would have to have a release from no less than the Governor himself. Some suspected that the reason Warden Lacy stalled the proceedings was that he wanted to be sure that John had recovered from the beating the guards had given him after the fight in the lunch room.

It took nine days to get the proper papers, but Bill finally was on his way to get his lifelong friend out of prison. Bill arrived at the prison and was escorted directly to the Warden's office.

Warden Lacy was still angry over some one forcing him to give one of his inmates an early release so he left his office when he knew Bill had arrived. He made up an excuse to go into town just to make Bill wait for him. Bill sat in the Warden's office for two hours and patently waited. The Warden finally returned and Bill gave him the release papers. Mr. Lacy looked the papers over looking for any excuse to deny the release.

The papers were in order, but the Warden made no effort to hurry the release process. After he had read them, he leaned back in his chair, put his feet on the desk, lit up his cigar, and starred out the window. Bill was furious with this arrogant jerk, but he knew it would not do any good to provoke him, it would only make things worse. Bill waited patiently. The Warden turned and glared at Bill in defiance. Finally, he picked up the phone and called the guard in charge and instructed him to bring inmate JH294763 to his office and hung up the phone. Without saying anything to Bill he picked up the morning paper and began to look through the sports. After thirty minutes, the door opened and in came John between two guards. John had shackles on his hands and feet. It was obvious that he had not bathed or changed clothes in weeks. He looked rough to say the least. Bill asks that the shackles be removed.

The, Warden said, "No. You can remove them when he is outside the Prison gates."

When Bill asks for some street clothes for John, The Warden sarcastically replied, "I do not dress inmates for a going out party. If you want him dressed, do it yourself. If your judge Carter wants him so bad I am sure you all can afford to dress him."

Bill stood up and asks, "Can we leave now?" The Warden motioned for them to leave and Bill, the Warden, two guards and John made their way to the outer gates of the prison. As soon as they were out of the gate, Bill demanded the guards remove the shackles. When they were off, Bill turned to the Warden and said, "You may need my help someday Warden. If you ever do, just remember this day and think long and hard before you ask for it. Have a good day sir." Bill said, "John lets go get you something fit for a free man to wear."

Bill had not talked to John at any time about the release so John had no idea what was going on. John had not spoken at any time during the release process.

As soon as they were in the sheriff's car, John turned to Bill and asks, "What is going on?" Bill explained what had happened with Shelia and how the Judge had overturned John's conviction. Bill then turned to John and said, "Old friend it is over. You are free. Now let's go and get you some clothes."

John hesitated for a moment and then said, "Bill forget the clothes and let's just go home."

"John, are you sure you don't want to get out of those prison clothes?"

"Forget the clothes Bill, just take me home."

At that request, Bill turned toward the interstate and they were headed for home.

The trip back home was awkward. Bill had tried several times to start a conversation with his old friend but John was not ready to talk. He answered all of Bill's questions with either a yes, no or no answer. It was obvious to Bill that prison had changed his old friend. He was no longer the happy personable friend he had known. His face was without expression no smile no frown nothing. John just stared out the window. Bill considered all that John had been through and decided to just let him alone to think. Bill hoped that with time, John would return to his old self. For the next few hours, Bill and John rode together in silence. About forty-five minutes from home John broke the silence by asking Bill if he knew who had the keys to his house. Bill told him he thought Jerry had them.

"I am sure Leigh asks Jerry to take care of things until you get out."

"Would you take me by Jerry's?"

"Sure." Bill replied.

After Bill and John picked up the keys from Jerry, Bill took John to his house. John got out of the car, said thanks to Bill, and went into his house. John was finally home, but......

CHAPTER FOUR

LEIGH IS GONE

John stepped into the house and closed the door. A house that had been filled with laughter and joy was now silent. The love of his life was gone and John felt loneliness he had never known. He and Leigh had been together since they were children. Leigh's parents and John's parents were good friends, and Leigh's parents moved next to John's parents when Leigh was four and John was five. They shared a common back yard where John and Leigh spent most of their time as children playing together. They became such good friends that when John was six years old and had to start to school, Leigh cried from the time John got on the school bus until he came home. John was so upset about his little friend Leigh's crying that his mother had to come and get him shortly after he got to school. It took lots of coaxing, bribing, pleading, and even some threatening on the part of both sets of parents to get John to go to school and Leigh to let him go. There was still a lot of crying, but the kids and parents managed to get through the first year of school.

However, the next year, when Leigh started to school, things got complicated again. The first day of school John took his little friend by the hand and they got on the bus. So far so good, but when they got to the school John took Leigh to his room and set her beside him. When the teacher came in to get Leigh to take her to her room John went with her. When the teachers tried to separate them, they both threw such a fit that their parents had to come and get them. It took more coaxing, bribing, pleading, and threatening before their parents could get these children to go to school in separate rooms. And then there was high school. John had to go to school in a different building. And it started all over again. Every time these two were separated there was trauma.

They started dating in high school and married when Leigh graduated from high school. After John graduated from high school he waited for Leigh to graduate. They married and went to college together. Where ever one of them went so did the other. John loved to go fishing, but if Leigh wouldn't or couldn't go, John wouldn't go either. Leigh loved to go shopping but she would not go without John. John's and Leigh's love for each other was more important than life.

John and Leigh had been together all their life, but now Leigh was gone and John was alone. His precious Leigh was gone forever and John was lost. For the first time in his life, John had no plans, goals, and no hope for life. He walked into the TV room and sat down in the love seat where he and Leigh had spent so many happy hours watching movies, talking about past events, planning new events, or just sitting and talking. It had been such a happy place for them, but now it was so empty and John could not stay there. He got up and walked into the kitchen, looked around and walked back into the TV room. He picked up the remote and sat down in a recliner and turned on the TV. After flicking aimlessly through the channels, he selected the late news. The news was depressing so he turned the TV off and laid back in the recliner. All his life John had lived according to his Christian 'upbringing', but now the Word of God haunted him. The word of God, the Bible said

"All things work together for good to those who love the Lord and are called according to his purposes."

John could not imagine how anything good could come out of what he was going through his life had been destroyed: his reputation was destroyed; his life's work with young people was ripped away from him, and worst of all, his precious Leigh had become seriously ill and he was not able to be by her side to comfort her.

John could not help thinking if he had been with Leigh when she had her heart attack, she would still be alive. They had been through a rough situation before when Leigh was young and had Rheumatic Fever. She had been so sick that even the doctor did not thank she would survive, but John refused to leave her side while she was sick. He slept on the floor and ate in her room until she was well. Had John not been hauled off to prison, He was sure he could have nursed his precious Leigh back to health. However, it did not happen. Leigh was gone. The love of John's life was gone forever. How could any good come out of this? John leaned back in the recliner and wept. All he could think was why. Why, God, why. Why has this happened?

CHAPTER FIVE

DIVINE INSTRUCTIONS

John had fallen asleep from sheer exhaustion. As he slept John had a vision or dream; he could not tell which. A man in a bright, white robe walked through the living room wall. As he stood at the foot of the chair where John was setting he begins to speak. "John, you have done a great work here. You have touched many lives. But your work here is done. Now leave here and go to a place where I will lead you." The man turned and walked back to the wall. He stopped, turn toward John and said, "Peaches' sends her loves." And then he turned and walked through the wall and disappeared.

John was stunned. 'Peaches' was the very private nickname John used to refer to Leigh when he was in a playful mood and wanted to tease her. But it was very private never in public. It was an act of affection when John called Leigh that. It was very private and John never used it in public so no one knew he called Leigh 'Peaches'. Who was this man and how did he know? What did he mean when he said, "leave here and go to a place I will show you"? What did all this mean? Suddenly, John was back asleep.

John was awakened by the sun shining through the living room window. Night had given way to daylight; it was morning. John lowered the foot rest and set up in the recliner. He sat there for several minutes thinking about the dream/vision that he had during the night. What did it all mean? Was this a man or Angel? Was it a messenger from God? Was God telling him to leave his home? Had this messenger used John's nickname for Leigh (peaches) as proof that he was from God, where he knew his Leigh was? It was all very puzzling to John.

John's stomach began to remind him that he had not eaten in two days. He got up and went into the kitchen to look for something to eat. The kitchen was no help. Everything was empty: the pantry, the refrigerator, and all the cabinets. Leigh's baby sister, Toni, had emptied out everything when she came up to take charge of Leigh's funeral. John just stood in the kitchen for a moment and then decided to go to a restaurant and eat. As he passed the mirror in the hallway he saw himself and realized he was still in the prison clothes. He stopped and began to thank about what else he needed to function in the real world again, his wallet with his driver's license, the keys to his truck, some money...a shower, shave, and definitely a change of clothes. Thirty minutes later, John was headed over to a neighboring town where there was a small dinner that served a respectable breakfast. John was hoping that he would not run into anyone that he knew. He was not ready to socialize yet. He sat down and ordered. While he was waiting for the eggs over easy, bacon, toast, and black coffee, he kept thinking about the dream/vision especially the part about leaving. What did it all mean?

After breakfast, John drove around for hours just thinking about the dream... The Cemetery John had not been to Leigh's grave. John instantly looked at his surrounding to see where he was. He was on Highway 132 about five miles from the cemetery, but going the wrong direction. John turned into the next driveway and turned around and headed the opposite direction.

As he drove he began to wonder if Toni knew about the cemetery plots that he and Leigh had purchased in the local cemetery and had she used it. After all that had happened, John realized he didn't even know where his precious Leigh was buried. He soon arrived at the cemetery and turned in hoping that he would find the final resting place of the love of his Life Leigh. As John drove slowly down the main street in the cemetery fear gripped him as he thought about the possibility that Toni had not known about the plots and had buried Leigh somewhere else. He traveled to the second road and turned right, traveled approximately three hundred yards and turned right onto the road the plots were on. As he approached the crest of the hill that hid the two plots his heart was beating so hard from fear, he could hardly breathe. Finally, he topped the hill and there it was: A new tombstone. Toni had done well. She had placed a beautiful double headstone on the plots: The right side had Leigh's information and the other side had John's information. In the top center of the stone was a silhouette of Christ with outstretched hands. The only thing missing was the rest of the information on John's side of the stone.

As John thought about it, he thought how wonderful it would be to just lie down by his beautiful Leigh and let them fill in his side of the stone. That sounded really great to John, but it was not to be at this time. John dropped to his knees on the grave and wept. As he wept, he ran his fingers over Leigh's name on the gravestone and softly repeated her name over and over. For the first time, John grieved over the loss of Leigh.

CHAPTER SIX

IT'S TIME TO LEAVE

The rest of Saturday was a blur in John's memory. He woke up early Sunday morning in the recliner in his living room. After leaning forward in the chair, he rubbed his eyes, stood up and stumbled into the kitchen where he managed to start a pot of coffee. Out the back door of the house was a porch where John and Leigh spent so many wonderful mornings talking and watching the sun come up. It was a cool brisk spring morning so John grabbed a blanket and his coffee and went out to watch the sunrise. As he sipped his coffee, the sun began to illuminate the sky like a huge fireball was coming over the hill. The trees appeared to be on fire and reminded John of the story of the burning bush in the Bible.

As John enjoyed the moment, he remembered it was Sunday morning and he had not been to Church for some time. He looked at his watch and noted that he had enough time so he went inside to dress for church. John got into his truck and headed for church.

He arrived at the church where he and Leigh had spent so many happy hours in fellowship with their friends. But, this time it was different: no one greeted him as he entered the church. One young mother gasped when she recognized him, turned around with her two teenaged daughters in tow and left the church. John stayed through the services but, it was not a pleasant experience. The people he had worked with, worshiped with, and fellowshipped with most of his life were now shunning him. He felt like a complete stranger.

As John was leaving the church, the pastor attempted to stop him in order to ask him when and how was he released.

He turned and pointed to Bill and said: "Ask Bill. He has all the details". John got into his pickup and went straight home.

Monday morning John had just poured a cup of coffee and was about to set down when he heard a car drive to the house. With a cup of coffee in his hand and the sound of an approaching automobile, John had a flashback to the morning that Sheriff Bill had come to his home to arrest him. He stood petrified in fear of what could happen. After the doorbell rang for the third time, John answered the door. Two men in suits identified themselves as members of the State police and needed to talk to John about the conditions of his parole.

John said, "I am not on parole. New evidence was given to Judge Carter and he overturned my conviction."

One of the officers said, "We don't know anything about your conviction being overturned, but we have the standard forms that Warden Lacy filed on you being a paroled pedophile and you have to register with the state registry for sex offenders.

John protested, "I am not a sex offender. My conviction was overturned by Judge Carter. Call him and he will tell you. Call Sheriff Bill. He will tell you."

The men ignored what John said. One of them handed him a packet and informed John that he had to fill out all the forms in the packet.

John picked up the phone and called his lawyer, Jerry and told him what was happening. Jerry wanted to talk with the men so John handed the phone to the officer that was doing all the talking.

After they talked for a while the officer seemed to be agitated and stated in a firm voice, "Regardless! We have no record of what you are talking about, but we do have orders and if these papers are not filled out and registered by Friday of this week we will be back to take John Henson back to prison". The man handed the phone back to John and the two officers got in their car and left.

John got in his truck and headed to Jerry's office. John and Jerry talked for several minutes and John demanded that Jerry call Judge Carter and get the mess cleared up, but Jerry informed John that he had tried to reach Judge Carter and he could not be reached; he was on a cruise ship and would not be back for two weeks. Jerry suggested that John fill out the papers and file them. Jerry assured John that it was just a matter of getting the right information to the right people and he would get it straightened out when the Judge returned.

John said, "No. I am not registering as a sex offender. If I do that it will become a permanent record that I will never get rid of."

Jerry tried to convince John that it would be alright. They needed time to work on the problem and if John would file the papers it would keep him from going back to prison until the judge got back. Jerry handed the papers to John, asks him to fill them out, and assured John that he would take care of everything. John thought for a moment and then put the papers back in the packet.

John said, "Jerry, let me think about it. I will talk to you tomorrow".

As John was going out the door, Jerry reminded him that the papers had to be on file by Friday or he would be back in prison and that would make the problem much worse. As John drove back to his house he thought about his options and he did not want to be on that sex offender's register and he did not want to go back to prison. At home, while John paced the floor and worried about what he should do, he was reminded of his dream, especially the part where the man told him to leave and go to a place where he would be led. As John was pondering whether he should register as a sex offender or go back to prison, he was now faced with a third option leave. Maybe that is the answer!

John stopped and said out loud, "Maybe I should load up my trailer and go hide in Alaska."

When he made that statement, John felt an overwhelming sense of peace come over him. He had not felt such peace and comfort since his mother rescued him from a snow storm when he was six years old. John had robbed his 'piggy bank' and sneaked out of the house to go to the local store for a candy bar for him and Leigh. Half a block from his house it started to rain mixed with snow. Within seconds, John was soaking wet and so cold he thought he would die before he could get home. Just when John was so scared, cold, and lost in the blowing wet snow that he didn't know what to do but stand and cry, he looked and saw his mother coming for him. She found the broken bank, guessed what John was doing and came looking for him. After 'mom' got him home, dried him, and put dry clothes on him, she wrapped him in a warm blanket. She then picked him up onto her lap. As she held him in her arms, she assured him that everything was going to be ok. John felt such an overwhelming sense of peace and security in that moment. Now he was feeling that way again. That was his answer. He was not going to register as a sex offender and he was not going back to prison. He was going to hide in Alaska.

He immediately sat down and began to plan his departure. He would let Leigh's baby sister have charge of the home. He made a list of everything he thought he would need to survive in the wilderness of Alaska and loaded into his truck and trailer. By Wednesday he had loaded his truck and trailer with all the tools, clothes and other supplies that they could hall and he was ready to go. Jerry called Wednesday morning to remind John that the papers had to be filed by Friday. John told Jerry he was not filing the papers.

Jerry said, "John, you will go back to prison".

John said, "Jerry how long will it take to get this mess cleared up".

Jerry responded, "I do not know for sure; Three maybe four weeks".

John said, "I will call you in four weeks".

"John, what are you going to do?" asked Jerry.

"Jerry, it is best that you don't know" and John hung up the phone.

John went to his truck he had prepared for the trip and set out for Alaska. The total trip was about four thousand miles and he could not make it before Friday. John's intentions were to get into Canada before the authorities knew he was gone. He had carefully planned his escape so that he could not be tracked. He turned off and took the battery out of his cellphone, GPS and laptop to disable the GPS devise in them. He also withdrew enough money from his bank account to pay cash for all the expenses of his trip so he would not leave a 'paper trail' from his credit cards that the authorities could track him by.

It was about fourteen hundred miles to Saskatchewan Canada and John thought he could make that in two days of hard driving. He was sure he could make it in three days. The authorities would have no reason to look for him until he failed to file the papers and that would not happen until Friday. By the time, they filed a warrant for his arrest it would be Monday and John would be well into Canada on the 'Trans-Canada Highway' headed for Alaska. John was comfortable with his plan and was on his way.

It was beautiful spring weather and the drive was very pleasant. Except for rain and light snow, the trip was uneventful. After six days and nights and approximately four thousand miles, John arrived in Fairbanks Alaska. He pulled into a rest stop just outside of Fairbanks to look at some brochures he had picked up that had information on camp sites. It was his intentions to find a camp site where he could park his truck and trailer get, some rest, and wait for Jerry to straighten out the mess back home. According to Jerry, John had three more weeks to wait till this could be done.

John found a campsite approximately thirty miles South South West of Fairbanks that had just opened for spring campers. There were only a few camp trailers in the camp. This pleased John because he did not want to attract any unnecessary attention until Jerry could clear him of charges if any had been filed. Now all he could do is wait.

The managers of the camp, Bonnie and Charlie, seemed nice enough and very accommodating when John ask for a site away from the crowd, they gave him a site at the back of the camp.

It was the middle of the week and John was getting set up for a three-week rest. He hooked up his camper to the campsite electric, water, and sewer supply. After setting up his satellite dish he had great reception for both his TV and computer. For the first time in months, John sat down and watched a program on TV.

CHAPTER SEVEN

THE SCAM ARTIST

Thursday morning John made a pot of coffee to go with his toast and sat down to read the paper he had picked up at the camp store. Just as John got interested in an article in the paper about a bear attack that had happened outside of a town north of Fairbanks, he heard a strange sound outside, a tap a short pause and another tap. After this happened three times, John got up and went outside to see what was happening. There was an elderly gentleman with a stethoscope that he was placing against the side of John's trailer. Every time he placed it against the trailer, it made a tapping sound. John was so puzzled by this strange action that he just stood on the porch of the trailer and watched the old man. The old gentleman would place the stethoscope against the trailer, tilt his head to the side, squint one eye and make a strange sound. Just when John thought to speak to him, a young lady came hurriedly across the camp grounds toward John's trailer scolding the old man for disturbing other campers.

As she took the older gentleman back across the campground, a man came over to where John was standing on his trailer porch. He begins to explain to John what was going on with the old man. He explained that the old man had Alzheimer's and that he thought everything strange to him was from outer space; he thought John's trailer was a space ship full of aliens. He explained that the old man had been a doctor and he was checking the trailer for alien heart beats. In between his explanations, He began to ask John personal questions like where he was from, what kind of work he did, where his family was...John was not comfortable with the questions and began to ask the man questions about who he was and where he was from. The man explained to John that he and the girl were brother and sister and the old man was their father. They were from Wisconsin and they had brought the old man to Alaska where he had lived most of his life. They hoped that familiar surroundings would help the old gentleman to remember. He then begins to question John again. John told the man to take care of that old gentleman and he excused himself and went back inside his trailer.

John was very disturbed by what he had just experienced. Something just did not seem right. As he sat there, he noticed the three were having a lively discussion over in their trailer. John was not a person who would spy on someone but these three were up to something. John got his binoculars from the drawer and begins to watch the three of them. Even though their blinds were almost closed, John could tell they were having a lively discussion that the old man seemed to be in charge of. It seemed obvious to John that the old man was faking the Alzheimer's. The question was why? Where they from the law checking on him or were they running a scam of some kind?

As John sat thinking about what he had just experienced and was wondering what he should do next, he remembered he had installed a very elaborate security system in his trailer. John and Leigh worked with the teens back home. They would take them camping at the wrangler's camp at the lake. They would set the trailer up and put the girls on the left and the boy' on the right. To keep them from sneaking into the wrong camp, John had installed a security system to catch anyone who tried. This security system was activated by motion and or sound. This security system would track a suspect day or night. And, it worked from either side of John' trailer.

John wondered if it still worked. He had not used it for two years. He jumped out of his chair and began to check it out. He opened the electrical panel and switched on the breaker for the system. The security control panel lit up and started a self-check operation. All systems checked out and reported the system was operational.

John began to plan how he could use the system to catch the three-scam artist in action. He set the sensitivity of the system to pick up anyone that came within fifty feet of the trailer track and record their activity. Should someone breach the lock system and enter the trailer, the system camera inside would pick up and record their activity. That evening John set the system to come on as soon as he left and he got in his truck and drove just out of sight of his camper and waited. It only took about thirty minutes for the three to go into action.

As John looked on with his binoculars the old man wondered over to John's trailer. The old man looked around as if to see if anyone was watching. When he was sure it was safe, he took something out of his pocket and "picked" the lock and entered John's trailer. John started his truck and drove to his trailer where he got out and went in. He caught the old man going through John's belongings. John had not given him enough time to find anything of value and so he took the old man sternly by the arm and took him back to his own trailer.

The brother and sister met them about half way between the trailers and began to make apologies for the old man's actions. John never indicated that he knew what they were up to, but simply told them to keep the old man out of his trailer. They suggested that it would help if John would lock his trailer any time he left it. Not wanting to attract attention to himself, John agreed with them and apologized for not locking his trailer. When the three were back in their trailer, John went into his trailer and viewed the recording from the security camera. There it was; the complete act of breaking and entering, in vivid detail—caught on tape. It was plane to John that this was not the act of a deranged old man, but was a deliberate act of a calculating, cunning thief.

John had all the evidence he needed to get these three arrested, but he did not dare get involved for his own sake. He could not take the chance that the authorities would arrest him and send him back to prison. He did not want these three to get away with robbing everyone in the trailer park but just could not get involved. He did not know what to do. He thought about giving the information to Bonnie and Charlie, but he didn't know if they were possibly involved also. After thinking about it long and hard, John decided to make a copy of the DVD from the security camera, write a letter explaining what he suspected the three were up to and leave it anonymously in the mail to the local Sheriff.

CHAPTER EIGHT

TIME FOR A NEW START

The next day John hooked to his trailer and left the campsite. After traveling close to thirty miles, John found another camp-site that was just opening for the season. The campsite was on the edge of wilderness capable of holding a hundred or more campers, but only had ten campers in it. This seemed like the perfect place for John to spend the next two weeks until Jerry could get things straighten out back home.

After four weeks had passed, John went into town where he could get a cheap track phone that could not be traced and called Jerry to check in. It was good news, Jerry told John the problem was taken care of and that John could come home. John thought long and hard about going back to Kentucky. He remembered how all the people had treated him in Church and there was the dream where he was to leave there. He decided to just spend some time in Alaska. He sat down to a good cup of coffee and began reading his paper. There it was on the front page! The local law enforcement, with the help of the FBI, had arrested three people who had been robbing trailer park campers in twelve states. The three consisted of a man and woman posing as brother and sister with their father who had Alzheimer's. That news article just made John's day.

After turning his phone back on and setting up his camper with TV. and computer, he began to search for land to homestead. About forty-five miles southwest of Fairbanks John found a section of land that could be homesteaded near a small town called Purgatory. The little town was not a very friendly town but John was not looking for friends at this time. He was just looking for a new beginning a place that would challenge his talents and give him time to forget. He set out early on Monday morning to look at the land he had found in the land office in Juneau. After driving as close as he could with his truck, John, not knowing what he might run into (bears or wolfs) got out his hunting rifle and three clips of shells and began to walk into the wilderness. After walking approximately two miles, he found a marker for the section of land that was laid out on the map he had gotten from the land office. According to the map, this marker was the southeast corner of the section of land. It was on the crest of a hill. Standing on the hill looking north there was a stream down in the valley about three hundred yards away. From the best John could tell the stream ran southeast toward the South West corner of the section of land. John took out his compass and walked the south border of the section of land until he got close to the stream. He found a place to cross the stream and followed it upstream until he came to a place where it disappeared into the hill at the base of a mountain. John climbed up the hill which was about twenty feet above the stream to take a look. The hill resembled a large 'toe' that stuck out from the mountain. John thought if he could flatten that 'toe' back to the mountain, he would have a good eight hundred by a thousand feet of square flat surface to build a nice cabin. John stood there for a moment reflecting on his thoughts. He turned and took two steps down the hill and stopped. He turned around to take another look. He then dropped to his knees and began to pray "Father God if this is your will for my life then give me peace about it and help me work out the details. In Christ's name, I ask this. Amen".

After resting for a while, John went down the hill to the stream and walked downstream to the place he had crossed and back to where he had parked his truck. It was now getting dark and John was getting hungry so he drove back to the little town to look for a restaurant where he could eat.

There were no restaurants in town, only a bar. John did not like bars so he decided to drive back to his camper. As he drove, he decided he would just drive into Fairbanks and have a good meal. At the edge of town, there was a small motel/restaurant that looked nice and John decided to stop and check it out. On the menu was country fried steak with mashed potatoes real ones and green peas. For desert, there was an assortment of homemade pies. Among them was a fresh chocolate pie. John was hooked. He loved chocolate pie.

The place was run by an older couple that seemed very nice—Don and Jenny. After dinner, John stayed and talked with Don and Jenny for more than two hours. The conversation was simple and non-specific. John learned through the conversation that Don and Jenny had lived in the lower forty-eight states and had come to Alaska for a fresh start much like John had done. John did not ask questions that would pry into their private affairs. He did inquire about precast yards in the area that might serve his needs in building his cabin. By then it was getting late so John rented a room in the motel and spent the night.

John spent several days in the motel while perusing his idea about building a precast lodge on the section of land he had looked at. In doing so he got to know Don and Jenny quite well. They were very knowledgeable about business in the area and that was very helpful to John. He learned where he could get the supplies and equipment he needed for his project. He became quite fond of Don and Jenny and stopped in to see them whenever he came to town.

The short spring and summer in Alaska did not give John much time to complete his plan before bad weather would set in. He had to work fast to get his cabin done before winter. He found a precast yard he liked and made arrangements for them to manufacture, deliver, and set up his precast lodge on his homestead. He rented a bulldozer and started the road to where the lodge would be erected. The precast yard had agreed to complete their work in a month so John had to work fast to build a road and flatten the "toe" of the mountain. He had a lot of rock to move so he hired a demolition contractor to come out and blast the rock away. After several days of blasting with three hundred sticks of (sixty present nitro) dynamite, John was able to cut a flat face on the mountain and to level an eight hundred by thousand feet flat spot at the base of the mountain for his lodge.

John had learned from weather charts and local residents that the stream could get deep in the winter storms so he decided to build a bridge over it that would get his road to the lodge above the flood waters. This would be another job for the precast yard. The month was up and it was time for the precast yard to do their work. John had designed the bridge so that it would be at least ten feet above the water during the worst storm condition that had occurred over the last one hundred years. This made the bridge twenty feet above the stream at normal stage. The bridge had to be one hundred and fifty feet long to tie the roads on both sides of the stream together.

The addition of the bridge to the precast contract extended the work and caused the precast contractor to take almost two mounts to complete. The precast work was done, the bridge and cabin were done, but it was now late summer. John had to work fast if he was going to get his cabin set for winter. He had to build a heating/cook stove; cut and store wood; install a water supply; build a food storage room, and there was that hole in the mountain where the cabin was set up. In the process of blasting away the face of the mountain to create a flat face to build the cabin against, John had uncovered a hole in the mountain about the size of a house door. The hole opened into a cave in the mountain that John knew nothing about. He did not know where or how far it went into the mountain or where it might come out. It could be a source for something or someone to get into his cabin and that was not acceptable. He built a steel frame anchored it into the rock wall and mounted a steel door that could only be locked or unlocked from inside the cabin.

The cabin was done. The road and bridge were done. Wood and supplies were in. Had he forgotten anything? John was setting in his new cabin, going over the list he had made of all he would need to survive a winter in Alaska. He was comfortable that he had provided well. He had spent almost all that he and Leigh had saved, but that was ok. He still had a small income from some investments they had made and he felt he could make it on that.

John did not know exactly how much wood he would need to heat his cabin and to cook with so in addition to what he had stored in the 'cage' (an extension of the cabin roof that was enclosed on three sides by precast walls and on the front by steel bars (to keep 'critters' out) he had cut down several trees. He stripped the limbs off and dragged the logs to the edge of the cabin clearing as a backup just in case he needed more wood. John was ready. And that was good because it was getting cold. One light snow had fallen and every day brought colder temperatures.

CHAPTER NINE

JOHN AND HIS CRITTERS

One morning while John was having his coffee he heard some-thing outside and went to see what the noise was. When he opened the door, and stepped into the cage he saw a large bear pacing back and forth in front of the bars of the cage. The bear would pace for a while then it would push against the bars as if to try to get in. When John yelled at the bear it startled the bear and it ran off. Two hours later the bear was back doing the same thing. John ran it off again and did not see it anymore that day. The next day the bear was back doing the same thing it did the day before. John did not want to kill the bear he just wanted it to leave and not come back. After thinking about it for a while he got his shotgun and loaded it with light loads. After John scared the bear off and when it was a safe distance away John shot the bear in the behind just to sting it so it would not come back. Two days went by without any sign of the bear. John hoped that was the end of the bear.

It was Friday and John did not know how many good days he would have before he might get snowed in so he decided to go to Fairbanks and spent the weekend at the motel with Don and Jenny. He packed a bag with clothing he would need and put it in the truck. He started to open the cage to get the truck out when he thought about the bear. Just to be safe he thought he should have some protection so he went back to the cabin and got his Desert Eagle forty-four Magnum with the shoulder holster. He put one clip in his pocket and one in the gun. He opened the cage and put the truck out of the cage. As he closed the cage, locked it and put the keys in his pocket he turned and saw the bear charging him. He had no time to do anything but try to kill the bear. He drew his gun, amid, and fired three rounds. The third round struck the bear in the head and killed it. The forward momentum of the running bear caused it to fall and pin John against the cage bars. He was so scared that he just stood pinned against the cage. When he finally got out from between the bear and the cage he just stood there in disbelief. He could not understand why the bear keeps coming back. John was not the kind of person that would just kill something for no good reason and he was so upset that he had to kill the bear. He did hunt and kill for food, but this was just such a waste. As he thought about what had just happened he remembered that there was a small settlement of local families he had met about fifteen miles from his place. He would call them. If anyone could use the bear for good, they could. He called them and told them what had happened. They were glad to get the bear because they said it would feed their families. John didn't eat bear meat and was glad it would be put to good use. He got his tractor and loader out of the cage and loaded the bear into his truck and took it to the locals. About a month later the locals brought John a beautiful bear skin rug. He did not know what to do with it, but he sure was not going to insult them by not taking it. He offered to pay them for it but they declined. John asks them to stay for dinner but they had to get back home and they left.

Two days after John had killed the bear, he heard a sound outside like something crying. After the third time he heard it, John went out to see what it was. Out near the woods was a pitiful little bear cub. It was scared and alone. He thought about it and realized that he must have killed its mother and he was just sick. He knew this poor little guy would starve to death if it was not mauled to death by some other animal. He thought about killing it to get it out of its misery, but John just could not do it. He picked the little fur ball up and took into the cage. John knew it had to be hungry so he made it a bed of old rags and went into the cabin and warmed some canned milk for it. He poked a hole in the finger of a rubber glove and filled it with the warm milk. The little cub sucked like it was starved. After its tummy was stuffed it laid back and went to sleep. John covered it with an old blanket and let it sleep.

John and the cub spent many hours together that winter. The bear cub was a great comfort to John.

He did not have to spend the winter alone. The little cub followed John around like a puppy and John grew to love it. He would set in the cage and talk to the cub. The cub would set on its hind quarters and listen to John just like it understood everything John was saying.

It was obvious that this little bear was not going to stay little for long. It had gained almost a hundred and fifty pounds over the winter and at times would get rough with John. John did not know exactly what to do with the cub. He had hoped it would revert back to the wild when spring came, but this just did not seem to be happening. One time, as John tried to correct Brutus, he bit John on the hand hard enough to cause his hand to bleed. John just could not put up with that so the next time he was in town, he bought the strongest 'Taser' gun he could find. The next time Brutus tried to bite John; John shocked the bear on the nose with the Taser gun. Brutus jerked backward, falling on his haunches and then ran as fast as he could toward the woods, screaming as he went. John did not see Brutus for three days. On the fourth day, John went outside to get some wood for the stove and he saw Brutus at the tree line. He stopped and watched the bear, but the bear would not come to him. John called to Brutus to come to him, but the bear went back into the woods. Two days later, Brutus came into the clearing again. John called for him to come to him and Brutus came about half the distance to John and sat down. John called again, but Brutus Just sat there with his head down swinging it back and forth. When John called the third time, Brutus just sat there swinging his head and groaning like he used to do when he was just a cub. As John approached, the bear lay down and rolled over on his back. John sat down and began to scratch the bear's tummy and talk to him like he did when the bear was a small cub. The bear stretched, squirmed, and grunted like he did as a baby. When John got up the bear jumped to its feet and bounced around John like a happy puppy.

John asks Brutus if he was hungry and the bear shook his head up and down as John had taught him to do. So, John went into the cooler and got a front leg from a deer he had harvested for his own use. The bear took the offering from John very gently. John scratched him behind the ear and left him to eat his meal. John did not know what he was going to do with this critter but for now, the friendship was mended and all was well.

Brutus became more and more independent as spring gave way to summer and summer gave way to fall. He would go out on his own and John would not see him for weeks. He never saw Brutus in July and August at all. When he came back in September he got rough with John and John shocked him with the 'Taser' gun as before. After a few days, the bear came back with an attitude of apology and the two made up again.

John was sure that Brutus was only coming around for a free meal and John was glad to give it to him. John enjoyed his company even if it was just for a short time. John was glad the bear was becoming more and more independent. John felt that Brutus had grown up enough to make it on his own and it pleased him that his friend was going to be ok.

During the spring when Brutus was venturing out on his own, John found another critter--an abandoned wolf pup. He named this one "Freddy the Freeloader". John did not think this one was ever going to make it on his own. He would not hunt. He always wanted a handout. When he got old enough and big enough John let him go outside for three days with no food to see if he would hunt own his own. It did not happen. Old Freddy just stayed outside of the cage and whined until John fed him. John could see rabbits running within twenty feet of him but this mutt just ignored them.

It was getting cold now and John was concerned about his critters. The bear was one year old now and John didn't see much of him. He was quite large, close to three hundred pounds, and John felt he could take care of himself, but would he hibernate through the winter? John just did not know enough about bears to know.

He thought it best to harvest enough meat to feed a hungry bear if he had to. Now Freddy was a different story. He was hunting on his own when he wanted to, but most of the time he just waited for a 'hand out'. John stored extra food for him, but when he feed him he would feed him more then he could eat at one time. He did this to force the mutt to stash the food and come back to it later. John would not feed him every day so he would learn to store what he had and or hunt on his own. John loved his critters but he wanted them to be able to survive on their own.

CHAPTER TEN

AND THEN THE FBI CAME INTO JOHN'S LIFE

One afternoon in late fall John was outside playing with his wolf pup when a helicopter landed on the plot in front of his cabin. Freddy ran off and hid as John stood in amassment. A man in a dark suit got out and approached John.

The man asked, "Are you John Henson."

John said, "Who wants to know?"

The man identified himself as Art Simpson with the FBI and began to question John about his past. John immediately became defensive and refused to answer his questions.

John said, "you obviously know my past and that I was acquitted of all charges so what do you want?"

Art said, "Actually, I want your help".

John responded, "You want my help with what"?

Art began to explain to John that the man that ran the town of Purgatory called "Slick Willy" was suspected of being a gun smuggler and that he wanted John to keep his eye on him and report any suspicious activities to him.

John stopped Art in the middle of his explanation and told him that he would not be his informant.

John reminded Art that while he was Interim Sheriff in Kentucky he had broken up a dope cartel that was operating there. He also reminded Art that after he had got his friend Bill elected to the post of Sheriff how he had worked with Bill to break up a car-jacking ring.

John said, "Mr. Simpson you know my skills as a detective and that I have the perfect cover: a retired engineer. So, if you really want my help, put me on the payroll.

Art answered, "I can't do that".

John said, "You Can't, are you won't"?

Art began to explain to John that he did not have the authority to make him an agent but he would sure like to have John's help. John told him he would like to help but that he was not going to put his life on the line without being compensated for it. John also told Art that he would not go into a situation that he did not have the authority to control.

After they talked for some time about Slick Willy and what he was doing John assured Art that he knew about Slick Willy and did not like him. He also said that he was not going to get involved without the authority to bring him down.

As Art was walking to the helicopter, He turned to John and told him that he would tell his boss about John's offer to help and what conditions had to be met if he did. Art got on the plane and left. John thought that was the end of the madder. But, three days later Art was back. He landed, got off the plane and immediately handed John a shield and gun.

"Welcome to the FBI", Art said.

John and Art spent the rest of the day talking about how they would get Slick Willy. They both agreed that they would have to catch Slick Willy in the act to make an arrest stick. They had to have a near perfect plan. They both agreed that John would need to spend time in Purgatory to watch old Slick and gather information. John would report to Art on his every movement so they could devise the plan and set the trap that would take this man down.

When John was not playing with the bear cub that first winter, he was exploring the cave in the mountain at the end of his cabin. He was sure that the cave was the hibernation place for Brutus' mother. If he was right, it would explain why the mother bear acted as it did. John was right. He found the hibernation place of the mother bear. That is not all he found. He found a trace of gold in the walls of the cave. He also found gold dust in the stream that was flowing out of the mountain. He did not think it was worth much, but it was something to do that long winter. Between gold mining and playing with the bear cub, John kept busy and enjoyed himself.

The more John thought about his new job with the FBI the more time he spent in Purgatory listening, watching and keeping a record of everything he could learn about Slick Willy's operation. Slick Willy was good about keeping his operation secret. After three weeks John had very little information nothing he could use. Willy was a big spender. Everything he had was very expensive, but he left no money trails. John and Art tried to track Slick Willy's finances but they could not find where he was getting his money and where he was keeping it. They could not find any bank accounts domestic or offshore. The only conclusion they could come up with was that Willy was running cash operation, a rather large one.

Maybe that was the answer. If Slick Willy was running a cash operation he would surely be interested in a gold mine if he thought one existed in the area. If he could create the illusion that he had struck gold Maybe Slick Willy would get greedy and come after the gold and slip up. John put several of the nuggets and a small bag of the dust he had panned in a bag. He planned to go to the hardware store in Purgatory and ask the operator of the store where the nearest assay office was. As John showed one of the stones to the operator he stated he wanted to get a value for his find. When the operator raised his eyebrows as he looked at the stone John knew he had struck a nerve; he had taken the 'bate'. John knew the man would tell Slick Willy. When the operator started asking questions about how much he had, where he got it and suggested that he be allowed to take it and show it to his boss John acted nerves and took the stone, quickly placing it back into the bag. He told the man that it would not be necessary he was going into Fairbanks and he would get it assayed there. John left the store.

CHAPTER ELEVEN

JOHN MEETS SARAH

There was a new restaurant in town. It was not much of a restaurant. It was just a small room with three tables and a booth at the window. The food was not much either. You could get a sandwich and a decent bowl of homemade soup. The coffee was hot and strong and John could not believe it she made good Chocolate Pie. The place was run by a very attractive young woman named Sarah. He was curious about Sarah because she was not married and such a 'loner'. John tried to talk to her several times but she was not very friendly. She was a good host, but she did not talk much. John was not sure if she was part of Slick Willy's operation or not. After three weeks of stopping into her place, John had not been able to learn anything about Sarah.

John had been to Fairbanks to see Jenny and Don and to pick up supplies for the winter. It was getting cold and the first big storm of the winter was coming in. He didn't stop in Purgatory as he headed to his cabin because he didn't know when the storm would get there. He did not want to get stuck in a snow storm. About three quarters of the way between Purgatory and his cabin he ran up on a stalled pickup. He stopped to see if he could be of assistance and found that it was Sarah. She had been delivering sandwiches to a Coal mine about twenty miles past John's cabin. She was not dressed for the weather that was coming in and this concerned John. She had on jeans, a shirt, a pair of sneakers, and a light jacket certainly not dressed for the incoming storm. When he asks her what she was doing out there she told him she had made a delivery and was on her way home. He asks her what had happened to the truck. She told him she did not know; it just quit. She had been there long enough that the truck was cold and so was Sarah. John suggested that she get into his truck and get warm while he checked out her truck. It was a nineteen fifty-three Chevy Pickup. He raised the hood and tried the starter. The engine was locked up. When he looked under the truck, there was oil on the ground and the oil plug was gone out of the engine.

John turned to Sarah and said, "Sarah your truck is not fixable and we have to make a decision fast about what we are going to do. We are fifteen miles from town and this storm is coming in fast. We cannot make it back to town before the storms catch us and bury us in snow".

Sarah said, "I must get back to town".

John said, "Impossible. If we hurry, we can make it to my place".

Sarah started to protest again, but John interrupted her and told her he did not have time to argue with her.

She said, "I can't just leave my truck".

He said, "Help me hook onto it and we will drag it to my cabin".

John rigged a makeshift tow bar and the two of them headed for the cabin. The snow was coming down fast and driving was getting hard. He knew he would not make it if he did not stop long enough to put the truck into four-wheel drive. By the time they got to John's section of land and started across his bridge, the snow was approaching six inches in depth and driving was really treacherous. When he made the turned at the end of the bridge and started up the hill to the cabin it was snowing so hard that John could not see the road clearly. The truck was losing traction and sliding from side to side on the road. They just made it to the cabin. After unhooking from Sarah's truck, John was able to get his truck into the cage and shut it.

It was obvious that Sarah was just plane scared. John tried not to do or say anything to cause any more fear. He tried to reassure her by telling her that as soon as the storm passed he would get her back into town. But, for now, they would be safe in the cabin. He opened the door and invited her in. When she stepped through the door and saw the head of the bear on the bear skin rug she jumped back into John. John caught her and steadied her. She was quick to get away from John. He showed her where the restroom was and told her where the clean towels were and invited her to freshen up while he got them something to eat. When she came back from the restroom she just stood with her arms folded and said nothing. He invited her to sit at the table but she just stood there without saying a word. John tried to engage her in conversation by asking her if she liked Venison stew.

She said, "I have never eaten Venison".

John said, "Try it and if you don't like it, I can open a can of soup".

She never responded. John knew he had to do something or it was going to be a very miserable night. He called her name. She ignored him. He called her name again. She turned and looked at him. Her face was blank.

John said, "Sarah, if there was any way humanly possible I would take you back to town, but it is impossible. That snow is at least a foot deep and still snowing. We cannot get there tonight. You are safe here. We have plenty food, water, and heat. You are safe here. Let's make the best of it. Now try to eat something".

She said, "I just simply cannot stay here tonight. I must get back to town".

"It is impossible. You saw how the truck slid all over the road when we were coming up the hill to the cabin".

"I saw a snowmobile out there where you parked your truck. Won't that go in the snow?"

"It will if you can see where you are going. Look out the window. You can't see your truck and it is only twenty feet from the window".

Sarah asks, "What window"?

John went over and opened the shutter to the bay window and turned on an outside spotlight so Sarah could see. The snow was falling so hard she could not see her truck. As she stood close to the window looking out, John's wolf pup jumped at the window. Sarah screamed and stumbled backward.

As she caught herself, she said in a loud voice, "What was that"?

John turned to see the wolf and said, "It is Freddy the Freeloader my wolf pup. Stay here till I feed him".

He told Sarah to stay in the cabin and keep the door closed. He told her the wolf was a wild animal and was not friendly with strangers. He went out to the cage and let Freddy in. He took him to his corner and fed him. When he came back in the cabin, it was obvious she was still shaken by the ordeal.

"What else have you got running around out there"?

About that time, Brutus stood up against the window.

Sarah was so scared she stood screaming and stomping the floor until John grabbed her and sat her down at the table to calm her down. After he sat her down he gave her a cup of hot chocolate. John started out the door.

Sarah demanded, "Where are you going"?

"Out to feed the bear".

"That bear will eat you".

"No, it won't. I raised him".

"Would you please close the shutter before you go out there," Sarah pleaded.

John closed the shudder, and went out and gave Brutus a large chunk of deer meat. When he came back in Sarah was sipping on the hot chocolate. She seemed calmer but it was obvious she was not comfortable. He served her a bowl of the stew with some home-made bread. He told her again to try it and if she did not like it, he would prepare her something else.

She reluctantly tried it. Paused for a moment and turned to John and said, "It is very good. Thank you".

They sat silently eating. John got up and poured Sarah another cup of chocolate and asks her if she wanted more stew. She declined. After the main course, John offered Sarah some of his home-made chocolate chip cookies.

He told her, "These are not nearly as good as your chocolate pie, but maybe they will do for now."

She smiled and took a cookie. After that, she took three more.

After dinner, he began to tell Sarah about sleeping arrangements. He suggested that she would sleep in his bed. Before John could explain his intentions, Sarah jumped up in protest.

She stated very sternly, "If you think I am going to sleep with you, you are out of your mind!"

John said, "No Sarah, no. I did not mean to imply that you would sleep with me. I am merely suggesting, as a good host, that you take the best I have and sleep in my bed. I will...."

Before he could finish, Sarah ask, "Where will you sleep?"

John replied, "I will sleep in this recliner..."

Sarah interrupted John again, "I am not going to take your bed and make you sleep in a chair. I will sleep on the couch."

"Sarah please!" John said. "Please take the bed. I sleep in this chair most of the time anyway. I set here working on my computer or watching TV and when I get tired I just cover up with this blanket and spend the night. I just changed the linens this morning and it is nice and fresh so please take it." He pointed to hooks in the ceiling and said, "I can hang blankets from the hooks and give you privacy. I can't do that around the couch or chair there are no hooks."

She reluctantly agreed and they began to hang blankets to give her privacy. John explained that he did not have any ladies clothing for her to sleep in but he offered her a pair of his sweat pants, a sweatshirt, and a pair of tube socks.

He explained, "These are too large for you, but they are very soft and warm. The pants have a drawstring so you can keep them on. If you want to you can cut the legs off or roll them up." John made sure there were fresh towels and wash clothes in the shower and let Sarah get ready for bed.

John, at five feet and ten inches tall weighing two hundred ten pounds and Sarah at five feet four inches tall and weighing maybe one hundred and fifteen pounds, was almost a hundred pounds larger than Sarah. She sure looked cute in John's clothes. She came out of the shower with the sweatshirt sleeves doubled up to the elbows so her hands would stick out and the legs of the pant pulled up to the knees so they would not drag the floor. John tried not to laugh, but she just looked so cute.

She looked at John and said, "laugh, you silly fool".

John trying not to laugh said, "I am sorry. I don't mean to laugh, but you just look so cute in that outfit."

She said sarcastically, "I am sure I do."

He snickered and said, "Good night Sarah. I will see you in the morning."

The storm raged for two days. On the third day, John managed to get his tractor out and he started clearing the road but it was impossible. The drifts were too deep and there was no place to put the snow. John knew that the only way he could get Sarah back to town was on the snowmobile and that it would be very dangerous. He went back to the cabin and told Sarah the conditions and asks her she wanted to try to make it back to town. She insisted that she had to get back. Sarah's lack of proper clothing was of great concern to John, so he instead that she wear some of his to keep her from freezing on the trip to town. He also got some blankets to wrap her in on the snowmobile. By noon they were on the road headed for Purgatory. It took an hour and forty-five minutes to travel the twenty miles from John's cabin to town. It was a miserable trip. It was very cold and the snowmobile would get stuck in the snow drifts. By the time they got to Purgatory, they were exhausted and Sarah was so cold she was shaking.

CHAPTER TWELVE

SARAH COMES UNDER ATTACK

After He dropped Sarah in front of her restaurant, John went to the hardware store to get caught up on the local gossip. There was a table in the back of the store where the locals would set, smoke, drank coffee and talk about everything that was happening in town. John didn't set down with them, but he did get close enough to hear them talking about the star attraction that Slick Willy was going to have in the new strip club he was opening up that night. One of the men asks who it was and he was told that it was Sarah who ran the restaurant. The man wanted to know how Willy talked her into doing that. John heard them talking about how Willy had had Sarah's truck sabotaged so it would break down and she would have to spend the storm at the coal mine camp. He had his assistant use that as an excuse to rent the restaurant space to someone else and to throw all Sarah's clothes away. He used her absence during the storm as evidence that Sarah had run out because she was behind on her rent. Willy's plan was that Sarah would have no choice when she came back. She would have to do what he wanted her to do. She would have no place to stay; no clothes; and no money. She would either dance at the strip club or be out in the cold.

John was furious over what he had heard. He did not know anything about Sarah. He still didn't know if she was part of Willy's gang or not. John was going to take the chance that she wasn't. He was going to give her help to get out of this mess if she wanted it. He bought a heavy wooly blanket to "hide" the reason he had come to the store and walked out.

When he got back to the restaurant he found Sarah sitting at the booth in front of the window sipping on a cold cup of coffee. Her bottom lip was quivering as though she was trying not to break down crying. He ordered fresh coffee and sat down across from her. He told her that he had heard about what had happened to her.

He told her, "Sarah, you can come back to my place and stay until you can get you a job and a new place."

What she said to John was out of pure hate and it was obvious she was hurting.

She said, "What is the difference between being Willy's whore or being yours?"

John just sat for a moment with his head down. Then he looked at Sarah and said, "One big difference: Sarah, I neither need nor want a whore, but I will help you if you want my help." He slid his chair back and got up. He turned and walked out of the restaurant. When he got to the snowmobile, Sarah came running out to where he was and stopped at the curb beside of the snowmobile.

She asks John, "Why do you want to help me? You don't even know me!"

He answered, "Two reasons; I don't like what they are doing to you and I don't like the people that are doing it to you."

She responded, "You don't understand. I don't have anything; no clothes, no money, nothing."

"I will take care of all of that. There will be lots of work here in the spring and when you go to work you can pay me back then. You need to decide quickly because your new boss is coming down the street."

She said in anguish, "What do you want me to do?"

He said, "Get on the snowmobile and cover up. We are going to take a long cold ride."

When she got on, John turned the snowmobile around in the street and headed for Fairbanks.

They could hear Slick Willy screaming in the background, "Go catch them! Get that bitch back here. She belongs to me!"

John opened his machine up. He ran as fast as his snowmobile would go and stay on the road. He had no intentions of letting Slick Willy's gang catch them.

It took three and a half hours to get to Fairbanks and Sarah was so cold she could not talk. John drove around town until he was sure that he had eluded the two men that were chasing them. He was not far from Don and Jenny's so he went to their motel.

When he got there, he went around back so he could hide the snowmobile. Then he and Sarah went inside. When he came through the door, Jenny met him and asks, "Who are you running from?"

He said, "Jenny I need your help."

She insisted, "John, what is going on?"

John sat Sarah down at a table in the back of the dining room. While Jenny was pouring them some hot coffee, John told her what had happened to Sarah.

He said, "Please tell me you have two rooms I can rent for a few days."

She told John that she only had one room, but it had two beds. He asks for a room divider to give Sarah some privacy. Jenny told him she had one.

John turned to Sarah and asks, "Can you manage with these arrangements until we can get our business done?" Sarah shook her head yes. John turned to Jenny and asks about a clothing store where he could get Sarah something to change into for the night. He explained his intentions to take Sarah to town tomorrow to shop for clothing for her, but for now, she needed something for tonight. Jenny told him that he didn't need to go to town. She had night clothing Sarah could wear. He explained that he still had to go to town to get him something to sleep in; he had not brought any with him.

Jenny told him, "I believe Don has something that will fit you. Now, what do you want to eat?"

"What do you suggest?" Ask John.

Jenny told them, "The special today is a baked pork chop, baked potato, and a tossed salad with your chose of homemade fried pies."

John turned to Sarah and asks. "How does that sound to you?"

She said, "I am not hungry."

John insisted, "Sarah, you have not eaten all day. You need to eat to keep up your strength. We are going to eat, rest tonight and tomorrow we are going to straighten this mess out. Now, will you try to eat something?"

She agreed and after dinner, Jenny set up the room and laid out night clothing for both of them. While Sarah was getting ready for bed, John and Jenny sat and talked.

John asks Jenny if she could use some help at the motel.

Jenny said, "I need help, but I can't afford to pay anyone."

"If you can use her I will pay her, but I want the money to come from you."

Jenny asks, "Why are you doing this? It is obvious that she has a lot of 'baggage', and that could cause you a lot of trouble. Why are you getting involved?"

John was careful about his answer. He had not told Jenny that he was working with the FBI. He did not want her to know. If she accidentally told someone, it might complicate his chances in solving the Slick Willy case. He was sure that he had his emotions under control concerning female company. However, he did enjoy the three days that Sarah was at the cabin. John said, "She is in trouble and I am just trying to help. However, she seems to be reluctant to take help from me. I told her I would give her the money she needs to get back on her feet and she could pay me back when work picks up, but she does not want to take anything from me."

"How much do you want to pay her?" Jenny asks.

"Offer her One hundred dollars a week with room and board," John replied. "I will take her to town tomorrow and get her some clothes. I will get you a thousand dollars for the first ten weeks plus whatever you need for the room and board."

"If she works at all she will earn her room and board. Just get me the money to pay her and we will be ok", Was Jenny's reply.

"I want you to ask her so she will think it is your idea."

Jenny agreed and the two went to bed.

The next morning John took Sarah to town to shop for clothes and supplies. John instructed Sarah to get at least seven sets of clothes so she would have a fresh change for every day. He explained that he only did laundry once a week. He told her he had to start the generator to do laundry so he only did it once a week. After three department stores, they had purchased seven changes of clothes for Sarah and two for John. Sarah reminded him that they had spent over three thousand dollars. John interrupted her by stating that they had not gotten her anything to wear outside in the cold. He took her to a sporting goods store and outfitted her with a good pair of coveralls, boots, a hood, and gloves something suitable for the cold snowmobile ride like they had just taken from Purgatory.

On the ride back to the motel, John went to the assay office and cashed in some of the gold dust to get cash for Jenny just in case Sarah took her up on the job offer. He left Sarah outside on the snowmobile so she would not see what he was doing. When they got back to the motel, Jenny had the lunch ready and was serving a full restaurant. Sarah immediately asks if she could help. Jenny gave her an apron and an order pad and sent her out to take orders. After three hours, the crowd had been feed and John, Sarah, and Jenny sat down to eat. It was then that Jenny asks Sarah if she was interested in a job. Sarah's eyes lit up. Jenny explained that she could not pay her very much. In keeping with what she and John had talked about, Jenny offered Sarah a hundred dollars a week with full room and board. Sarah immediately turned and looked at John.

John said, "You are looking for a fresh start. It isn't much but come spring when the work picks up I am sure it will get better." When Sarah turned back to Jenny to accept the offer, John winked at Jenny in approval. Jenny and Sarah talked about the work Sarah would be expected to do while the two prepared the evening meal. John helped himself to a cup of coffee and a piece of chocolate pie. He went into the lounge and watched the evening news.

The next morning John loaded his stuff on the snowmobile and was ready to leave for the long ride back to the cabin when Sarah through her arms around his neck and kissed him on the cheek.

She said, "Thank you so much for your help. I will pay you back for the clothes. I can't pay much right now but I will pay a little a week till I get it paid."

John said, "Don't worry about paying me right now. Just get yourself taken care of for now and when you are more stable we will talk about payback. Right now, you have too much to think about to worry about a few thousand dollars' worth of cloth. I am not worried about it in the least. I know you will pay me back. Right now, take care of yourself."

He then turned to Jenny and said, "I don't know when I will get back in town, but if you need me for anything call me."

The three of them exchanged "small talk" for a few minutes and John started for the cabin.

CHAPTER THIRTEEN

JOHN INVESTIGATES SARAH

On the ride home, John had a lot of time to think about Sarah and he was still concerned about the possibility that she could be somehow connected with Slick Willy. If she was, what had he gotten Jenny mixed up in?

When he got back to the cabin he took the glass Sarah had used to drink from and took her fingerprints off of it. He then got on the FBI website and ran Sarah's prints through their database. She was Sarah Pritts from Los Angeles. She had been married to a Carl Pritts who was in prison for killing a man. The man he killed was thought to have been part of Carl's gang who had robbed a bank. The police could not get enough evidence to convict the gang of the robbery so they were still living in LA. And operating their strip club called the Zombie Hut.

According to the FBI file on the robbery case, eight hundred and fifty thousand dollars' worth of bearer bonds had been taken in the robbery and had not been recovered. Carl and three other men, suspected of being in his gang, had been captured on the bank security cameras. They were never seen in the bank at the same time, but all five of them had been seen in the bank over a four-week time period. The fifth man, the man that Carl had killed, had been a teller in the bank. The gang had broken into the bank vault from an underground abandoned storm drain. They were in and out of the bank in less than two hours. The bearer bounds and two hundred thousand dollars in cash were taken. None of it was ever recovered. When they left the bank, they set a bomb to go off just before the bank opened for business. The bomb closed the storm drain and did a good job of covering up the evidence.

There was nothing in the file that directly linked Sarah to the robbery, but she was a person of interest. The FBI wanted to question her, but she left town before they could get to her. John wanted to know why so he called Art.

Art answered the phone, "Hello John. What is new and exciting?" Art acted as if he didn't know that John had accessed the FBI database but John knew that he did know.

John asks Art, "What can you tell me about Sarah Pritts?"

Art said, "Who is Sarah Pritts"?

His response aggravated John because he knew that any time he accessed the FBI database that Art was alerted and that He would get a report on everything John looked at on the database.

John asks Art, "Are we going to work together on this or are we going to continue to play twenty questions"?

There was a pause on the phone line and then Art ask, "Why do want to know about her"

"Art, when you are ready to share with me what you know about her give me a call." John hung up the phone.

Art must have talked with his boss about the matter because it was twenty minutes before he called John back.

When John answered the phone, Art said, "John this is an on-going case and we need to know what interest you have in it".

"Art, I am involved in the case and I am looking for some answers. The question is whether I find them on my own or do I search for them as an FBI agent."

"John, you are supposed to be working on the Slick Willy case..."

"Art, there is a possibility that they are connected. Sarah Pritts was in Purgatory."

Art started to ask John some questions, but John interrupted him by telling him his intentions to go to LA to look around and see what he could find out about the case, and maybe get some answers to his questions. Art started to tell John he would notify the LA office that John was coming but John stopped him.

"I believe I will have better success if I go down without anyone knowing I am coming or who I am. I will give you a full report when I get back."

"Where is Sarah now?"

"I will give you a full report when I get back."

By the time, John got his road cleared of the snow, the county road crew had the roads cleared enough that he could use his truck to go to town. John packed his bags and headed for the airport in Anchorage. From there he flew to LA. He arrived in L.A. around three PM. After he got settled in the motel, He got in the rental car and took a ride to the Zombie Hut.

The Zombie Hut occupied the corner of two connecting streets, Diagonally across from there was a playground. In John's opinion, this was not right, a playground so close to a 'strip club'. He drove around and parked on the opposite side of the playground where he could see through the playground and watch the strip club. After two and a half hours he had taken several hundred photographs of people entering and leaving the club.

Back at the motel, John placed the chip from his camera on his computer so he could view the pictures. He had taken several pictures of a young lady that came out of the club. He was troubled by her because she looked too young to be in a place like a strip club and she looked like Sarah. He ran her picture through the facial recognition database of the FBI but got no results.

John was not able to let this go; she looked too much like Sarah there had to be a connection. John estimated the girl to be around fourteen to sixteen years old and started searching for birth records for Carl and Sarah Pritts. And there it was: they had a Daughter Patty Pritts.

According to the birth records, she would be fifteen years old. But what was she doing in a strip club? Had one of Carl's gang members taken her in? John had to know. The next morning John called Art to see what he could tell him about Sarah and Carl's children. Art told him that the couple had one daughter named Patty and that Sarah had been two months pregnant with a boy. The night Carl killed his partner he also beat Sarah so brutally that she had to be rushed to the hospital for an emergency hysterectomy. He had beaten and kicked Sarah so brutally he had ruptured her uterus. She had to have the surgery to stop her from bleeding to death. While she was recovering, her daughter was placed in child protective custody.

Art thought that Sarah was afraid of members of Carl's' gang. He explained to John that while she was in the hospital she had several visits from members of the gang. Art told John that he thought that Sarah might have had information about the bank robbery that the gang wanted. He believed that is why she snuck out of the hospital, cleaned out her bank account and left the area. John could not imagine why a mother would run off and leave her ten-year-old child. Was she so afraid of the gang she left without taking her child or was she so selfish she was just running to save her own self?

The last thing John wanted to do was to spend time in a strip club watching a naked woman squirming around a steel pole. But, there were just too many unanswered questions. He had to get the answers and to do that he would have to visit the Zombie Hut. The next morning, he sat in the motel restaurant sipping coffee and thinking about what he was going to do. He had been warned by Art of the security system that the Zombie Hut had and that presented some problems for John. He wanted to get some pictures of the inside of the club but he was not sure he could get them. He would use the small camera that Art had given him to use in the Slick Willy case, but he was not sure he could get it passed their security system. The camera looked like a shirt button, but it had an electronic 'footprint' that he was afraid would be detected by their security system. He needed something else that had a similar 'footprint'. He could not use a cell phone; they were not allowed in the club. After thinking long and hard, he thought that maybe a set of hearing aids would do the trick. The hearing aids would present an electronic "footprint' and maybe would keep the camera from being detected. It was worth a try. He bought a set of hearing aids, turned them down low and placed them in his ears. With the camera in his shirt, the hearing aids in his ears he headed for the Zombie Hut.

When he arrived at the club he was asked if he had a cell phone and that was all that the security guards checked. John was surprised. Art had warned him of the security at the club and John expected a much more elaborate examination at the door. That just did not happen. He went in, walked around looking at, and taking pictures of everything he could without drawing suspicion to himself. He sat down at a table near the stage.

One of the girls came over and asks for his drink order. He ordered a coke. The girl asks if that was all he was going to drink. He made an excuse about having a bad liver and that he could not enjoy the "good stuff".

John pretended that he was there to meet a friend and asks the waitress if she had seen his friend Jack McCarthy. He made up a description of his friend. He described him as six feet tall weighing two hundred and fifty pounds with a scar over his left eye. He also told the girl that Jack had a glass eye.

John sat sipping on his five-dollar coke and thinking about the lack of security in the club. He noted that there were several security cameras in the club, but he got in too easy. Was he being set up? Was he under surveillance? He had arrived at the club around three P.M. by his plan. The night crew had not arrived yet and the club was almost empty. He wanted to look around before the night crew came in. This would give him time to study the place without a crowd in the way.

While he sat there thinking a voice from behind him asks, "Mister would you like to donate to my dance?"

He turned around to see Patty Pritts standing there in a pair of panties and a tank top. His first thought was to take his belt off and give her a grand good whipping for running around in public without being properly dressed. He kept his thoughts to himself. He handed her a twenty-dollar bill, but she pulled the top of her panties forward and invited John to put the money in them. John was appalled.

He asks her, "What is your name?"

"Patty".

"Patty what?"

"Patty Pritts".

John said, "I knew a George Pritz. How do you spell your name?"

She replied, "Pritts".

"It must be a different group. He spelled his name with a 'z' in it. When are you going to dance?"

"In twenty minutes," She replied.

"I am afraid I won't get to see you dance. I have another meeting and I have to leave. Maybe I will see you the next time. But here is the twenty anyway. You put it anywhere you want to."

John was not going to stay there and watch Sarah's daughter make a fool of herself. John stopped the waitress that had been waiting on him and asks her to give a message to his friend Jack if he came in the club. He explained to her that he had to leave for another meeting and ask her to tell Jack to call him.

He went out of the club and started to call a cab when he noted that one of the men in the club came out close behind him as if he were following John. Instead of calling a cab, John walked down the street toward town. As he walked, he kept an eye on the man by looking at him in the reflection of the store windows. Sure enough, everywhere John went the man followed him. John walked casually down the street toward a store at the end of the block. When he got in a store, he got out of the man's site and ducked into the restroom. In one of the stalls, he reversed his reversible jacket which turned it from light tan to a black. While in there, he but on a fake beard and glasses. He also put on a ball cap he had in his jacket pocket. The disguise worked. John walked right past the stalker unnoticed.

When John got back to his motel room he called Art. One of the first questions he asks Art was how he knew the club had a good security system. Art explained that every time they tried to get someone in the club, they knew they were coming before they got there. John asked Art if he had considered the possibility that someone in the FBI was tipping them off.

Art paused for a while and then asked, "Why would you say that?"

John replied, "I walked in without any security check of any type. They ask me if I had a cell phone and when I said no they let me in. Art someone must be tipping them off. I was followed after I left the club. Make sure they do not run my picture through the system and find out that I am an FBI agent."

Art said, "Let me call you back."

An hour later, Art called John back, "You were right John. I just blocked a search for your identity in the system. I created a false identity for you. You are now in the system as John Mark, An art collector from Florida. Be careful John. They are a mean bunch. Did you learn anything of value?"

"Art, I have done everything I can for now. I will be home as soon as I can cover my trail down here."

John spent the next two days checking on Patty. He found where she lived. He discovered that she had a new baby, a little girl named Abigail. And, she was not married. He found out that her bills were being paid by the members of her dad's gang. She had no bank account and no credit cards. Everything she bought was with cash. Her rent was paid by the club.

As John flew back to Alaska he thought about what he had learned and put that together with what Art had told him about Sarah. He was afraid that Sarah had left for her own safety. He was afraid she did know something about the robbery maybe where the money and the bonds were. If he was right, the gang wanted to talk to her as well as the FBI. Maybe the gang was using Patty for bait to catch Sarah.

As soon as John got back to Alaska he went straight to Art's office. They talked for hours about what John had seen and experienced in La and about the possible connection between the two cases John was working on. They could not find any connection between the two cases except John working on both cases and his involvement with Sarah. John asks Art to allow him to continue to work both cases. He convinced Art to not call Sarah in for questioning, but let him deal with the mater. He would find out what Sarah knew about the bank robbery. They concluded their meeting and John left for his cabin.

On the way back to the cabin John was going to stop in Purgatory at the restaurant that Sarah used to run but it was closed down. He went to the local hardware store and played a game of checkers with one of the locals while he caught up on the local gossip. While he was letting the opponent beat him, he was listening to all the local news being discussed by those around the 'Smoke pit' as John called their gathering place. About an hour of that was all he could take. He passed his seat at the checkerboard to one of the locals, bought a box of wood screws to make repairs on his kitchen cabinet and left for home.

CHAPTER FOURTEEN

SARAH'S STALKERS RETURN

Three and a half weeks after John set Sarah up to work with Jenny he got a call from Jenny. Sarah was in trouble. Men from Slick Willy's gang were hanging around Jenny's and Sarah was scared so bad that she would not come out of her room. John told Jenny he was on his way and to tell Sarah to stay out of site till he got there. He told Jenny to tell Sarah to put all her clothing in large garbage bags. When he got there, he would park around back of the restaurant and block the line of sight of the guy watching the back of the restaurant. When he got there, he told Sarah to sneak into the back seat floor of his truck and he put the bags of clothes in on top of her to hide her from the man that was watching the place. After she was in and secured he closed and locked the truck. He then went into the restaurant. While he and Jenny were making small talk, they were watching for the man to see if he would check the truck out, he did. Sarah was well hidden and the man went back to the place where he was watching the restaurant. As John was getting into his pickup, Jenny said, "Thanks for taking care of all the clothes for me."

"Not a problem Jenny. I have just the people to give them to." As John drove away he looked back in his mirror to see if he was being followed, he was not.

As soon as he knew it was safe and he was sure they were not being followed, John called out to Sarah.

"Are you ok?"

"I can't breathe. These bags are crushing me."

John pulled over on the side of the road and pulled the bags off of her to let her get up.

"Sarah, I think it is clear. The two 'goons' are not following us. Why don't you get into the front seat?"

Sarah asks, "Where are we going?"

"Back to the cabin until we can come up with a better plan. Do you have any good ideas?"

"No, I don't know what to do," said Sarah, "I am at my wit's end. I just don't know what to do. I wish I had the guts to just shoot them."

"I can teach you to shoot and get you a gun if you are sure that is what you want to do."

John went on to explain to Sarah that if she decided to try using the gun she needed to be sure that that is what she wanted to do. He explained that if she started she would have to finish it. She would have to be sure she killed everyone that attacked her or they would surely kill her. She would have to be ready to shoot every one of them, maybe two or three times to be sure they were dead.

Sarah said, "I just don't think I could do that. I just cannot stand the thought of killing someone, even if they do deserve it."

John said, "Let's go back to the cabin and get some rest and think about it. We will come up with something"

"What will keep them from sneaking up to the cabin and attacking us… me there?" She asks.

John thought about her question and wondered if he should tell her about his security system. He was still not sure of Sarah's position in the Slick Willy clan. Was she part of it or was she a victim of it. She was genuinely scared when he picked her up at Jenny's. Her heart was beating rapidly, she was clammy and cold and she was having trouble breathing.

While he was thinking about it, Sarah asks, "Did you hear my question?"

John replied, "Yes I heard you. You do not need to worry about that." He decided that it would not do any harm if she knew about the security system.

"Sarah, I have a very elaborate security system around the cabin. Anyone that gets within a thousand yards of the cabin is picked up on the system."

"How do you know if it is a man or animal?" she asks.

"When I get an alarm, I can pick it up on the camera and see it on the computer." He answered.

"Then what will you do. Run and hide while they destroy the cabin looking for us?"

"No Sarah. I am not like you. I will do what I have to do if I feel my life, or yours, is threatened. I am very good with a high-powered rifle."

"You mean you would actually kill someone?"

"Yes, I will kill if I have to, to protect us." He replied.

"I sure don't want you mad at me,"

"I don't think you have anything to worry about. You haven't tried to kill me yet. Have you?"

"I couldn't kill you, John. I would not have anyone to come to my rescue when I get into trouble." She replied.

She turned toward John when she said that. John turned and looked at her and chuckled. That brought out Sarah's beautiful dimples.

John could not resist himself. "It is good to see you laugh Sarah. You are so beautiful when you are happy. Well, you are beautiful all the time but you are especially beautiful when you are happy."

That embarrassed her and she looked away. But, John could see her blushing.

At this time, John was convinced that Sarah was just a victim of Slick Willy's evil scheme. She was a simple young woman; she laughed when happy, cried when hurt, and ran when threatened. She was being threatened and He intended to help her any way he could. He did not know why she had left her child, but he was sure he would know when she was ready to tell him. In the meantime, he would take care of her. He would be her friend. He would watch, listen and respond accordingly to the information that he gained. John was sure that this course of action would lead to catching Slick Willy and maybe even lead to a solution to the bank robbery as well. He felt that Sarah was the 'common thread' to both of these cases. Willy was after Sarah and Sarah were running from the Bank gang.

Toward the end of the day, they were approaching Purgatory. John did not want anyone in Purgatory to see Sarah and tell Slick Willy so he asks Sarah to get down on the floor where he covered her with a bag of cloth from the back seat. As they drove through, John was observant to who was on the street and whether or not any of Willy's gang was watching. Everything seemed to be ok.

When they got out of town, John took the bag of cloth off of Sarah so she could get back into the seat.

Within a few minutes, they were going across the bridge to John's land. The closer they got to the cabin, the more anxious Sarah became. She kept looking in every direction

John asks, "Sarah, what is wrong? You seem tense. Are you ok?"

Sarah replied, "Where is your bear?"

John chuckled, "You need not worry about old Brutus. He is still in hibernation for another three months. Now old Freddy is a different story. He most likely will aggravate us continually. But, you don't need to worry about him. I will not let him hurt you."

When they got to the cabin, John told Sarah to stay in the truck while he opened the cage. He drove into the cage and closed it behind them and locked it. He then opened the truck door for Sarah and helped her out of the truck. John suggested that Sarah go into the cabin while he got her clothes.

He said, "Sarah, remember when you walk in the door there is a huge bear head just inside the door. Don't jump out of your 'hide'."

She tilted her head as she turned toward John and smirked at him as she walked in. She stepped over the head of the bear on the bear skin rug and went on into the cabin. It was a much more relaxed atmosphere than the first time John brought her to the cabin; that pleased him. His thought for the first time that he would be able to work with her and help her in the process. They might even become good friends.

Sarah stood in the main room and saw that John had built walls around the bed.

She said, "You have built walls around the bed. Were you expecting me back or is this for someone else?"

He replied, "Neither one. I just finished the original plan of the cabin. I have to admit; I was embraced the last time you were here that I didn't have anything more private for you then a blanket hung from the ceiling. So, I finished the two bedrooms."

"Two bedrooms?" She asks.

"Yes. Come and see. They are complete with chest and dressers for your clothes."

"Which one is mine? I mean which one do you want me to use?"

"Take your pick. The one against the left wall has a window."

"I had just as soon not have a window. I am afraid that darn bear will jump at me and I would just die if it did. I will take the one on the right."

"Ok. We will put your stuff in that room. While you are unpacking, I will start dinner."

While Sarah was putting her clothes away, John fried two steaks, baked two potatoes and made a tossed salad for dinner. Just as he was finishing up, Sarah came in the kitchen area and sat at the bar.

"What can I do to help?" She asks.

"Make a chocolate pie." He replied.

"I know you want to wait for dinner while I make a pie." She said.

"Not really. We will have peanut butter and jelly on toast for dessert tonight." He replied.

"I love peanut butter and jelly. That was my favorite food when I was a kid."

"You are still a kid." He said.

"Ok old man can we eat now?"

They sat and enjoyed the meal and talked about everything but each other's past. There were a lot of questions Sarah had about John but she would not ask him. John was waiting for her to tell him about her past and Patty but that night was not the time; she did not say a word about either.

CHAPTER FIFTEEN

THREE MONTHS OF WINTER

Stuck in a cabin for three months is hard on anyone. But, for a gal that was from LA, it was especially rough. The winter was harsh. There were several days when the snow storms were so severe that it was impossible to get out of the cabin. When it was not snowing, it was so cold that it was dangerous to stay outside.

Sarah could not go into town because of Slick Willy's gang and John would not leave her alone. They managed to get in to see Don and Jenny twice in three months. The first time they went out of the cabin to go to town, Freddy the Freeloader John's wolf charged Sarah and scared her so bad she almost passed out.

John knew that Sarah would not survive if he didn't think of something to keep her occupied so he asks her if she would like a buckskin coat. John had become a very good seamstress with Caribou hides from the Caribou he had harvested for himself, Freddy, and Brutus. He had made himself a very nice coat that he showed to Sarah and asks her if she would like one. She did not believe that He had made it, but he convinced her that he had and that he had enough hides and all the other material they needed to make her one. She said yes and that became their project for the winter.

Sarah was not a seamstress. She kept sticking herself with the needle and had no idea what a thimble was or what it was for. John was patient with her. She was a hard worker very prescient to learn. When she made a mistake, John would take out the stitch or piece of material and suggest that she try again. A coat that would have taken a good seamstress about a week took them almost six weeks.

She would get so intense with the task that she would make, in John's opinion, cute faces. One time she would make an 'o' with her mouth. The next time she would just squint her left eye. And later she would make a very sincere frown. John got so tickled he had to leave the work table and go into the next room. He was afraid if he stayed he would start laughing at her. All of those facial expressions were just too cute.

John had bought a red fox fur from the locals who tanned the hides for him. They used the fox fur to make a fur collar for the coat. He had taken antlers and sawed them into very thin, round, shapes to use for buttons. He then polished them and coated them with a clear epoxy. The buttons were a perfect complement for the coat.

Finally, after six and a half weeks the coat was finished: The fur collar was on; the full-length zipper for warmth was sown in, and all the buttons were in place. It was time for Sarah to model it. John held it up for her to put on; first her right arm then her left arm. It fit her shoulders just perfectly. Just enough room for a heavy sweater without sagging and snug enough to be very comfortable. The fit was absolutely perfect. Sarah stood in front of the marrow turning from right to left for almost ten minutes.

"John." She said, "I have never seen such a beautiful coat. I certainly never dreamed of ever having one. Is this really mine?"

John chuckled, "Of course it is yours. You don't see anyone else around that it will fit, do you?"

John watched her inspect it inch by inch. She put her hands in the pockets. Zipped up and unzipped it. She took it off and put it back on. She inspected every one of the stitches. Laid it down on the work table and checked the extra liner and put it back on. After she pulled her hair out from under the collar, she turned and ran to John and through her arms around his neck and kissed him.

She said, "Thank you, thank you. This is so beautiful. I can't wait to wear it in public."

John said, "As soon as it gets warm enough, we will go into town and buy you a complete outfit to go with it and we will go to the best dinner club in town. Maybe even go dancing."

She took a deep sigh and said, "That would be so much fun. I am not much of a dancer but I will sure try just to get to show off my coat."

It was getting time for supper so they joined effort and fixed the evening meal. After supper, they sat down to watch a movie when they got an alarm from the security system. John pulled the pictures up from the security cameras on his computer. There were two men over the creek from the cabin on the edge of the woods. They were setting something up but from the angle of the camera, John could not see what they were doing. He switched to a different camera to get a better look. They were setting up a mortar tube. John knew that if he did not act quickly, they were going to shoot mortars at the cabin. He ran out of the cabin with his high-powered rifle with a night scope to get in position to shoot back if they tried to shoot mortars at the cabin. When he got into position where he could get a good shot at the attackers, he called Art to tell him what was happening. Art told John to do what he had to do to protect himself and that he was on his way in the helicopter. John set his rifle on a rest where he could see the two men and get a good shot if he had to. One of the men picked up one of the mortars to load the tub and he dropped it. Both of the men tried to run but there was an explosion. When the smoke cleared, John could see both men lying on the ground about twenty feet from where the explosion occurred. They were not moving.

John had told Sarah to hide in a closet while he took care of the situation so when Art arrived John went outside to meet him. The two of them went over to where the attackers were. The explosion had killed both of them. What remained of the mortar tub and extra round that did not explode was of great interest to Art. He identified them as being part of an arms shipment that the FBI had been tracking. They suspected Slick Willy had them, but they could not prove it. John recognized the two men as the two that had been after Sarah, but he did not tell Art. He did not want Art to know that Sarah was with him. He purposely kept Art outside the cabin while they talked. They both agreed that they didn't have enough evidence to tie Slick Willy to the attack and decided to gather the evidence and cover up the attack so no one could tell that it had happened. This way Slick Willy would think that his two men had just run off with the mortars. Maybe that would cause Slick Willy to make a mistake while looking for them to get his 'stuff' back. Art gathered up everything he could use including the two bodies and John agreed to bury the rest. Art left for the office.

John went back into the cabin but Sarah was still hiding. John went to the closet to get her. She was so scared she just sat on the floor in the closet. He reached down and took her by both hands and lifted her up. She began to cry. John put his arms around her and told her it was over. The two men were gone. She just continued to cry. John tried to console her, but she kept crying.

She asks, "When is it going stop John? When is it going to stop? Are they ever going to leave me alone?"

"Those two will not bother you again," John replied. "They blew themselves up.

"They are dead?"

"Yes, they are dead."

Sarah asks, "Who were the men with the Helicopter?"

"They are with the FBI," John answered.

Sarah got very quiet; then she asks, "Why did the FBI come out here?"

"Mortars and Mortar launchers are not legal for the general public to have. That is why I called them."

"Did you know the FBI men?"

"Yes. I did some work for them once."

"Do you still work for them?"

"I would help them if they needed my help."

John was afraid that the questions were leading into subjects that he was not ready to share with her so he changed the subject.

"Would you like some popcorn to go with our movie?" He asks.

The question distracted Sarah's train of thought. John restarted the movie and they sat down to watch.

Sarah got the feeling that John did not want to talk about his involvement with the FBI. She was curious, but she was afraid to ask any more questions. She was afraid that it might have something to do with her past. She knew that the FBI wanted to talk with her. What she did not know was that John was hiding her from the FBI so they would not interrogate her about the bank robbery. John was hoping that he could find out what she knew about the robbery without her having to go through the stress of an FBI interrogation.

John was convinced that if she knew anything it was of a passive nature. He was sure she had not been part of the robbery. He was concerned about her because of the stress she had been through and was still going through. She did not sleep that night and John stayed up with her watching movies. He fixed hot chocolate and a small snack. The hot chocolate seemed to calm her nerves and around five A.M. she finally lay down and took a nap.

The next morning John got up early and took his tractor and loader out to the spot where the explosion occurred. He loaded everything that was left of the explosion and took it back into the woods and buried it. After he dressed the spot to hide the evidence he went back to the cabin. Sarah was still asleep. She came walking into the kitchen still half asleep just after eleven A.M. John handed her a cup of coffee and ask her if she was hungry. She shook her head yes.

John asks, "Breakfast or lunch?"

She said, "It doesn't matter."

John fixed her an open-faced roast sandwich with mashed potatoes and gravy.

She asks, "Did I have a nightmare last night or did someone try to blow us up?"

"You lived a nightmare last night. Someone did try to blow us up. It was those two guys from Slick Willy that were watching you at Jenny's place. But, like I told you last night, they blew themselves up."

"Is it over John? Are they finally going to leave me alone?"

John was reluctant to answer because there were too many unanswered questions. There had to be more to the reason Willy was chasing Sarah then him wanting her to dance in his club. He could have hired a dozen dancers for what he had spent chasing Sarah. There had to be another reason he was chasing her. John wondered if there might be a connection between Slick Will Jack, his smuggling operation, and Carl Pritts, and the bank robbery.

Sarah asks, "John did you hear me?"

"I really don't know" He replied

"What do you mean? Do you think he will try to get me again?"

"I just don't know Sarah. It just does not make any since. Why would Willy spend so much time and effort to get a dancer for his club?"

"I don't know either," Sarah replied. "I have never met the man. I have only seen him twice and one of the times was when he chased us out of town. I didn't even meet him when I rented the restaurant. I rented it from an employee of his. I don't know why he is chasing me but I am really tired of it. I just want it to stop."

As if life wasn't completed enough, the last storm of winter came in and dumped two feet of fresh snow everywhere making it impossible to get out and go anywhere. John was quite happy with spending time in the cabin, but Sarah was about to go "stir crazy". Two weeks later John knew he had to get her to town for some relief so he got out with his tractor and started clearing the road. After two days of pushing snow, he could get the truck out. If the state had done its job they could go to Fairbanks.

While John was finishing his work with the tractor, Sarah was standing inside the cage watching him when Brutus (out of hibernation early) came running up to the cabin. When Sarah saw, him she let out a 'blood curdling' scream and ran into the cabin, slammed and locked the door. John got off the tractor and greeted his old friend. After scratching his ear and getting him something to eat, he went in to check on Sarah. She had locked herself in the closet. When John opened the door, she would not come out.

"Is he gone? Is he gone? Please tell me he is gone." She cried.

"Sarah, he is just a big old pet. Come out and meet him." John pleaded.

"No! No! No! She cried. I hate him. I am afraid of him. Please make him go away!"

John wanted to laugh but he knew her fear was real and he did not want to make it worse for her.

"I have fed him and he has gone back into the woods so it is safe for you to come out now." He told her.

"John, I can't take any more. If Willy's 'goons' aren't trying to blow me up your darn bear is trying to have me for lunch. Make it stop John. Please make it stop. I just can't take it anymore." And she began to sob bitterly.

John put his arms around her and just held her. It took him fifteen minutes to calm her down. He reassured her that he would not let anything happen to her. He took her over to a recliner, sat her in it and put up the footrest.

He said, "Set there and rest while I fix you something to drink. What would you like to drink something hot or cold?"

"Something hot…your hot chocolate would be good." She replied.

"Hot chocolate it is. Give me just a few minutes."

He served her a steaming hot cup of chocolate and sat down in front of her with a cup of his own. Sarah just sat there with her head down staring at the cup of hot chocolate. When she finally looked up at John her face was stained with tears. John reaches over and gently rubbed the top of her foot.

He told her, "Sarah, we are going to get through all of this and there will be better days."

"When John? When will it get better?" She sobbed.

"As soon as the county road crews get the road cleared, we are going to go in and spend a few days with Jenny and Don. Maybe go out for that dinner and dance that we talked about." While he was talking to her John got up and got a blanket and covered her up to her waist in the chair. He suggested that she set there and rest while he went out to shut and lock the cage and put wood in the stove. He said he wanted to get everything secure before it got dark.

A week went by and the county road crew had not cleared the road. John was not ready to subject Sarah to another ride on the snowmobile so they waited.

CHAPTER SIXTEEN

THE PRISON BREAK

Sarah and John passed the time for the next two weeks watching movies, talking very little and reading books. John had convinced Sarah to start reading the Bible. They did spend a good deal of time discussing the Bible. She had never read the Bible and had all types of questions which John was happy to help her with.

On Thursday morning the day, John had set as laundry day they were stripping the beds when Sarah asks John if she could ask him a personal question.

He said, "Sure ask away."

She asks, "Does a homosexual man ever have feelings for a woman?"

John was stunned by the question. He stopped what he was doing and just stood still for a few seconds. He then turned toward her and asks, "Why are you asking me that?"

"Aren't you homosexual?"

"Good Lord no", He stated. "What made you think that?"

"Well, we have lived in this cabin for three months. You have measured every inch of me for the coat and you have not even tried to… to even kiss me." She replied. "Don't' you think I am attractive?"

John responded, "Sarah, I was married to the same beautiful woman for thirty-five years, and yes I think you are very attractive. As a matter of fact, I think you are 'drop dead' gorgeous."

Sarah ran and pushed John down on the bed, landing on top of him. She said, "You mean you are a normal man and we have lived in this cabin together for three months and we could have…" She paused and said, "You know."

John gently rolled her off of him and while they lay facing each other John told her, "Beautiful lady, I am very attracted to you. In fact, I have been in love with you from the first time I saw you. But, I am twenty years older than you and it would not be fair to you. And, I do not believe in sharing a bed with a woman unless I am married to her. So, if you want to 'you know', as you but it, we will have to get married.

Their conversation was interrupted by a phone call from Art. He called to inform John that Carl Pritts had escaped from prison and Art was concerned that he was on his way to get Sarah.

"How could he know about Sarah being here?" John asks.

"Come on John." Art said. "Willy knew, I knew. Do you think it so hard that Carl would know as well?"

"We will discuss the details later. What do you suggest we do right now?" John added.

Art told John he was going to place guards around the cabin until Carl was caught.

"Art, the man is a killer. Do you think your men are up to the challenge?" John asks.

"The two men I am sending are young, but they are good agents. Carl is an artist at dismantling security systems and getting past locks so watch out for him."

"How many men are with him and when do you expect him to get here?"

Art replied, "I don't know how many men he has, and we think he is here now. My men will be there in fifteen minutes."

John stopped everything he and Sarah were doing and he started running a check on his security system. Everything checked out for the time being. But, John was not comfortable with the situation so he kept scanning with all the cameras for the next two hours. He picked up the two guards Art had sent out to guard the cabin. This concerned John. If these two could not hide from John's cameras, how could they hide from someone as skilled as Carl?

While John was checking his cameras one of them quit working; then a second one quit; then a third. He immediately called Art.

"Art, Carl is here. He is shutting down my security system." John told him.

Art immediately told John to go to their secure phone system. John switched phones and grabbed Sarah. He put a coat on her, put her inside the cave and told her not to come out until she heard his voice. After turning off all the lights, he grabbed a rifle, a night scope, and his Desert Eagle. He went outside to a place where he could hide but still see the cabin. From there he could watch the cabin and see anyone that tried to approach the cabin. From the hiding place, John scanned the woods for any sign of movement. He spotted the two men Art had sent to guard the cabin they were both face down in the snow. He also spotted two other men crossing the creek and moving toward the cabin. Just then he heard Art's helicopter approaching so did the two men. One of them ran back to where they had hidden something. John watched as the man took out a shoulder held rocket launcher. It was obvious what his intentions were and John had to stop him from shooting Art's plane down.

John sat his rifle on the tripod and took careful aim. He could see through the night scope that the man had on body armor so John took aim at the man's hip. He knew that if he could hit the man in the hip his rifle was powerful enough to put the man out of commission to where he would be unable to fire the rocket launcher; it worked. The man was rolling on the ground in obvious pain. The other man tried to run but John got him in the leg also. Just then Art landed the helicopter just across the creek from the cabin. John called Art and told him what had happened and that two of them were on the ground just across the creek. Art sent agents to check on his men and to get the two escaped convicts. The two men were Carl Pritts and one of the men that had escaped with him. Both of Art's guards were dead, their throats had been cut.

While they were securing the scene, and getting the convicts ready to transport, Art ask, "Where is the third man?"

John asks, "What third man?"

Art said, "According to our Intel, there were three men headed out here. Where is the third man?"

Before John could answer, there was a blood-curdling scream that came from the cabin area; then a loud rower. John looked at Art and then turned to Carl and said, "I guess you missed that part of my security system. It is called a twelve-hundred-pound Grizzly. And right now, your friend is in a lot of trouble if he is still alive."

This made Carl extremely angry: he struck one of the FBI agents and took his service weapon. Just as he turned to fire the weapon, John discharged his Desert Eagle, striking Carl in the right shoulder. The force of the round from John's gun was just enough to cause him to miss his target. He missed John but just barely nicked Art's shoulder. John was not taking any chance that Carl would try to fire again so he shot him in the other hip. That took the fight out of him. The agents quickly cuffed him so he was no more threat, and came to help Art.

Art turned to John and said, "John you need to check on the third man and see if there is anything left to take back with us."

When John got to the cabin, He broke out laughing.

Art hollered to John, "What is so funny?"

John hollered back. "Art, you have got to see this. Brutus has the man lying on the ground and he is just sitting beside him. Every time the man tries to move, Brutus bounces on him with his front paws until he is no longer trying to move. It is hilarious Art."

Art and all the agents laughed. One of them said he would like to see that but not enough to get around a Grizzly in the night.

Art hollered back to John, "Can you get the man to us or do you need help?"

John called back and said, "I think I have plenty of help. Brutus will hold him while I cuff him. Then I will point him in the right direction and let Brutus run him to you."

"John, please keep the bear at the cabin," Art pleaded.

John instructed Brutus to roll the man over and Brutus took his paw and rolled the man onto his stomach. He then instructed Brutus to hold the man down. Brutus put his right paw on the man's head and smashed the man's face into the snow. Needless to say, the man did not resist when John pulled his hands behind him to cuff them. When he got the cuffs on him, John instructed Brutus to let him up. John helped the man to his feet and pointed to the lights where Art and the rest of the FBI agents were, and told him to go to them.

John said, "You have one chance and only one chance to get there without doing something stupid. If you mess up in the least; your fault, my fault, or nobody's fault, I am going to turn this bear loose on you and he will take your head off. Do you understand?"

The man in a panic said, "Yes, yes I understand mister. I won't cause any trouble. Please just keep that bear away from me. Please! Can I go now?"

John said, "Get."

When the man was about half way down the hill to the creek, John just could not resist; He told Brutus to growl. Brutus stood on his hind feet and let out a rower that shook the woods. The man dove into the creek face first and came up screaming for help. The FBI men were laughing so hard they couldn't get to him until he had thrashed himself against rocks in the creek and had run into two trees. This man was so glad when the FBI took him into custody.

John called Art on their phone and asks if he could handle things. Art said he could and John went in to check on Sarah. John turned lights on in the cabin and opened the door to the cave. In his haste to get outside, John had not turned on a light in the cave for Sarah. She had been in the cold, totally dark cave for almost two hours. She was sitting on the floor with her arms around her knees and her face buried in them. She sat there sobbing; so distraught that she did not move when John spoke to her. John reached down and picked her up in his arms. As he came out of the cave he kicked the door to the cave closed with his foot and took Sarah to the recliner. He sat down with her in his lap. He put the foot rest up and covered them up with a blanket. She sobbed and sobbed until she finally went to sleep. John held her in his arms the rest of the night.

CHAPTER SEVENTEEN

JOHN AND SARAH TRY TO MAKE A NEW START

For the next three days, Sarah was like a Zombie. She went through the motions of life but she said very little. On the third day as John was fixing supper Sarah sat on a bar stool across from where John was cooking.

Sarah said, "John before all this mess occurred with Carl, You and I were talking about going to Fairbanks. Can we still go?"

He replied, "Yes we can if you feel like doing that. I believe the roads are finally cleared enough that we can get out."

"John, was I dreaming or did you ask me to marry you?" She asks.

"I told you that I was twenty years older than you and that it would not be fair to you to ask you to marry me because of that. But if you don't mind the age difference, then yes. I did ask you to be my wife." John replied.

"I guess you want me to sign one of those marriage 'thingies', don't you?" She asks.

"I think you should. Don't you think so?" He stated.

I don't mind signing the thing and I do not care how old you are. You are the only man who has ever tried to take care of me. And. I am tired and afraid. I do not want to be alone ever again. So, when can we do this?" She asks.

John replied, "Let us get a good night sleep tonight and tomorrow we will pack our bags and go to town. We will get all the paperwork in order, get married, go dancing and go on a honeymoon. How does that sound?"

For the first time in a week, Sarah smiled. Her beautiful dimples just blossomed. She said, "It sounds wonderful."

John reached over, took her hand, kissed it on the top and said. "My lady let's eat."

That night when they were ready for bed Sarah ask, "John I know you won't share the bed with me until we are married, but will you stay in the room with me tonight? I haven't slept for two nights. I am just so afraid."

He told her to get ready for bed and when she got into bed he laid down beside of her and put his arm around her. She picked up his hand and kissed the back of it and said, "Thank you, John." And she went to sleep.

That night John did not sleep. He was so concerned about Sarah that he just laid there beside her and watched her sleep. For the first time since the loss of Leigh John thought that maybe there was hope for happiness again in his life. He was so hopeful that they could have a good life together. John knew he had to close the two cases he was working on and clear Sarah of any involvement in them for that to happen.

The next morning John was hurrying through all his chores so he could get packed for their plan to go to town and start their life together. Sarah, on the other hand, seemed very distracted. She would pack a piece of luggage and unpack it. She did this three times. John noticed but thought that she was just excited like he was. When they were finally ready to go, John took their luggage and put it in the truck and they were off to get married.

The road was not completely cleared. There were places where the snow had drifted and John would have to run through the drifts. One time he hit a drift that threw so much snow on the windshield that John could not see the road. He slammed on the breaks and slid to a stop just before they went over a cliff. John just sat there for a while to let them both regain their composure. Then he slowly backed up the truck to get it back in the road. The rest of the trip was very quiet neither of them spoke a word.

By the time they got to Fairbanks, the roads were almost clear. There were about two inches of packed snow on the roads, but it was a good surface to drive on and they made it to town without further incidence.

By noon they had gotten a prenuptial agreement written, and signed. They had their marriage license and found a judge to marry them. All through the morning, Sarah did not have much to say. John knew she had been through a lot so he didn't think much about her silence. He took her to the best restraint in town and they were seated at a table with a beautiful view of a snow-covered mountain.

They ordered their meal and had started planning the activities of their honeymoon when they were interrupted by a man in a very expensive suit. He introduced himself as Tom Cane, Vice President of Jackson Mining Co. He told John he knew who he was and that he was interested in buying his goldmine.

He said, "We are prepared to offer you a million dollars for your mine."

John replied, "Mister Cane, we were just married and I am not interested in talking about business of any kind. So, would you please leave us alone?"

The man was persistent in talking about the mine and it angered John. John stood up and demanded that the man leave. Sarah excused herself and went to the lady's room. The man gave John a business card and asks him to call when he was ready to talk. He excused himself and left.

John sat there thinking about the man's offer and wondering where Sarah was. Just when he started to go looking for her, he saw her coming back to the table. He got up and pulled her chair out and asks if everything was ok. She sat down, but never answered John. The waitress brought their food and just as John was about to start eating:

Sarah said, "John please don't be angry with me, But I can't go through with this."

"Can't go through with what?" He asks.

"I can't go through with this marriage." She replied. "John, I just don't know you. Just about time, I think I know you something new comes up. Like this man wanting to buy your gold mine. It is just too confusing. There is just so much that I don't know about you."

"I lived fifty-five years before I met you, Sarah. Sure, there are things about me, but I do not have anything to hide. If you have questions, just ask. I will tell you what you want to know." He replied.

She said, "John, I need time to think. Please don't be mad."

Sarah had done or said things that hurt John before but nothing like this did. This was so hurtful that he just sat eating in total silence. He could not finish his meal.

Sarah said, "John say something. Please try to understand. The last thing I want is to hurt or disappoint you, but I just need time to think. Please try to understand."

John said, "Sarah, finish your meal."

"I am not hungry." She said

"Are you ready to leave?" He asks.

"Yes. Where are we going?" She asks.

John did not answer her. He paid the bill and they got in the truck. He drove to a local bank and set up a bank account with ten thousand dollars in his and Sarah's name John and Sarah Henson. He then drove to a suburb where there were some nice efficiency apartments and rented one in their names.

Sarah asks, "John, are you going to tell me what you are doing?"

"I am going to give you some time to think. The apartment is paid for, for a month. There are ten thousand dollars in a joint bank account. Here are some counter checks and some cash. The cash should take care of your needs until the new checks come in. And here is a cell phone with my number programmed in it." He replied.

"What are you going to do?" She asks.

"I am going back to the cabin and take care of some unfinished business." He replied.

She asks, "Can I call you if I need to talk?"

"You need to take this time to relax and sort out your feelings. Calling me is not going to help you do that. If you have an emergency, call and I will do all I can to help. I hope you know that." He told her.

She said, "Well, I guess this is it." And she kissed John. "You are a very good kisser, John Henson."

"How would you know?" He asks.

"I just kissed you." She said.

"That was not a kiss." He put his arms around her and gently pulled her to him. He gently but passionately gave her a kiss that lasted for fifteen seconds. When he turned her loose she took a deep breath and sided.

"John that is not fair. You kiss me like that and now you are going leave."

"Sort it out, Sarah. When I come back I want you to be ready to give me a definite answer. Whether it is yes or whether it is no, I want you to be absolutely sure of your answer. I love you kid." And he turned, got into his truck and left.

Sarah stood and watched him drive away. She was never more confused than at that moment. What had she done? Had she run off the only human being that had ever cared for her? Just before John got into his truck, he turned and looked at Sarah and tried to force a smile. It felt like someone had stabbed her right in the heart. She knew she had hurt this beautiful man, the only one that had ever been good to her. And, now he was leaving. All she could do was stand there with tears running down her cheeks.

"What was I thinking? How could I have ever done this? Will he ever come back? Will he ever forgive me?" She just stood there weeping. "I just hurt so badly." She went into apartment and sat down and wept.

John drove away broken hearted. The hope for a future that was so strong the night before seemed to be shattered. He was alone again and all the hurt he had known after the loss of Leigh was back. He did not have any idea what Sarah's answer would be when he returned he feared the worst. As he drove, he was half heartily praying and asking God why? The answer he kept getting was 'All things work together for good… It just did not help.

He thought, "I can't think of Sarah now. I have to concentrate my time to solve the two cases I am working on. I cannot think of her now."

CHAPTER EIGHTEEN

THE GOLD MINE SAGA

In the confusion of trying to help Sarah, John had left his coat at the restaurant and was headed back to get it. When he got to the restaurant, he was met by Tom Cane from Jackson Mining.

He greeted John, "Mr. Henson when you are ready to talk, give me a call."

John was already aggravated and Mr. Cane's present did not help the situation. John turned toward Mr. Cane and snapped, "Mr. Cane, until you are ready to pay me one hundred million dollars after taxes for my mine, leave me alone."

"A hundred million is not much for a good mine. Show us what you have got." He replied.

"It is a hundred million after taxes." John snapped.

"Show us what you have," Tom said.

John stood staring Tom 'eye to eye' for about fifteen seconds without saying a word. Then he said, "If you want to see the mine, be here in the morning at eight AM."

Tom said, "I will see you at eight AM."

The two men parted company and John set out for his cabin.

The next morning, John met Tom at the restaurant. He told Tom to follow him into the restroom. In there, he handed Tom a bag and told Tom to strip.

83

He said, "Take off everything you have on and put the clothes and belongings into the bag."

"What is this all about?" Tom asks.

"You are not getting anywhere near my mine with any type of GPS device," John replied.

"I don't have any GPS devices with me." Tom protested.

"You either do it my way or we do not go. What is it going to be?" John asks.

"Ok. What do you want me to do?" Tom asks.

"Take off everything you have on. And I mean everything, from your watch down to your socks. Here is a new pair of coveralls, boots, coat, hat, and gloves. Anything else that you need will be provided for you when we get there. You can put your belongings in one of the lockers here in the bathroom." John instructed him.

After Tom had changed his attire to John's satisfaction, they got into John's truck and headed for the cabin. When they went through Purgatory, John handed Tom a hood and told him to but it on and not to remove it until he was told to. To do so would terminate the visit to the mine.

When they got to the Cabin John opened the cage and drove in. He locked the cage behind them and they went in the cabin. All the way, John watched Tom very carefully to make sure he did not remove the hood or sneak a peek at their surroundings. John led Tom through the cabin and into the cave still under the hood. Fifty yards into the cave, John told Tom he could remove the hood. He stood for a few seconds until he got used to the light in the cave. He turned to John and said, "I need some tools to take…"

John interrupted him by handing him a canvas bag with a head light, magnifying glass, chip hammer, camera, writing tablet with pen, and sample bag.

He said, "I think you will find everything you need in the bag."

Tom put the light on his head and began to inspect the gold in the mine walls. For two and a half hours he chipped rocks from the walls, took pictures, and all sort of measurements.

He asks John, "How far does the cave go back into the mountain?"

John told him he had been about four hundred yards into the cave, but he had not found the end of it. At three hundred yards, it split into three corridors and he had not examined all of them yet.

"Are there any other entrances to the cave?" Tom asks.

"There has to be more because there is fresh air in the cave, but I have not found them yet," John replied.

"Well, I have seen enough," Tom stated. "I will need to take these samples with me for analyses."

"I expected you would," John replied. "We will weigh them on the way out and you can give me a receipt for whatever they weigh."

When the two finished their business in the cave, they reversed the procedures and headed back to town. When they got to Purgatory, John told Tom he could remove his hood. John let Tom talk and ask questions as they drove to Fairbanks. When they finished their meeting, Tom told John he liked what he had seen and that he would like to talk to John in a couple days.

John said' "I will meet you here in two days. But, if you are thinking of trying to get me to lower my price of a hundred million after taxes it will not happen. I will see you in two days, and you are buying lunch."

Tom said, "Sounds fair to me. I will see you in two days."

Two days later John and Tom met and settled on the conditions of sale of John's gold mine, the time John had to vacate the premises and the security of John's Pet Brutus. Brutus was not to be harmed in any manner. John agreed that he would come and get Brutus if he was spotted around the cabin after John moved out.

CHAPTER NINETEEN

A NEW PLACE TO LIVE

P art of their agreement allowed John to move the cabin to a new section of land John had homesteaded. The new section of land joined and overlooked a large lake that was part of a game reserve. John immediately engaged contractors to prepare the site and the precast yard to move the cabin and build a two-story precast lodge. The old cabin would be used for storage and temporary living space until the lodge was complete. The bottom floor of the lodge would have three sides underground with the front facing the lake. The top floor of the lodge would have a living room/meeting room that had a glass wall all across the front that overlooked the lake. There would be two full baths upstairs and downstairs; large spacious bed rooms; a library and a room dedicated for a study/computer room for John. Outside, the back would have a large yard surrounded on one side with the old cabin made into garages. The opposite side of the yard would be a wall of precast panels. The third wall where the entrance to the lodge is would be made of twelve feet high steel bars. It would have double sliding gates that were electronically controlled. John had purposely designed the courtyard large enough that a helicopter could land in it. Everything was in motion. The contractors were working hard and everything was ahead of schedule.

John had made several trips back to the old cabin site to check of Brutus. He had picked Brutus up twice and brought him to the new lodge site. Brutus quickly learned that the new lodge was the place to be with John and he and John watched the construction together. Brutus' presence was very unsettling to the workers, but John keep them separated and all went well. Brutus explored the new location and soon made it his territory.

CHAPTER TWENTY

TIME TO CLOSE THE CHAPTER ON "SLICK WILLY"

It was the middle of the summer and the new construction was going well when John's thoughts turned to Sarah. He thought it time to go and check on her and get her answer. One way or another he had to know and close this chapter in his life. Brutus was spending more time in his new territory So John felt he would be ok. John loaded his truck and headed for Fairbanks. He made it to Jenny's for dinner and was eating with them when he got a call from Sarah.

All she said was "Help me. John, they are after me again." The phone went silent. John ran to his truck and sped across town to the apartment where Sarah was staying. He got there just in time to see two men dragging Sarah, bound and gagged, out of her apartment to a waiting van. John took a club from under the seat of his truck and ran to the men, striking the one in front of Sarah and knocking him unconscious. The second man dropped Sarah and attacked John with a knife. When he tried to stab John, John struck him with his club. The man staggered and fell on his knife. The knife penetrated his heart and killed him.

John checked him and when he knew he was dead, he went to the first man who was waking up and proceeded to tie him up. When he had him bound tightly, he dragged him to the truck and put him in the bed of the truck. He then went to Sarah and loosed her from her ropes. He gently removed the 'duct tape' from her mouth. Neither of them spoke. Sarah just sat on the ground with her head down sobbing. John picked her up and placed her in the passenger seat of his truck and got in the driver side.

As they were driving, John called Art to tell him what had happened. He told Art where the man was that was dead and that he had the other one with him. When Art ask John where he was taking the second man John told him to meet him at the county dump north of town and hung the phone up. By the time, Art caught up with John, John had staked the man to the ground at the edge of the dump where bears were known to visit. The man was pleading with John to let him go. He told John he was terrified of bears and begged John to just shoot him. John got out his duct tape and was going to tape his mouth shut when he told John he had information that would make him a lot of money. He had information about Slick Willy that would bring a big reward and if John would let him go John could keep the reward.

John asks, "What information could you have that would be of any interest to me?"

He said, "Let me go and I will tell you."

John in a very rough manner put the duct tape over the man's mouth and started to leave.

The man started screaming as loud as he could with tape over his mouth, "I'll tell you! I'll tell you!

John ripped the tape off his mouth and said, "Start talking and it better be good because you are not getting another chance."

The man started talking as fast as he could. "Willy has an arms shipping coming into the port in Anchorage in three days. It is coming in on a cargo ship in container number 1326. The boxes in the container are marked 'ham' but the boxes are double lined. Between the inner and outer lining is a space of three inches. The space is filled with AK47 rifles and ammo. Keep the reward, but please let me go."

About that time, Art drove up. He got out of his car and looked at the man staked out on the ground and asks, "What are you doing now, John?"

"I am just fixing lunch for the Polar Bears," John replied.

Art said, "John you cannot do suspects that way. Now let him up."

John went over and put the tape back on the man's mouth and told him, "If you make a sound I will get the bears myself."

"John, you need to let him up." Art protested.

"He is all right. We need to talk about what we are going to do about the ocean container that Willy Jack is bringing in with guns in it. Just confiscating the container will get the guns, but unless we can tie Willy to the container we will not get him." John told Art.

"What is your plan?" Ask Art.

"I am going to re-route the container to Sumbawa to feed the hungry in the famine. We will send a telegram to Willy saying. "Your shipment was mistakenly loaded with ham. Everybody knows that you do not send 'ham' to a Muslim country so we know it had to be a mistake. We have re-routed this container and will check to see what has happened to your shipment. Please accept our apologies for this mistake."

"When Willy tries to calm the container, we will have him," John explained.

"Your idea is just crazy enough to work." Art said. "But let me handle it."

"Art, you must not let this man get a message to Willy. If you do, he will warn Willy and he will get away. Before you say anything about his rights, He is involved in selling guns to the terrorist so that makes him a terrorist. Treat him like one. Hide him for the next three or four days to keep him from talking with Willy. The ball is in your court, Art."

"John, I will take care of everything. Now, are you going to let that man up?" Art asks.

John went over to where the man was staked to the ground and put a handcuff on his right wrist and cut that wrist loose. He then stepped over the man and jerked the man's arm so hard that it flipped the man to his stomach.

When the man tried to protest, John said, "Shut up! I really wanted to kill you for putting your filthy hands on my wife. If you ever touch her again, I will feed you to the bears." John pulled the man's hands behind him and cuffed them together. He cut the man's feet loose from the stake, but they were still tied together. John picked the man up to his feet and dragged him, hopping to where Art was standing.

"He is all yours," John stated.

John left Art to deal with the situation and turned his attention to Sarah. When he got into the truck Sarah was just sitting with her hands in her lap and her head down staring at the floor. When he tried to talk to her she did not respond. He asks her if she would like to stop somewhere and get something to eat or drink. She just shook her head no. After driving in complete silence John pulled into a parking lot of a store that had closed for the evening and stopped the truck. He reached over and put his arms around Sarah and she began to sob.

To say that Sarah had been subjected to very stressful experiences was a gross understatement. She had been tortured for the last six months by Willy and his gang. If Art did not get him this time, John did not know what he was going to do. As he held Sarah in his arms and felt her trembling as she sobbed and sobbed he made up his mind he was going to put a stop to the torture. One way or another he was going to stop Willy if he had to use his rifle on him. He really wanted to take him out to the lodge and introduce him to Brutus. If Brutus slapped him around and bounce on him maybe that would make him leave Sarah alone. At least he would know how much he was terrifying Sarah. His train of thought was interrupted when Sarah ask John if he would take her home.

"You want to go back to the apartment?" He asks.

"Please don't say that John. That is not my home. If I don't have a home with you, I don't have a home. You ask me to make a decision about us when you left. When I saw the hurt in your eyes as you turned and looked at me just before you got in the truck and drove away, I knew the answer. I was such an awful fool. I don't know what I was thinking. I thought I had lost you forever. I was afraid you would never come back. My answer John is if you will still have me…" She began to sob. "I love you so much and I will be the best wife if you will give me a chance."

John gently pulled her tear-stained face to him and kissed her and said, "Well then, it is settled. Meet Mr. and Mrs. John Henson. Let's go get your stuff and we will find a room for the night and get some rest. Tomorrow we will start over."

As he held his new wife in his arms he began to thank God for Sarah and ask God to bless their lives together and let them be a blessing to others.

Four days later Art called John and told him that his plan had worked. When Willy Jack got the fax that his cargo container had been re-routed, he stormed into the shipping office at the shipyard and demanded to see the dispatcher who had re-routed his shipment. When he was asked to identify the shipment as it appeared on the manifest and he was asked to sign the manifest, he signed it, threw it in the dispatcher's face and demanded that his shipment is brought back immediately. The dispatcher, an undercover FBI agent, looked at the signed papers and called in his backup officers and arrested Slick Willy for trafficking in illegal firearms.

Art said, "Good job John. Now you are officially retired from the FBI."

John asks, "What About the bank robbery job?"

"The boss does not want you involved with that job.

His exact words were, "Tell John to stay away from the L.A. case. If I hear of him dabbling around in it, I will throw him in jail. John, he is very serious about you leaving that case alone. Do you understand John?" Art asks.

"Art, I am going to do what I have to do to clear Sarah from that mess whether your boss likes it or not. But you don't have to worry; I will not do anything illegal." John replied.

Art warned John again, to stay away from the L.A. case and told him that the FBI needed to talk to Sarah.

John said, "Art that is not going to happen. She has been through enough trauma and you are not going to traumatize her further by putting her through an FBI interrogation. If you insist and try to force her, I will have her lawyer up and anything she may know will be lost to the FBI forever. If you will leave us alone, I will pass any information I learn on to you. Art, we have been friends up till now and I would like for it to stay that way, but if you insist on harassing Sarah we will not be. I will drop my gun and badge off at the office tomorrow."

CHAPTER TWENTY-ONE

THE HONEYMOON

John and Sarah got up the next morning after he had rescued her from the latest attackers and went to have breakfast with Don and Jenny. John was very pleased to tell Don and Jenny that he and Sarah were officially man and wife.

Jenny looked at Sarah and said, "I am glad to hear you made the right decision."

John asks, "What is that all about?"

Sarah told John, "I came over here and told Jenny what I had done about telling you I needed time to think and she ripped me apart. She really let me know what an idiot I was. And she was right. And, Yes Jenny I made the right decision. Thank God he took me back."

John said, "Enough of that kind of talk. Let's talk about a honeymoon. Where would you like to go?"

Sarah said, "I don't know. Where do you want to take me?"

John answered, "I would like to take you to the moon and back, but I suppose that is out of the question so why don't we start with a site seeing train ride and think about it. There is an excursion train that runs from White Horse, Yukon to Skagway Alaska. It takes two days each way and runs through some of the most beautiful country in the world. How do you like that idea?"

Sarah replied, "That would be lots of fun. Can we take pictures?"

John handed her a small, but a very nice pocket camera and said, "I thought you would like to do that."

When she took the camera, Sarah gasped and said, "John, this must have cost a fortune."

"My love, the look you have on your face right now makes it worth ten times what I paid for it," John told her.

"You will have to show me how to use it." She told him.

"It will be my great pleasure." He replied.

John and Sarah packed their clothes and headed for the first leg of their honeymoon. By this time in their relation, John was very much in love with Sarah and wasted no time in showing his affection to her. When she came into the room where he was he would reach out to take her hand. If he walked in the room where she was he would walk to where she was and put his arm around her. This seemed to disturb Sarah. Once when she was on the observation deck of the train, John walked up behind her and put his arm around her and she pulled away from him. This disturbed John. He knew that she had never had anyone that had loved her or shown her any type of affection. Her birth father had been killed in a drug deal that had gone wrong and her mother was a drug addict. As a child, she had to fend for herself and love was not to be had. She married young to get out of the horrible home she was living in. The man she married was a self-centered selfish person who did what pleased him. Many times, this included beating Sarah. John knew he needed to give her time to adjust to his gestures of kindness and love.

It was after the train ride that John got the word that the FBI had arrested Slick Willy and John was no more part of the FBI. John considered this a blessing because now he could concentrate on getting his new life off to a good start. He could concentrate on teaching Sarah to accept being loved and appreciated.

After the train ride, they went back to Don and Jenny's place and spent two days. John left Sarah with Jenny while he went to check on the construction of the new lodge. While he was gone, Sarah began to tell Jenny about the train ride and share the pictures she had taken. Sarah began to tell Jenny how John was always touching her, taking her hand, and putting his arm around her.

She said, "Jenny he is smothering me and I don't know what to do about it."

Jenny looked at Sarah with a blank stare and said nothing. After about two minutes she got up and got another cup of coffee. When she sat down she 'unloaded' on Sarah, "God help you girl. He is just trying to tell you and show you just how much he loves and appreciates you. If you screw this marriage up I am going to wring your neck. If he reaches out to take your hand, give him both of them. If he wants to hold you hug him back. If he puts his arms around you melt in his arms. This man is the very best thing that has ever happened to you. Don't you love him?"

Sarah put her face in her hands and began to weep. Jenny reached out and took Sarah in her arms.

"Sarah honey, I know you have never had anyone to love you and I suspect you don't know how to love anyone either. But, having a man like John to love you like he does is the greatest thing you will ever experience. You have a very good, loving man that will show you the happiness you can't even dream of if you will just let him. Honey, when he reaches out to you accept it and embrace it. It is just his way of saying Sarah, you are the most important thing in my life and I cherish every second I get to spend with you."

"Jenny, you are right, he is the best thing that has happened to me and I am so afraid I will mess it up. Please help me."

"You are not going to mess it up if you just let him love you and remember to always love him in return. When he comes near you reach out and take his hand…"

Before she could finish, Sarah said, "Jenny if I do that I will break down and start crying and he will think I am stupid."

"No, he will not think you are stupid. He will think you are finally tearing down the wall of fear that is keeping his love out of your life. He will take you in his arms and comfort you and he will thank you for letting him in. He is willing, but you must let love happen. Do you understand? Now let's talk about where you are going to go next on your honeymoon."

"Well, I have always wanted to go to the Niagara Falls but I don't know if he wants to go there."

"Good grief girl, he has asked you a hundred times where you want to go. Just tell him. He wants –more than anything–just to please you. So, tell him where you want to go."

It was getting toward dinner and John walked in the door.

Sarah turned toward John and asks, "Can we go to Niagara Falls?"

"Absolutely!" John replied.

"See how easy that was," Jenny said to Sarah.

The next day John started making preparations for their trip to Niagara Falls. Three days later they had obtained a passport for Sarah and they were on their way. At the falls is a lookout tower that stands over seven hundred feet tall. John bought tickets to go up to the lookout tower. Sarah did not tell John that she was afraid of heights. When she got on the elevator to go up in the tower she went to the back of the room in the elevator. What she did not know was that the elevator was a glass elevator and twenty feet up the tower the elevator rose above the tub at the base of the tower and the wall Sarah was standing against was a glass wall looking over the falls. She was so terrified she would not open her eyes. When the operator of the elevator saw, she was not opening her eyes, he stopped the elevator at three hundred feet and announced that the elevator was not moving until everyone had taken a good look and had taken pictures if they wanted to. Sarah just stood there.

John trying not to laugh whispered to her, "Honey if you don't take a look we will be here all day."

"I can't, John. I just can't. I am afraid of heights."

"I have got you. Just turn around and take a quick peak so the man can get the rest of these people to the top."

While she faced John, and clutched his jacket in her fist she demanded that John holds her tight.

He said, "I have got you and you are ok now take a look." She turned her head to the right and opened her eyes for just a second.

As she buried her face in John's chest she said, "I looked! Now can we go?"

John motioned for the man to go on to the top of the tower. At the top were several souvenir shops and a restaurant. Sarah was occupied with the souvenirs and picked up a pin that had a girl in the handle. She turned to John and said, "This is cute."

John told her to turn it upside down. When she did the girl's clothes came off and she was naked. She threw the pen back in the display box and protested, "That is horrible. Why did you let me do that? Why didn't you tell me that was going to happen?"

"I could have let you buy it and take it home and show it to everyone and then tell you," John said.

"John, you are horrible. You knew that was going to happen and you let me turn that pen upside down anyway."

About that time, Sarah staggered and John caught her.

She said, "John this thing is moving!"

John said, "of course it is moving. Any tall structure like this tower sways in the wind. If it doesn't sway it will collapse."

"I don't like this. Please take me down. She pleaded.

John said, There is a great restaurant up here. Are you sure you don't want to stay and have lunch?"

"John, please don't tease me. I am so scared I am shaking. Please take me down." The tower swayed; Sarah staggered; John caught her and Sarah squealed, "Please take me down."

One good thing came out of the tower experience: Sarah did not mind it that John held onto her while she was on the tower. In fact, she demanded that he do so.

The rest of the Niagara Trip was very enjoyable for both of them. John took her to a real nice restaurant that overlooked the 'Falls'. They had a seat next to the window where she could eat and watch the Horse Shoe Falls at the same time. They took the 'Maid of The Mist' boat ride and saw all the displays that were related to the Niagara Falls.

After a week at the Niagara Falls, they returned to Fairbanks and Jenny's place. It was obvious that Sarah and John had a good time. John was happy because Sarah had a good time. Jenny described Sarah as 'glowing and giggly'. Her happiness just bubbled over and she could not wait to tell Jenny all about the trip. After two hours Sarah finally ran out of stories to tell and she ended her presentation by saying, "Wonderful, wonderful, wonderful. I have never been so happy."

Jenny asks her, "Is the honeymoon over or are you going to go somewhere else?"

"No, it is not over. John said we are going to go somewhere but, it is a secret and he has not told me yet. I am so excited I am about to burst and he will not even give me a hint."

They stayed at Jenny's for two days and left for the last part of the honeymoon the third day. On their way to Anchorage Sarah squirmed, tapped her fingernails on the seat arm and continued to quiz John about where they were going. He would just laugh and tell her it was a surprise.

She finally asks, "How do I know if I have the right clothes packed if I don't know where I am going?"

John laughs and said, "If you don't have what you need I suppose we will have to go shopping. But, it is a secret. You are going to have to wait."

When they arrived at the waterfront there was a huge ship with a sign that said, Hawaiian Crouse.

Sarah looked at the ship sign and gasped, "John I told you this would happen. I don't have a thing to wear to Hawaii. I don't even have a swimsuit."

John cocked his head slightly to the right and said, "Pretty lady it is two and a half hours before we have to board the ship and I am sure we can find a shopping mall where you can find the proper attire for the trip."

"I guess you want me to get a bikini, don't you?" She asks. "Absolutely not!" He replied. "That will expose too much of you. I do not want anyone to see that much of you but me."

"Well, I could get a one-piece suit with legs that go on my knees, long sleeves and blouse drawers. Would that suit you better?"

"You keep messing with me, girl, and I will buy you a suit made of paper. And, the first time you get wet you will be standing there with nothing on but your imagination." He told her. Of course, he was kidding and Sarah knew it.

She said, "You are a horrible old man and I love you." And she kissed him on the cheek.

John remaindered her that they were going to be on the ship and the islands of Hawaii for two weeks and that anything she bought she would have to carry so be wise with her purchases. That was never a problem with Sarah. Getting her to buy the things she needed was a problem for John. Sarah had been deprived of the things she needed all her life. Getting her to purchase something she wanted never happened. Even though John had assured her that they had plenty of money she would not buy anything without asking him first. One day on the cruise they were going to attend a semi-formal dinner and she needed an evening dress. At the boutique, she would look at the price even before she would look at the size. When they found a light blue dress that John really liked he took out his pocket knife and cut off the tag and put it in his pocket.

"Try this one on." He pleaded.

"John." She said, "Have you looked at the prices of this dress? The cheapest one I have seen is over three hundred dollars. We can't afford that can we?"

"Sarah my precious lady, if you are half as beautiful in this dress as I think you will be, we are going to buy it if it cost ten thousand dollars."

She said, "But John..."

Before she could finish her protest, John gently put his index finger on her lips and declared, "My precious wife, no 'buts'. Tonight, you are going to feel like and look like what I know you to be; the most gorges woman in the world. Now please try the dress on if you like it." He pleaded again.

When she came out of the dressing room she said, "John I can't get the top hook to fasten. Can you help me?" She turned her back to John and used her right hand to pick her hair off her neck. John took hold of the two clips on the dress to fasten them but, before he did he bent down and kissed her on the back of her neck.

She gasped and squealed, "John." She turned around facing him and said, "What are you doing?"

He chuckled and said, "You just look so luscious I just could not help myself. Come here and let me hook that thing."

She said, "No." And she began to laugh. "You nut. I don't trust you. I never know what you are going to do. You are so crazy and I love you so much." She put her hands in back of her neck in an attempt to close the latch when John put his arms around her and pulled her to him and took the latch out of her hands.

She protested, "John people are looking."

He said "I don't care. Let them look. I want the whole world to know you are my lady and that I love more than life its self."

When he finished the clasp and released her, she stepped back and looked at John. Her bottom lip was quivering. It was obvious that she was trying to hold back her emotions.

John broke the tension by asking her if she liked the dress. She turned and looked at herself in the mirror, turning from side to side. She told him that it fit perfectly and she loved it.

Then she asks him, "Do you like it and how do I look in it?"

He told her, "It compliments your skin tones. It highlights your beautiful blue eyes and you look perfect in it. Now let's get everything you need to go with it. And please promise me that you will forget about price."

"John, you know that is against my nature, but for you, I will try." She answered.

The evening was a perfect romantic time of laughing, talking, dancing and just sharing with each other their feelings. About half way through the night the 'MC' for the night began to announce the couples that were on their honeymoon and ask them to come to the microphone and tell about themselves. When they got to John and Sarah, she would not talk. But, John got up to the 'mike' and sang her a love long. The song was named 'Have I told you lately that I love you'. When he finished, there was not a dry eye in the room. They all gave him a standing ovation. Sarah just stood there with tears streaming down her face.

When they stuck the microphone in Sarah's face and ask her how they met she said, "This beautiful man rescued me from a snow storm and he has been rescuing me ever since." And she pushed the microphone away.

They concluded the evening by walking the observation deck hand in hand. They would stop from time to time and lean on the handrail and look at the ocean and the stars. When John would reach out to take her hand, she would gladly take it with both of hers.

For the next week, as they enjoyed the beaches, attended cook-outs, toured the islands and took in the sights of Hawaii together, not only did their love grow but so did their friendship. However, Sarah's insecurity continued to show. The night before the ship docked at Anchorage they were standing on the observation deck when John came up behind her and started to but his arms around her she started to move away from him. Then she stopped, reached back and took both of John's hands and pulled his arms around her. She leaned back and relaxed as if to melt into his arms.

She said, "John please forgives me for pulling away. I have never known anyone like you and I have certainly never had anyone love me like you do. What I want more than anything is to please you and be the perfect wife. Honestly, I don't know how. Please be patient with me while I learn."

John replied, "My darling wife I have seen firsthand how much you have been mistreated and I intend to change all that. I will provide all your needs and as many of your 'wants' as I can. I will always love you and cherish every second I get to spend with you. As our lives become intertwined together we will learn to share with each other our deepest feelings. And, my desire is to always put your feelings before mine. Always remember this: letting me hold you like I am now will make any bad feelings that may have occurred go away. I love you Sarah and I will take every opportunity to show you that I do."

CHAPTER TWENTY-TWO

THE NEW HOME

When they got back to Anchorage John ask Sarah if she wanted to go to see Jenny and she replied that she just wanted to go home. Instead of traveling through Fairbanks, John plotted a course that would take them just east of Purgatory. When he turned through Purgatory he asks Sarah if she wanted to stop and check her old town out. She just frowned at him. He chuckled and went through the town and headed for home. When they got to the place where John would have turned off the main road to go to the cabin he drove past the turn-off.

Sarah said, "John didn't you just miss your turn?"

Without any other explanation, John answered, "Nope."

Sarah paused for a few seconds and ask, "What are you doing now, and where are we going?"

He answered, "We are going home."

"You missed the turn to the cabin. Please tell me where we are going. I am really tired and I just want to go home and rest. Can we do this tomorrow?"

About the time she asks the question, John turned off the main road and drove up the hill to the new lodge. When he got to the steel gates he took out the opener and pushed the button. The two steel gates opened and they drove in the yard. John closed the gates behind them and opened the garage door where he parked the truck.

He instructed Sarah to leave the bags and he would come back for them. When they got to the back door of the lodge, John opened the door and turned around to Sarah. He put his right arm around her waist and scooped her up with his left arm.

"John, you nut! What are you doing? Put me down." She protested.

"Not until I carry my new bride over the threshold of our new home." He answered.

When he put her down he turned and closed the door he turned on the lights. Sarah just stood there.

"Honey this is our new home. Do you want to see it?" He asks.

She just stood there. John took her hand and led her through the kitchen to the dining room and into the combination living/family room where the end wall was solid glass. From there the view overlooked the large lake where a large flock of Geese was landing.

She just stood looking out the window at the Geese. Then she turned and ask, "John why are we here and not at the cabin? When did you…What is going on?"

"Well like I told you this is our new home. I sold the cabin and built this for us. Do you like it?" He asks.

She paused, looked around and said, "There is no furniture."

"Well, I wanted my new bride to have the privilege of helping with the furnishings. I thought it would be fun if we did it together. We have what we need to get by for two or three days until we get the furniture. We have the bedroom furniture. We have a TV. We have the loveseat to set on and the kitchen is fully functional. If you want to you can start Dinner and I will get our luggage from the truck. There are steaks in the freezer, canned vegetables in the pantry, and some fresh veggies in the bottom of the refrigerator.

"If it is ok with you I would like a bowl of soup. Do we have any soup?" She asks.

"Yes, there is soup and that sounds good. I will have some soup also." He answered.

John got the luggage while Sarah warmed two bowls of chicken with rice soup and the two of them sat down on the loveseat and watched a John Wayne movie. About halfway through the second movie "Ghost in the Darkness" Sarah went to sleep. John quietly got up and turned the covers down on their bed. He tried to pick Sarah up without waking her.

On the way to the bedroom, she said to him, "You think you are going to get lucky tonight, don't you?"

John knew that question was an invitation to an intimate moment with his lovely wife. John believed that intimacy between a husband and wife was a gift from God and he cherished every intimate moment he got to share with Sarah. That night he knew his 'lovely' was very tired and his concern for her caused him to replied, "Beautiful lady when you said "I do" and agreed to spend the rest of your life with me I became the luckiest man alive. So, to answer your question, I am already lucky." He laid her on the bed and put a cover over her. Before he could get ready for bed she was sound to sleep he gently kissed her on the check and joined her in bed. John fell asleep thanking God for the beautiful mate God had given him.

The next morning John got up early and left Sarah still asleep. Before he left the bedroom, he leaned down and gently kissed her on the cheek. About the time he got the coffee started and was mixing the blueberry pancakes she came into the kitchen and sat down close to where John was making breakfast.

She said, "You put me to bed last night in my street cloth and I didn't take a bath."

"Why don't you take a bath while I am cooking breakfast?" He asks.

"That is a good idea." And she, still half asleep, shuffled her feet toward the bathroom. "John, there is a hot tub in the bathroom. Am I supposed to take a bath in that?"

"No, you nut. You are in the hot tub/sauna room. Go to the next door to the left and you will find a bathroom. Hurry up or your pancakes will be cold."

She had not unpacked her clothes from the trip so she came out of the bathroom with John's bathrobe around her. John was reminded of the first time she spent the night with him at the cabin the night he rescued her from the snow storm. She was so cute that night in John's sweat pants and shirt and now she had done it again. There she stood with John's bathrobe on that was so big on her that it dragged the floor and her hands were lost in the sleeves. She had a towel on her head and John thought she was just precious. He just could not let this picture get away. Her camera was on the table and before she could protest John had it and was snapping away. When she saw what he was doing she hollered at him to stop and tried to run and hide in the next room. She would not come out until he promised not to take any more pictures. John took the card out of the camera and put it back on the table. She peeked around the corner to see if he was going to take more pictures. The camera was on the table and she ran and got it. John anticipated that she would try to erase the pictures so he hid the card.

"John what did you do with the card out of my camera? If you show those pictures to anyone I will just die. Please let me erase them."

John took her in his arms while she was still pleading with him to let her erase the pictures and told her, "My beautiful lady don't you know that I would never deliberately embarrass you in public. Those pictures are for my eyes only. Let's eat and we will look at them together and if I can't convince you to let me keep them for me to look at only, we will get rid of them."

"You promise?" She begged.

"I promise." He answered.

After they ate John took the card and downloaded the pictures from the card to his computer. He then hooked a cord up to the fifty-four-inch flat screen TV and started a slide show. They had taken more than two hundred pictures on their three trips. The slide show held so many beautiful memories. Everything was wonderful until Sarah's picture popped up on the screen in John's bathrobe.

She jumped up and said, "John that is horrible. They are just horrible. Please get rid of them. Please, please get rid of them."

He reached up and pulled her into his lap and told her, "Honey if they bother you that much I will erase them." After John had erased the pictures from his computer he reminded Sarah that she would have to delete them from her camera.

John and Sarah spent many happy hours together planning, picking out, and placing the furniture in their new home. They made several trips to Fairbanks which always included stops at Jenny's. Sarah would ask Jenny's advice and the two would talk for hours. John would drink coffee and eat all of Jenny's chocolate pie.   Every time Sarah and Jenny would come up with what they considered a good plan for the living /family room, John would remind them that it had to include the bear skin rug. He was not demanding that the rug had to be in their living room, he just loved to pester Sarah. She still did not always know when he was joking or when he was serious. The truth was that John would have sold the rug to make Sarah happy, but she did not know John that well yet. The third time he reminded them about the rug Sarah slapped her hands on her lap, took a deep breath and let it out hard and fast in sheer frustration. Jenny broke out laughing. Sarah said, in disgust, "What is so funny?"

Jenny replied, "Honey can't you tell that he is just messing with you for the fun of it?"

Before she could reply, John came over to where they were sitting and sat down beside Sarah and said, "My lady, do you remember what I told you about how I wanted the downstairs big room decorated?"

"Yes, you want it decorated to be a hunting lodge." She answered.

"I also told you that Brutus' mom the bear skin rug would be down there. Didn't I?"

Sarah paused for a moment and then replied, "Yes you did. So why are you pestering me about putting it upstairs?"

"Because," He said, "You are almost as beautiful when you are angry as you are when you are happy."

Jenny laughed hysterically at the two of them.

Sarah sat there for a moment trying not to laugh, but her Beautiful dimples gave away her pleasure with what John said. She turned and pointed her finger at him and said, "You horrible old man we have work to do. So, go get yourself another piece of pie and leave us alone." She jumped up out of her chair, reached over and kissed him on the cheek. That was her way of telling him he was forgiven but not to do it again. She said, "Now will you let us do our work?"

John grabbed her and kissed her passionately with a kiss that lasted for ten seconds. When he sat her back down he said, "Go back to work if you can." She took a deep breath and just sat there.

Jenny was laughing so hard she couldn't get a breath. She said, "You two are worse than two love sick teenagers."

John was very pleased with Sarah's interior decorating skills. As it turned out she was quite good at it. The large living /family room where she focused most of her attention was absolutely beautiful. She had the walls painted satin white. She took several of the pictures they had taken on their honeymoon and had them enlarged to poster size. John made solid wood picture frames to hang them in and she placed them on the walls as part of the decor. Sarah and Jenny had picked out a couch and love seat that was covered with light tan leather. Both of the pieces had recliners built into them. Sarah complimented them with solid cherry wood end tables, a coffee table, and an entertainment center. She used these pieces to create a TV viewing area in the north-east corner of the living/family room. The southwest corner of the room was set up so that several people could sit in recliners and visit while observing the activities on the lake, or just look at the sunset. Sarah had hung a curtain across the window that could be closed in the evening to block the setting sun if it was too bright.

She had added lighting trays along the north and south walls that would project the light on the ceiling and reflect back down in the room to create a 'soft' light effect. She complimented the lighting with a large multilayer chandelier in the center of the room. John added controls that would allow the lights to be turned on or off and dimmed or brightened from a remote control.

Because all the colors in the room were soft pastel colors when a bouquet of flowers was placed on one of the tables it really became a centerpiece. The bright colors of the flowers became dominate in the space that surrounded them. And, Sarah loved flowers so there were always flowers on the tables.

She and John placed a small table in the North-West corner of the room so they could sit and have morning coffee and look at the lake. They spent many hours at the small table sipping coffee, talking and watching Geese and Ducks landing and taking off from the lake.

Sarah saw her first Moose when it came to drink from the lake. It was a large bull and Sarah got so excited she had to take a picture of it. John grabbed his camera with a telescope lens and set it up on a tripod so she could get several shots. She was so happy she took twelve shots. She got one shot of the Moose when it turned and looked directly at her camera. She had that one enlarged. John made a frame and she hung it on the wall.

CHAPTER TWENTY-THREE

TIME TO BRING PATTY AND ABIGALE HOME

John and Sarah finished their home decorating and were settling into enjoying their new home. Summer was over and it was starting to get cold. John was busy checking supplies for the winter but Sarah seemed very distracted. After three days of her shutting John out of everything she did, John got concerned and went to her where she was staring out the window at the lake. When he tried to put his arms around her she pulled away. He reached out and took her arm and sat her down at their small table in front of the window and asks her what was wrong?

She answered, "Nothing is wrong. Why do you ask?"

John said, "Sarah, don't tell me nothing is wrong. You have ignored me for three days. You have been moping around here like you are in a fog. You are not talking to me or hearing anything I say. Now tell me what is wrong."

She looked at John for almost twenty seconds without saying a word. Then her bottom lip began to quiver and her eyes filled with tears. She sat there without saying a word and tears began to stream down her cheeks. John reached over and took her in his arms and pleaded with her to tell him what was bothering her.

She said, "John you told me if you held me in your arms that bad feelings would go away. Please make these feelings go away. They hurt so much."

He pleaded with her, "Honey, tell me what is hurting you and I will do everything humanly possible to make it stop."

She said, "John I have got to tell you something and I don't know how. And it just hurts so much because I should have told you already. I am afraid you will hate me."

"I could never hate you, Sarah. So, what is it you need to tell me?" John asks.

She said, "John I have…" and she began to weep so violently she could not get her breath. She caught her breath and repeated, "John I have a daughter that I have not seen or heard from for five years. You must thank I am awful."

Before she could say anything about her daughter John said, "If you are talking about Patty, I know about her."

She pulled away from John and looked right at him and angrily asked, "How long have you known and why didn't you tell me you knew?"

He reminded her that he had been with the FBI and part of his job was to investigate anyone that was involved with Willy Jack. She was part of the investigation. She jumped up from the table and went over and stared out the window.

With her back to John, she angrily asks, "Well, are you going to tell me about the investigation?"

He answered, "When you get over your 'hissy fit' and come over and sit down, I will tell you all I know about the investigation."

She came over and sat down at the table and demanded, "I am setting down, now talk. When did you find out about Patty and why didn't you tell me?"

"Well to answer your first question," he answered, "After I took you to Jenny's after the snow storm I went to L.A. to investigate you. I met Patty and saw her daughter Abigail. And the reason I did not tell you was that it was an ongoing investigation. And besides, she is your daughter. Why didn't you tell me about her?"

"Don't try to put the blame on me. You have been out of the FBI for almost two months and the investigation is over. Why haven't you told me? Did you say Patty has a daughter?" She began to cry again.

John reached over and took her hands and said, "Sarah, honey we can set here and argue over who should have told who what all day and get nothing accomplished. Or, we can do something about it. The question we need an answer to is, what do you want to do about Patty and Abigail?"

"John! I want to see my daughter. Can we go see her?" She begged.

"No Sarah. That is a dangerous idea." He answered.

She pulled her hands away from John in protest and asks, "Why can't I go see my daughter."

When John tried to reach out and take her hands, she pulled them up to her shoulders where he could not reach them.

John got up out of his chair and forcefully took her hands and said sternly, "Sarah you have got to listen to what I am going to tell you. What I learned in the investigation is that your ex-husband's old gang wants to get to you and they are using Patty for bait. They think you have something that is theirs. If they get you they will torture you until they get it or they kill all of you. I will not let you go down there and take that chance. I cannot stand the thought of losing you."

"Why John, why do they want me? I don't know anything and I don't have anything. Why won't they leave me alone?"

"Sarah, I know this is going to be painful but I need you to tell me what happened the night of the robbery," John stated. "I know about the beating Carl gave you but I don't know what 'set him off'. Were you there when he killed Tim and did you see him do it? I want you to think back to that night and tell me exactly what you saw."

Sarah started telling John what she saw. She said, "I did not see Carl and Tim fighting. I saw Carl roll Tim's body in a rug…" She paused and said, "Wait, I saw Carl go through Tim's pockets and he took a key out and laid it on the hall table before he carried Tim's body out of the back door of the club. Just when I picked up the key, I heard someone come in the front of the club. I knew the key was important to Carl so I hide it to keep anyone from getting it."

"Where did you hide the key?" He asked.

She paused for about thirty seconds and John asks her again where she hid the key.

She replied, "There is a large picture of a bullfighter and I put the key between the backing and the picture. I put it in the lower right corner. Surely they have found it by now."

"No, they have not found it. They thank you have it. That is why they are after you." John told her. "If I am right, this will all be over soon."

"What about Patty and Abigail?" Sarah pleaded.

"Sarah, do you trust me?" He asks.

She paused for a few seconds and said, "Yes I trust you. What are you going to do?"

"I am not going to tell you because if you are questioned by the FBI you will not have to lie to them because you will not know. But, I will remind you several times in the next few months that you said you trust me. Life is going to get very tense and if we are going to get through this you will have to trust me completely. You will see your daughter and granddaughter, but it must be my way. So, I ask you again, do you trust me?"

"John, I don't know what I am getting into, but you have always treated me good. So yes, I do trust you." She answered.

John picked up the phone and called Art. When he tried to tell Art about the key, Art stopped him and reminded him that he was not to get involved with the Bank robbery case in LA. Art's attitude made John mad and he told Art, "I have information that will help you solve the case. Do you want it or not?"

There was a pause on the line and that let John know there was someone else listening to their conversation. John just hung up the phone.

Fifteen minutes later Art called John back. "John, how did you get the information?"

Before Art could ask any more questions, John told him that if he was going to treat him as a suspect they were through talking and hung up the phone again. Ten minutes went by and Art called again, "John please don't hang up again. I am interested in the information you have. Please tell me what you have learned."

John told him, "I learned that Carl Pritts and Willy Jack are first cousins and that they talked several times just before the bank robbery. I believe that Carl was going to use the money from the robbery to 'buy into' Willy's operation."

Before John could tell Art about the key, Art ask, "Can I ask you how you obtained that information?"

John stated in a firm voice, "Art you are doing it again. I am not a suspect. I learned about them being cousins through Ancestries. com and I still have friends in law enforcement. They obtained the phone records for me. Art, I have not broken any laws and I have not disobeyed you or your boss's directive about the case. Now, if you will be quiet for just a minute, I have something important to tell you."

Art said, "John I am listening."

John told art, "Sarah remembered that the night that Carl killed the bank teller Tim that he took a key out of Tim's pocket. Carl laid the key on the hall table before he rolled Tim's body in the rug and took it out the back door of the club. Sarah hid the key to keep it safe for Carl in a painting that is still on the wall in the club. If my hunch is right, that key is to a safe-deposit box in the bank and I believe that is where you will find the money and bonds from the bank robbery. If you get a search warrant for the club and find that key, you can tie every one of the gang to the robbery and solve the case. But before you make a move you had better find the 'leak' in the FBI office in LA."

Art said, "John that is very good information. If we can find that key, we just might solve the case. Now, will you let me take it from here?"

John replied, "Art I will stay out of it if you will let me know if you find the key."

Art said, "I will let you know."

John turned his attention to Sarah. He said, "Sarah I am going to be gone for as many days as it takes to do what I am going to do. Before I go I am going to get an older couple from the local village to stay with you. They will be downstairs decorating the big room. I have made arrangements for them put up trophies and other decorations to turn the room into a lodge. They are a lot like Don and

Jenny. Their names are David and Robin Cots. David is the one who made the bear skin rug we have. They are both locals who know the area and will take care of you. We will go to their village tomorrow and meet them."

John took Sarah to the village and they spent the day with David and Robin. Sarah seemed very comfortable around David and Robin and that pleased John.

The next day John made arrangements to go get Patty. He knew that Patty would not come with him of her own free will so he made special arrangements to bring her back whether she wanted to come or not. When he got to LA he rented a cop car that had been used on a new movie and waited until Patty came out of the back door of the Zombie Hut. As she walked toward her baby setter's apartment two of John's helpers dressed as policemen got out of the cop car and arrested Patty. When they got her in the car one of them drugged her with a sedative from a ring that had a needle attached to it. One of the police impersonators was a nurse John had hired to make sure Patty was ok for the trip back to Alaska.

After they had Patty, the two dressed as police officers went into the baby setter's apartment and told the babysitter that Patty had been arrested and charged with prostitution. They said they were from Child Services and were there to get Abigail. As soon as they got Abigail in the car they headed for a small airport where John had a private jet waiting to take them back to Alaska. When they got to Alaska and landed at a private airport just out of Fairbanks John transferred the two to an unmarked ambulance and headed for home. The nurse had put an IV in Patty's arm to keep her sedated until she was at the lodge. Abigail slept through it all. As soon as they were secure in the lodge John's two helpers took the ambulance and left.

John thought he was going to have to sedate Sarah. She was excited but crying hysterically. It was all He could do to keep her away from Patty and Abigail. The last thing he wanted was for her to wake them up. John finally got her calmed down, but the only ones that got any sleep that night were Patty and Abigail. Sarah would look at Patty and cry. Then she would look at Abigail and cry. This went on all night.

CHAPTER TWENTY-FOUR

PATTY GETS AN ATTITUDE ADJUSTMENT

John had told Sarah that Patty had told him that she hated Sarah for running off and leaving her. He did not know just how much she hated her mother until Patty got up the next morning. John and Sarah were in the kitchen playing with Abigail and drinking coffee when Patty walked in. When she recognized Sarah, she called her every filthy name she could think of and then she turned to John and started cursing him. She said, "Get your filthy hands off my daughter." And she started toward Abigail. John intercepted her before she could get to Abigail and grabbed her by the hair on her head. He dragged her by the hair and threw her out the door on the back balcony. He went out behind her and closed the door. It had snowed during the night and the tempter had dropped down into the low teens. When she tried to get back in the lodge, he blocked her from entering.

She shouted, "Get out of my way. I am freezing out here."

"You had better get used to it. If you don't learn to respect your mother and me and clean up your filthy language you will be out here permanently." He told her.

Standing there in her nightgown and house shoes, this gal from LA was no match for the Alaska cold and she quickly gave in to John's demands.

"Ok, ok." She said. "Now please let me inside."

John let her in, but stood between her and Sarah and told her to apologize to her mother.

She looked around John and said, "Bitch I am sorry for…"

Before she could finish what she was going to say, John through her back out in the snow and slammed the door. He said, "If you think I am joking just keep it up." When he let her in again he sat her at the table and wrapped a blanket around her to stop her from shivering. He told her, "Patty these are the conditions you will adhere to: You will not ever swear in my presence or your mother's presents ever; you will respect me and your mother, and you will respect this as your home. You may never love either of us. You may never like either of us that is your right. But, however, you will respect both of us. Do you understand?"

"I have a home in LA and I want to go back. Why didn't you just leave me alone?" She stated very hatefully.

"That place where you were jumping around naked in front of a bunch of dirty old men does not exist anymore. It was raided last night and all of the operators were arrested. The Zombie Hut is shut down."

"You must have enjoyed it that is where I met you." She said very sarcastically.

"I was there on FBI business. If you remember I did not stay and watch you make a fool of yourself." John replied.

Just as the argument was getting started it was interrupted by a phone call from Art. "John the information you got us was what we needed. We found the key. We have arrested the whole gang and connected them to the robbery and therefore to the murder of the teller. We have got them, John. Good work. However, we did not find Sarah's daughter. Do you know anything about what happened to her?" John ignored the question and thanked him for the phone call. He said, "Good Art, I guess it is finally over. Now maybe Sarah can get some rest without having to always wonder who is after her. This is good news. Thanks for the call Art." And John hung up the phone.

Patty wanted to know who John was talking to. John told her it was his FBI friend who had shut down the Zombie Hut and put her friends out of business. And he told her that she had two choices: She could make the lodge her home or go back to LA and live off the streets.

She said, "I am not going to stay here."

John said, "You do what you want to do. You are twenty miles from the nearest town or another house and you have just tested the tempter outside. Whatever you decide, Abigail is not going with you. That baby disserves a chance at life and you cannot give it to her."

"She is my baby and I will do with her as I see fit…"

Before she could finish her remarks in the hateful tone she was talking, John jumped up and grabbed her and started dragging her to the door. He asks her if she would like to spend some more time outside. When she said, she had had enough he sat her back down at the table. She just sat there not saying a word.

John knew this was not the end of the matter. Patty continued to push the limits of the conditions John had laid out for her and kept to herself as much as she could. She would not talk to either John or Sarah, and it was breaking Sarah's heart. Two weeks went by and it just got worse. Sarah was so upset that she was not sleeping and she would spend hours in her room with the door closed. John knew she was crying and he could not comfort her. He knew he could not let this go on or Sarah would have a complete breakdown.

He set the 'stage' to break Patty before she broke Sarah. John had very carefully kept everything away from Patty that would give her any 'edge' in the ongoing battle of wills: guns, keys to the truck, phone, and the computer with internet. He completely isolated her from any connection with the outside world.

But, at the start of the third week, John set her up to try to escape he left the keys to the snowmobile hanging on the key rack. After he had taken a ride to hunt for meat for the freezer he deliberately left the keys in plain sight. He watched the keys to see if Patty would take them—she did. Early the next morning John was up watching to see what Patty was going to do. Just as he suspected she was in the yard opening the gate to try to run. John was thankful that she did not try to take the baby. She got on the snowmobile and started out the gate. John had 'rigged' the snowmobile with a remote control shut off switch. As soon as Patty got out the gate, he shut the snowmobile down and shut and locked the gate. Brutus had not gone into hibernation yet and he was part of the plan. John stepped onto the balcony and blew the silent whistle he used to call Brutus and waited. Patty tried frantically to start the snowmobile but, John had it shut down completely. After about five minutes Patty turned to John who was staring at her from the balcony and began to scream cuss words at him.

John let her throw her 'fit' for about another five minutes until he saw Brutus coming up the drive. Without saying a word, John just pointed at Brutus. When Patty turned around and saw Brutus coming toward her she went hysterical. She screamed and squalled; she tried to climb the fence; she begged John to let her in the gate. About twenty feet before Brutus got to her John opened the gate and let her in. He was down at the gate and grabbed her and dragged her downstairs where he threw her in a 'root cellar' and locked the door.

After going back up to the back lot he fed and played with his old Friend Brutus.

After twenty minutes, he went back to the root cellar to check on Patty. When he opened the door, Patty had taken off the cold weather clothes and thrown them on the floor. John picked them up and told Patty when she learned to live by the rules he would think about letting her out and he slammed the door with her locked inside. John had prepared this room like the solitary confinement room he had been in, in prison. If anything could get Patty's attention this would.

John had spent his life working with teens, especially troubled teens. He loved young people and Patty was no exception. He had no children of his own and he had always wanted them. He had such a compassion for all children and he loved all of them. What he was doing to Patty was going to be hard on Sarah, Patty, and him. But, he knew he had to tear down the wall of hate that Patty had between her and her mother. He knew what Patty and Sarah had been through and wanted more than anything to see these two love each other again. He knew how much Sarah loved Patty and because she was Sarah's daughter, John loved her too. He hated what he was doing to Patty. He just wanted to take her in his arms and hold her and tell her everything was going to be alright and that he and her mother just wanted to help. The tough character that he had to be was just an act. He went twenty feet down the hall and sat down and wept.

After a half an hour, John went upstairs and started breakfast for Sarah and Abigail. He did not know how he was going to tell his beloved Sarah what he was doing to her daughter. He knew in his heart that what he was doing—breaking Patty—was the only way he could salvage her. She was so hardened in her hatred for Sarah leaving her that she would not listen to reason. His greatest desire was to see Sarah and Patty reunited as mother and daughter. His greatest fear was he would destroy Sarah in the process. The last thing he wanted was to hurt Sarah, because she had hurt enough. It was a very tense moment when Sarah came in the kitchen.

She came in and sat down and asks, "Where is Patty?"

John said, "Sarah a few weeks ago I ask you if you trusted me. I ask you the same question twice. You told me that you did trust me. Now I am asking you to do just that trust me."

She demanded, "What have you done to my daughter?"

John replied, "This morning she stole the snowmobile and tried to run away. I caught her and she is in the root cellar. That is where she will stay until she learns to abide by my rules."

"How long do you plan to leave her down there?" Sarah asks.

"She will stay there as long as it takes to get her attention." He answered. "When she is ready to listen to my rules and agree to them I will let her out, but one second sooner."

"How long John?" Sarah pleaded. "One day? Two Days?"

"Sarah, you are just going to have to trust me with this. It may take weeks. I just do not know how long she will rebel against rules...

Before John could finish Sarah asks, "You are going to let her out to use the bathroom and to bathe, aren't you?"

"Absolutely not!" John replied. "I want her to be as miserable as possible without inflicting bodily harm on her. The more miserable she is, the quicker she will break and listen to reason."

Sarah protested in a loud voice, "John that is absolutely disgusting and I will not allow you to do that to my daughter!"

John calmly said, "Sarah if you want your daughter back you are going to have to trust me with the way I am handling this. If we do not get her to change her ways she will not be fit to be around Abigail and I will not allow her to live in my house the way she is acting. I will take her back and dump her on the streets of LA where I found her. Now, if you will just trust me I believe I can 'salvage' your daughter. I ask you again do you trust me?"

Sarah jumped up out of her chair and ran to the bedroom. She slammed the door and locked it and would not come out the rest of the day. For the next three days, John saw very little of Sarah. He would try to talk to her but she would not listen. He would cook for her but most of the time she would not eat what he fixed for her. She would fix something herself and go back to the bedroom and shut the door.

John devoted his time playing with Abigail and thinking of Patty. When he tried to feed her the evening of the day he put her in the cellar she cursed him and tried to throw the food at him. He slammed the door just before the food hit him.

She screamed, "I have to go to the toilet!"

John said, "There is a drain in the middle of the floor. You can use that."

She screamed again, "I am not using that. What do you think I am?"

He answered, "I know what you are, but we are not going to discuss that right now." And he walked away. John had built a small sliding hatch at the bottom of the main door to the cellar. After the first day, he slid her food through the sliding hatch door and would not speak to her. For the first week, she cursed John every time she heard him coming to open the hatch. He would not respond. On the second day of the second week, she said 'please' when John came to feed her. John was excited about that but that was just the start of what he expected from her before he would let her out. On the third day of the second week, John caught Sarah trying to open the lock and let Patty out. When he pulled her away from the door she turned and slapped at John. John caught her hand and tried to reason with her. She pulled away from him.

She stomped the floor and screamed at him, "Let her out of that horrible place! She is not an animal! She is my daughter and I want her out! If you care anything about me, you will let her out now!" When John tried to reach out and console her she pushed him away and screamed, "I hate you for what you are doing to Patty! I hate you!" And she ran away crying.

The next two days were hard for John. Sarah would not have anything to do with him. She was keeping Abigail away from him to hurt him. Patty was not talking she was not even cussing him. Even his old friend Brutus was in hibernation. John had no one to talk to. He did not hate Patty. He actually loved that little girl and wanted more than anything to see her and Sarah love and appreciate each other as a mother and daughter should. He certainly did not want to hurt Sarah. She had shut him out completely and he could not get through to her.

In his efforts working with troubled teens, he had been very successful at reaching some very tough ones. But, now he began to question himself about what he was doing. He was no longer sure that what he was doing with Patty was the right thing to do. He walked out to his truck and would have driven away but, it was starting to snow hard. He sat in his truck and wept for almost an hour. He could not do this any longer. He decided he would let Patty out and as soon as he could he would leave and let the two of them, Sarah and Patty, work out the differences.

He got out of the truck and went to the cellar to let her out. When Patty heard him, she began to plead with him to open the door and let her talk to him.

She said, "Please let me talk to you John. I promise I will not cause any trouble." Her voice was very calm and submissive.

John stood at the door for a short time when he heard her plead again. He opened the door. She was a mess. Her face was streaked where she had been crying and tried to wipe it with dirty hands. Her clothes were nasty and she stunk. The whole room stunk. John looked at her and felt so ashamed for what he had put her through. He wanted to get on his knees and beg her to forgive him but this was her 'hour'.

She said, "John I will respect you and mother. I will respect your home and I will not cause you any more trouble if you will let me out. I would not blame you if you threw me out of your house. If you let me stay I promise I will not cause you any more trouble."

John said, "Stay here while I go get you some clean cloth. There is a shower down the hall. I will leave the door open. You may come out if you want."

She said, "If you will get me a bucket of water with a sponge and some soap I will clean this room."

He told her to leave it and they would clean it later. He returned with the clean cloth for her and showed her where the shower was. He told her to take as long as she wanted to. He told her there was a new toothbrush and toothpaste in the medicine cabinet. Along with the cloth, he brought a hair dryer and comb. He instructed her that when she finished she was to come upstairs and he would fix her a decent meal. Thirty minutes later she came into the kitchen where John was. He served her a bowl of venison stew out of the slow cooker he had prepared that morning. With the stew, he served homemade bread and a glass of milk. This reminded him of the night when he rescued Sarah from the snow storm. He had served her the same meal. To make it complete he had to have some chocolate chip cookies. He was in business: he had made some that morning for Abigail.

She started to eat when she stopped and asks, "Aren't you going to eat?"

He replied, "Honey I have already eaten." When he called her honey she instantly turned toward John and stared at him. After a few seconds, she slowly turned back to her food and began to eat. At that moment, John realized that was the first kind thing he had ever said to Patty and he felt so ashamed.

He really loved this little girl. She was the daughter of his wife Sarah whom he adored. She was a beautiful child. She had long auburn hair that hung down in flowing ringlets that splashed off her shoulders. She had sparkling blue eyes with long eyelashes. Her flawless skin still carried the tan from the LA sun. All of her features were just right. She was a younger version of John's beloved Sarah and he wanted so much to be able to be a father to her. For her to be the daughter he never had. He wanted her to love her home because she wanted to not because she had to.

At this time, he just did not know what to do next. He would show her as much kindness as she would receive. He would provide her with all her needs and hope she would respond in kindness. If he never gained her respect or love he would be satisfied if she was reunited with her mother. John firmly believed that a mother and daughter should love, respect, and need each other.

Sarah had not spoken to John in two days. The last thing she said to John was that she hated him and Patty heard it. Patty was not the hateful, hard-hearted person she had pretended to be. She actually was a very loving person, but she had not had anyone to care about her in five years since Sarah left and did not know how to love anyone. She heard how Sarah reacted to John when he would not let her out of the cellar. Patty knew she was the cause of Sarah not speaking to John and it troubled her.

CHAPTER TWENTY-FIVE

THE FOUR OF THEM WORK ON RESPECTING EACH OTHER

The next three weeks were an imitation of life between the three of them. John went about doing the things necessary to run the home. He and Patty were working at the task of respecting each other. They spoke when they needed to but they had not begun to try to get to know each other. Patty was respectful to both John and Sarah and she was not swearing. However, she was not making any attempt to 'make up' with Sarah her mother. She cleaned her room and did her laundry, but made no effort to help with any other work in the house. She would take care of Abigail when she could get her away from Sarah or John. Sarah wandered around the house like she was in a fog; she was not having anything to do with John; she spoke very little to Patty, but she would hold and play with Abigail. Abigail was enjoying all the attention. She loved everyone. She was the 'common thread' that bound the rest of the gang together.

Patty watched John interact with Abigail with great interest. He was very patient with Abby. He would pick her up when she was throwing a 'baby fit' and console her by taking her to the front window and showing her 'critters' on the lake or just sitting with her until she would calm down. He was always patient with her and never raised his voice. He would never refuse to pick her up when she held up her arms. John would sit and talk to her and play with her for hours and Abby loved all that attention. Her first word was 'Gam Pa'. That was her attempt to say 'Grandpa'.

One evening Patty had just fed Abigail and was wiping the food off her face so she could get down from the chair and play when John walked by. Abby who was very impatient and wanted to get down reached her arms up for John to get her out of the highchair and called Gam Pa. Patty said, "If she calls you Grandpa does that mean I can call you Dad?" John turned around and asks, "What did you say?" Patty quickly sat Abigail on the floor and ran to her room. John came to the door that was ajar and knocked. She did not respond, but he could see that she was standing looking out the window. John walked up behind her.

He said, "Patty if I heard you correctly and you want to call me Dad. I would be so pleased and honored. I will do everything possible to earn your respect and love. I will provide all of your needs. I will provide you a home and do everything humanly possible to make you feel that you are loved and that you belong here. I will constantly remind you of what a very special young lady you are."

She turned toward him with her tear streaked face and said, "I have never had a Dad. That man that caused me to be born was neither a Father nor a Dad. He was just pure evil. I am getting very attached to you and I hope you don't let me down."

John replied, "Patty honey, I had rather die than let you down or hurt you in any way. I have grown attached to you as well. I see a potential in you that is beyond anything I have seen in a young person in a long time. I want so much to have the chance to help you develop your potential." He opened his arms to give Patty a chance to come to him. After they hugged for a while Patty asks if she could talk to John. He asks her what she wanted to talk about.

Patty asks, "Do you know why mother ran off and left me?"

John replied. "Honey it was not her choice. She was running for her life." John sat and talked to Patty for over an hour explaining to her what had happened to Sarah. He told Patty about her father robbing a bank, killing a man and beating Sarah almost to death. He told her that while she was running for her life, Sarah had tried to get Patty back from child services but every time she called, her call would be traced. Then the FBI and Carl's gang would come looking for her and she would have to run again. She wound up in Purgatory where Carl's cousin Willy Jack was.

John told her, "I rescued her from a snow storm when Willy Jack set a trap for her and I have been rescuing her from Willy's gang, your father, and his gang ever since. The only reason you had a place to stay is the gang at the Zombie Hut was using you as bate to get Sarah 'out in the open' so they could catch her."

Patty just sat there with her head down without saying anything for over thirty seconds. Then she turned toward John and said, "John I mean Dad, I did not know any of that. I didn't know Carl (she did not refer to him as her Dad) killed my little brother. I didn't know he almost killed my mom. I knew he was in prison but I didn't know why. You are right about them wanting to get mom. I heard a conversation between two of them about her having or knowing where the money was. I didn't know then what they were talking about, but now it makes sense.

Dad, will you help me talk to Mom about why I have acted so horribly toward her? Will you explain to her that the reason I acted so awful to her was that I didn't know what she had been through? All I knew was that she deserted me." Before John could answer she said, "And one more question." She raised her voice and asks, "Why did you put me in that awful box? Why didn't you tell me what you just told me? Where did you ever get such a horrible idea to lock me in that cellar?"

John answered, "Would you have listened to me if I tried to tell you about your Mom?"

She stared at him for a while and with a sheepish grin on the face, said, "No I probably wouldn't have. I was too mad at you two. But that was a horrible experience. Where did you get that idea?"

"Patty it is a fair question that I think your mother would like the answer to also. Why don't we go get your mother and I will tell both of you at the same time?" They went into the living room where Sarah was watching Abigail and sat down next to her.

John said, "Sarah, patty ask the question about where I got the idea for putting her in the cellar and I thought you would like to hear the answer." She did not answer him, but she did turn toward him and Patty as if to hear what John had to say.

John began to explain, "When I lived in Kentucky my first wife and I had no children of our own and we loved children. So, we worked with teens in the area. I counseled troubled teens as part of our work. One of the twelve-year-old girls I counseled accused me of having sex with her. I was convicted of statutory rape and sent to prison. While in prison I got into a fight that landed me in solitary confinement for six months. Solitary confinement was a concrete box like the cellar you were in Patty. I was in there nine weeks before the judge got the proof that the little girl was lying and overturned my sentences. My wife died while I was in that box. I was not allowed to go to her funeral."

Patty and Sarah just sat and looked at John in unbelief. And then Patty spoke and said, "You mean nine days don't you John? Surely you weren't in there nine weeks."

"No Patty I mean nine weeks. I was in there eight weeks when the guards took me out and washed me with a fire hose, made me put on dry clothes, and put me back in for another week. I was in the 'box' for a total of nine weeks." Patty started to ask a question when John interrupted her. He said, "I don't want to talk about this anymore right now. It brings back some very painful memories." John got up and went out to where his truck was parked. He did not want Patty and Sarah to see his tears and know how badly the memories hurt him.

Patty and Sarah just sat in silence and stared at each other. Patty spoke to Sarah but Sarah just looked away. Patty spoke again, "Mother did you hear me?" Sarah still did not respond. Patty pulled her chair close to Sarah and put her hand on Sarah's and said, "Momma I need to talk to you about John."

Sarah replied, "What about John?"

Patty asks, "Momma do you love this man?"

Sarah put her face in her hands and began to weep. "Of course, I love him." She replied through her tears. "He is the most wonderful thing that has ever happened to me. I have been so caught up in my own grief that I never thought about what he has been through or what he is going through now. I haven't even thanked him for bringing you and Abigail home. I am so ashamed of myself...."

Before she could say anything else, Patty interrupted her and said, "Momma he thinks that the best thing he can do is to leave and let you and me work out our differences. Momma if you love him you need to go tell him now. He is going to leave if you don't stop him."

Sarah jumped up and ran into the bedroom where John was packing his luggage. She said, "John you promised you would never leave me again." He just kept packing. Sarah said, "John you can't just run off every time we have a disagreement."

"Sarah," He replied, "Disagreements do not bother me. We are not going to agree all the time and that does not bother me. But, when you ignore me and shut me out of your life completely like you have done for the last three Weeks I can only draw one conclusion: you don't want me in your life anymore."

She took his hands and pulled him around so he had to look at her and began to plead, "Please, please don't do this. John, you know that is not true. You are my life. I cannot make it without you. Every good thank that has happened in my life has been because of you. Please don't take that away from me." She put her arms around him, buried her face in his chest and begins to weep. He put his hands on her shoulders and started to gently push her back so he could talk to her, but she pleaded, "Please don't push me away from John! Please don't push me away!"

He put his arms around her and held her.

After several seconds, she looked up at John and said, "Thank you for bringing my girls home. Please forgive me for not trusting you like I said I would. Please forgive me, John. Please tell me you can forgive me."

John gently put his hands on her shoulders and pushed her back to arm's length and said, "Sarah if I am going to stay I have to have a reason. You have to give me a reason to stay."

Sarah looked at him with a puzzled look on her face and said, "John." She paused for a second and said again, "John I love you." And she began to sob. "I can't make it without you. John, I love you and I need you. Patty needs you. Abigail needs you. Aren't we a reason enough for you to stay?" She continued to sob.

When John pulled her to him and said, "Yes, your love and all of you are a good reason to stay. Thank you for telling me you love me. I needed to hear that from you." When he embraced and kissed her she was comforted.

After they held each other for a while, Sarah said jokingly, "Besides, if you leave, when that darn bear of yours wakes up, and you are not here to feed him he will have us for lunch."

John laughed and said, "Blame it on poor old Brutus."

The two of them walked hand in hand back into the kitchen. Patty had found some canned tomato soup that she warmed up and was making grilled cheese sandwiches for everyone. Abigail was taking the cheese off the sandwiches faster than Patty could grill them. John grabbed her and distracted her while Patty finished the grilling. After they ate John started a movie and the four of them sat down as a family and watched it together. Abigail went to sleep in John's arms half way through the movie and he gently put her in her bed. While he was up he popped some popcorn for everyone and served it with cold tomato Juice, Sarah's favorite snack. That night was the start of a new beginning for John, Sarah, Patty, and Abigail.

CHAPTER TWENTY-SIX

A FAMILY IS FORMED

The four of them spent the next two months sharing the lodge, it was still too cold and wintry to get outside. John and Sarah started their Bible study again and invited Patty to join them.

Patty asks, "Is this a requirement or do I have a choice?"

John replied, "Patty, God does not require anyone to study his word and we will not require you to do it either. Sarah and I enjoy studying the bible together and thought you might like to join us. But, it is strictly up to you. You do not have to join us if you don't want to."

"Well I am not much for this God stuff so I think I will pass."

Patty went in the living room and sat down to watch TV. Abigail who was starting to talk a little climbed up into John's lap. Most of her vocabulary consisted of the words 'why' and 'what'. When John and Sarah started a conversation that contained the word God she asks, "What God?"

When John started to explain to her that God is the creator of all things Patty came into the kitchen where they were. She told John that she did not want him 'brain washing' Abigail. This angered John, but he held his thoughts and his anger.

He turned to Patty and said, "I am not 'brain washing' Her. I am answering her question…"

Before he could finish, Patty intruded, "You are forcing your religion on her and she is too young to make a choice for herself. Dad, I call that 'brain washing'."

John held his thoughts for a moment and answered, "Patty I will never hurt this child. But, when she asks a question about anything I will answer her as truthfully and as honestly as I can. And, I will not ask your permission to do so."

Patty thought for a moment before she responded to what John had said. While the tension between her and John had lessened from what it had been, she did not think of him as the monster that threw her in the cellar, but she did not want to anger him. The stern voice he used when he told her he would not ask her permission, frightened her. She walked out of the room and stopped to look out the front window at the lake. After a while, she went back into the room where the three were studying the Bible and sat down.

When John and Sarah looked up at her she asks, "Can I ask questions and will you answer me honestly as well?"

John answered, "Of course you can and yes I will."

"Why do you believe in God?" She asks. "Scientists don't. They believe in Evolution."

"That is not exactly true." He replied. "The last time I checked, more than fifty percent of the scientist surveyed said that they believe in God. I am an engineer. That is a scientific field and I believe in God. Evolution is said to be a theory, but it is more like a religion to me. A person has to believe in it because there is not a shred of evidence to support it. According to evolution nothing exploded and became everything. That just does not make any sense to me. I believe the Bible from cover to cover. I even believe the cover on my Bible, it has my name on it." John held up his leather covered Bible and showed Patty his name on the front of it.

Patty said, "You can't prove there is a God either."

John got up and took Patty by the hand and led her to the front window. He said, "Patty look out there and tell me what you see."

She answered, "I see the lake." She paused and then continued, "I see trees, and snow. Why do you ask?"

John told her, "If you will pay close attention, you can see an Otter about three hundred yards out on the left edge of the lake. It has two babies with it. Another hundred yards is a Moose that has come to the lake to drink. On the right side of the lake about the same distance as the Moose, a Snow Leopard is hunting. And there is a flock of Geese landing. The lake has fish in it. We had some for dinner two nights ago. There are omnivores, carnivores, and herbivores that depend on that lake. In other words, the lake is a complete ecological system. What do all the critters have in common?"

Patty said, "I don't know, Dad. You lost me when you started talking about all those 'vores'. I don't know what you are talking about."

John chuckled and said, "Patty an omnivore is an animal that eats both grass and meats. A bear is an omnivore. A carnivore is an animal that eats only meat. That Snow leopard is a carnivore. And the Moose is an herbivore it eats grass. And by the way, you and I are omnivores. We eat vegetables and meat. Now, what do we all have in common?"

"Dad I don't know. What is the point?"

"We are all unequally different but complex creations. We all have our own unique lives yet we all require food, water, and oxygen or air. If you study our uniqueness it should become clear that it cannot be an accident that we are on this earth. There has to be a master creator. God is that master creator."

Patty did not respond. She went back and sat down to watch TV. John went back to where Sarah and Abigail were and the three of them continued reading and studying the Bible. Three days went by and Patty kept to herself while Sarah and John studied the Bible. Abigail ran between the three of them: staying where she got the most attention mostly with John. On the fourth day, Patty came in and sat at the table where Sarah and John had just sat down and started to read. For a while, Patty just sat there without saying a word.

John asks her if she would like to have a Bible so she could read with them or just follow along with what he and Sarah were reading. She said she would like to follow along so John went and got her a Bible.

Patty looked at it for a moment and asks, "Who is Leigh?"

John had given her, a Bible he had given His First Wife Leigh for her twenty-first birthday. It was a soft leather bound, red letter, reference Bible with Leigh J. Henson embossed on the front, right lower corner. John explained to Patty that Leigh was his first wife.

Patty said, "I can't use this. It is obviously very expensive and I don't want to damage it."

John replied, "Yes, it is expensive. I had it made special for her. But, as much as she loved children, she would be very honored and pleased for you to use it and take care of it."

Patty looked at it and gently ran her fingers over the cover and traced Leigh's name with her index finger. She opened the front cover and there were all the important dates in Leigh and John's lives together. She looked at the information. When she realized what she was looking at she closed the cover quickly.

She said, "Dad, this is you and Leigh's family Bible. I can't use this. I can feel her looking at me!"

"Honey," John replied, "If you can feel her looking at you, you can see her smiling." She loved children. You, Abigail, and your mom are my family too. And when you are ready, there is room in that Bible for all of you.

It was quiet in the room for what seemed an eternity and Patty said, "Dad you have not told me..." She paused and asks, "Mom has he told you about Leigh?"

Sarah answered, "No he has not."

Patty interrupted, "Dad will you tell us about Leigh?"

John sat with his head down for a moment and got up to get a cup of coffee. When he turned around to set back down they could see his eyes were teary.

Patty said, "I am sorry Dad. I didn't mean to bring up a painful subject."

"It is ok honey," John answered. "You all have a right to know. Where would you like me to start?"

Sarah answered, "Start at the beginning. How did you two meet? When did you start dating? Did you rescue her from a snow storm like you did me? I hope you did not scare the crap out of her with a wild bear."

John chuckled and before he could answer, Patty wanted to know what Sarah was talking about.

John turned to Sarah and said, "Honey this is your part of the story. You can answer that question." Then he turned to Patty and said, "The first time I held your mother, that bears' mother scared her into my arms."

Patty thoroughly confused asks, "Will somebody tell me what you two are talking about?"

John and Sarah sat there laughing.

Patty started to get up and leave when John told Sarah, "Honey, tell her about how we met and I will fix us a snack. When you are done, I will tell you two about Leigh and me."

Sarah talked for an hour telling Patty about the snow storm. Then she told her how much the bear head on the rug scared her when she started through the door to the cabin. She told her that she jumped back into John's arms and when John caught her it scared her worse.

She said, "I was in a strange place with a bear in front of me and a strange man grabbing me from behind and I just about lost it." Sarah said, "I tore away from him, jumped over that darn bear head and stood in the middle of the cabin floor shaking."

In between her laughter, Patty said, "Mom it couldn't have been that bad."

Sarah said, "I saw your reaction when that bear was coming up the drive toward you. I saw how brave you were."

"But mom, that bear was alive!" Patty answered.

"He was alive when he stood up against the window three feet from where I was standing in the cabin!" Sarah exclaimed.

John said, "Tell her about the night gown you wore that night."

"John, you have a big mouth," Sarah said.

"What is he talking about momma?" Ask Patty.

Sarah told her, "I did not have any clothes with me except what I was wearing. He offered me a pair of his sweat pants, a sweat shirt, and a pair of sox to sleep in."

Patty replied, "I bet you looked cute in that outfit."

Sarah said, "That is exactly what he said and I called him a fool. I really felt stupid in his cloth, but they were warm and comfortable." Sarah went on to tell Patty about how she and John shared the cabin through all that had happened to them and how John had protected her from Willy Jack, Carl, Carl's gang, and the FBI. And through it all how they had fallen in love and married. She told her about their honeymoon and every place they went.

When she was done, Patty said, "Mom, I think Dad is a 'keeper' don't you? And, I want to see all the pictures you two took on the honeymoon."

"Yes, he is a 'keeper' and we will look at the pictures tomorrow. Right now, I want to hear about Leigh and John." Sarah replied.

John came back to where the girls were with a tray of milk and cookies. When he sat the tray down on the table Abigail stood up in a chair and before anyone could stop her she grabbed a cookie and tried to dunk it in one of the glasses of milk. She spilled the milk everywhere sending the three adults scrambling to clean it up. Abby was undaunted by the excitement. She stood in her chair dunking her cookie in the milk she had spilled on the table. She had made a gooey mess with crumbled cookies and milk. Patty was scolding her while John and Sarah were laughing hysterically. Sarah picked Abigail up and sat her on the kitchen sink to clean her up while John and Patty cleaned the table and floor.

Abigail held up her little hand full of crumbs to Sarah and exclaimed! "Cookie!"

She did not want to give up her cookie long enough for Sarah to clean her up. Sarah had to get her another cookie to calm her down. Patty was mortified, John and Sarah were still laughing and Abby was happy as long as she had her cookie. After spending fifteen minutes cleaning up the mess they finally sat down to enjoy their snack.

While they were enjoying their snack, John began to tell them about Leigh and him. He started with his parents and Leigh's parents being good friends and moving beside each other when he was five and Leigh was four. He told them how he and Leigh had grown up together and had become lifelong friends. For the next hour and a half, Patty and Sarah listened without saying a word. When he finished, John got up and went into the bathroom to wash his face.

When he came back to where the girls were, Patty said, "Dad Leigh sounds like a very special person. I wish we could have met her."

John said, "You will meet her."

Patty did not understand what John was saying, but Sarah knew he was talking about when they got to Heaven they would meet Leigh.

It was time for bed and Abigail was already asleep. Patty took Abigail and went to their bedroom. John and Sarah did the same thing. When they got in their room, Sarah put her arms around John and said, "John you have been through so much and lost everything, but yet you found the strength to save me and my kids. You are so special and I thank God for bringing you to me. I love you with all my being. You are so good to us."

He replied, "Honey I thank God for you also. You and the children have given me my life back. I am alive again because of you all. You all are my life now."

The next day Patty joined the Bible study. For the next two weeks, the three of them had a time of sharing and learning together. This brought them closer as a family.

The weather was beginning to clear so that they could get out and go to town. John and Sarah had planned to go to town and do some shopping. While they were in town they planned to go to church. When they ask Patty to join them she was reluctant. She claimed she didn't have proper clothing to wear to church. John asked her, "Patty have you looked through the clothes in your closet to see if there is anything you can wear?"

She asks him, "Dad, who do those clothes belong to?"

He answered, "Honey, all those clothes were bought for you. We did not know what you liked or what size you wore so we quested at it. You need to go through them. If you can't wear any of them or you don't like any of them we will take them to Goodwill when we go to town. Saturday, we will go shopping for some new clothing for you."

She stated, "Daddy there are some very nice, expensive clothes in that closet. They were here when I got here. You bought all of them for me before I got here?"

John replied, "Yes honey, your mother and I bought them for you. Our hopes and prayers were that you would accept our love and become a willing part of this family as you have done. We thank God for you every day."

Patty began to cry. She couldn't find words to express her feelings and she just stood and cried. Then she said, "Momma, Daddy I love you two so very much. Thank you for loving me when I was unlovable." She continued to cry.

John and Sarah quickly went to her and embraced and kissed her. While they were reassuring Patty that they were so glad she was now part of their family, Abigail stood pulling on Sarah's skirt with up lifted hands crying, "Up, up, up." The three of them picked her up between them. They took turns tickling and loving her until she got tired of it and demanded, "Down, down, down!" The little squirt ran and picked up her baby doll and got in the rocking chair that John had made for her and started rocking. The happy mood they shared continued as the three of them laughed at Abigail's little stunt.

That Friday they all loaded into the truck and headed for Don and Jenny's. They arrived just in time for Sarah to help Jenny with the evening meal. Patty volunteered to help as well. John played with Abigail. Don was out working on a pipeline. The next morning after breakfast, they were all ready to go shopping when John handed Patty three hundred dollars in twenty-dollar bills. He told her that it was for personal spending money. He told her that he would pay for any clothes or supplies she wanted to buy.

She took the money and said, "Oh goody! I can get a tattoo!" The look that John gave her let her know that would get her thrown right into the cellar. She concluded, "Or maybe not!" She said apologetically, "Dad I was just teasing."

John walked beside of her and with his right arm he hugged her and said, "No tattoos in my house ever! Please."

"You don't have to worry about that from me, Dad. I think they are stupid. I can't imagine someone putting something on their body they can never take off. To me, it would be like never being able to change my under wear. So, Dad, you don't have to worry about me getting a tattoo."

John pulled her to him and hugged her again and told her, "Precious child I could not love you more if you were my very own flesh and blood. You do not know how much that means to me to hear you say what you just said. Thank you so much."

They had a great time shopping, but Patty was like her mother she looked first at the price tag before she would look at the dress. Just as she reached for a tag on a cute dress John grabbed her hand and said, "Will you let me worry about the cost and you just pick out something you like?"

She said, "Dad what is my price limit?"

"You just pick out the clothes and I will let you know if it is too much."

She deliberately looked until she found the most expensive outfit in the store and held it up. She sheepishly said, "What do you think of this one Dad?"

John looked at her and the outfit and grinned. Then he said, "Try it on and let us see how you look in it."

She asks, "Don't you want to know how much it cost?"

He replied, "Try it on."

It was a light tan pleated skirt with an attached white, short sleeved top and a matching jacket. When Patty came out of the dressing room looking adorable she asks, "What do you think?"

John looked and turned to Sarah. Sarah grinned with approval and John asks Patty, "Do you like it?"

Patty said mischievously it goes good with my boots. Don't you think?" She was still wearing her winter boots certainly no match for such a beautiful dress.

John looked at Sarah and the two of them were trying to remain serious and not laugh at Patty's attics. John turned to Sarah and said Honey, will you help this nut (he gestured toward Patty) pick out what she needs to complete the outfit? I am going to take 'fizzle britches' (talking about Abigail) to get her a toy before she has another fit. I will meet the two of you at the food court at the end of the mall in thirty minutes." They all agreed and John and Abigail left for the toys.

After John had spent over a thousand dollars on Patty's clothes she felt guilty and refused to buy anything else. Sarah had concluded her shopping and Abigail was tired and getting fussy, they concluded their shopping and headed for Jenny's. After dinner, Jenny wanted to see what Patty had bought to wear to church. Patty put on her new dress with all the extras and came out to model it for all to see. She looked like a living doll. She was absolutely beautiful.

Jenny said, "John you and Sarah had better carry some very large sticks with you tomorrow. You will have to fight the boys away from her any place you take her in that outfit."

Patty was embraced by what Jenny said and quickly went and changed back into her jeans. The rest of the evening was filled with laughter and fellowship. And, Abigail was entertaining everyone with the battery powered kitty cat John bought her. It had a feature that repeated everything that Abigail said. When she got tired of it repeating everything she said she told it to 'shut up'.

When it repeated "Shut up" to her, she grabbed it and ran to John and complained, "Gam paw', it talks too much. Make it stop." Everyone laughed while John turned the toy off. Abigail then took it wrapped it in a little baby blanket and proceeded to rock it. She soon fell asleep and she and her new toy were put to bed. The rest of the crew soon followed her.

CHAPTER TWENTY-SEVEN

PATTY MAKES A LIFE-ALTERING DECISION

Sunday morning John took his new family to the church he had been attending when the weather permitted him to go. He introduced everyone to his new family and led them to the third row on the left of the church where he always sat. The service started with the usual singing and then preaching. About half way through the sermon which was very lively the preacher came off the stage into the congregation. As he made one of the strong points in his sermon he gestured by extending his hand-held microphone towered where John was holding Abigail. Before he could pull back the microphone,

Abigail said in a loud voice, "You talk too loud." When it was picked up by the microphone and filled the church the church erupted in laughter.

The Pastor (who lost his train of thought) replied, "I do not!"

When he went back up to the pulpit he had to pause for a moment to regain his composure. When service was over, John tried to apologize to the Pastor. The Pastor laughed and told John that was the first time he had been told that he talked too loud. While John was still trying to apologize the Pastor reassured John that it was ok.

He told John, "You cannot get upset with the honesty of a child. I thought what she said was rather cute."

While Sarah and John were exchanging conversation with the Pastor and his wife Abigail was trying to hide from the Pastor.

The Pastor asks Abigail, "Are you going to shake my hand?" She tried to hide from him. But, when he turned to talk to another Church member, she reached out to hug and kiss him on the check.

While the Pastor was still in shock, Patty pushed by everyone, shook the Pastor's hand, told him it was good to meet him and hurried to get into the truck. When John and Sarah got into the truck they both turned around and looked at Patty in the back seat.

Sarah who thought Patty's actions were rude asks, "What was that all about?"

Patty replied, "Momma, those guys are staring at me…"

Before she could say anything else, John asks her, "Are you bragging or complaining?"

Patty answered, "Daddy, I don't like them staring at me. Can we just go now?"

John turned around and started the truck and drove out of the church parking lot. When he was on the road he said to Patty, "Did you ever stop to think that those boys were just admiring your beauty? You were the most beautiful girl in the church today you know."

Patty replied, "Mom and Dad can we change the subject? I did not mean to be rude, but those guys made me feel so uncomfortable."

Sarah said, "Honey you are a very beautiful young woman and you are going to attract the attention of most of the young men you see. Just be yourself and be polite and everything will be ok."

Three weeks later in church, everybody found out that Abigail could not whisper. Right in the middle of the sermon, she pulled another one of her little 'monkey shines'. She stood up in the seat, cupped her hands over her mouth as if to whisper into John's ear and ask in a loud voice, "Grandpa, why is he always yelling at us?"

The Pastor got so tickled with her that he could not continue his sermon. After the laughter died down he asks everyone to stand so that he could close in prayer and the service was ended.

That Sunday several of the young people came to Patty and introduced themselves to her and she was more comfortable in the church from then on.

The next day John was out cutting wood while Sarah, Patty and Abigail were inside enjoying some venison stew that John had started in a slow cooker early that morning. All things considered, it was a normal family day. The rest of the week was a good week for the family except for Patty. Patty showed signs of depression she was keeping to herself and not interacting with the family. Thursday evening Sarah and John were taking turns telling Abigail stories until she fell asleep. Patty was in the TV room by herself watching a move. Sarah took Abigail in the bed room where she and John sleep and put her in bed. John and Sarah got in bed with Abigail. John asks Sarah if she knew what was wrong with Patty.

Sarah replied, "I don't know but I am concerned about her. She has not said a dozen words all week." Patty started into their bed room to get Abigail when she heard John and Sarah talking about her. She stopped just outside the room to listen to what they were saying.

John said to Sarah, "That child has been through more and suffered more than anyone should have to suffer in a life time. I do not know how she has survived this long."

Sarah replied, I know and I feel so ashamed that I deserted her for five years."

Before she could say more John interrupted her and said, "Honey you could not help that. You were running for your life. Had you been caught you could have been killed. Then where would Patty and Abigail be? We can't change the past, but we can give her a chance for a future. What we need to do now is make sure she knows she is loved and appreciated. We need to reassure her every day that this is her home and we are glad she is here."

While John and Sarah continued to talk about Patty, she went to her room. She went to the edge of her bed and knelt down. She said, "God I don't know if you are real or not and I don't know how this Prayer thing works so I am going to just talk. The Bible says you love everyone. So, can you love someone like me? I mean can you love someone that has done all the bad things I have done? God if you are real then tell me if you love me. Well, I don't hear anything so I guess I am done." She went to John and Sarah's bedroom and knocked on the door.

Sarah said, "Honey, come in. Do you need something?"

Patty said, "Mom I just came to get Abigail to take her to bed."

Sarah replied, "Patty, honey she is fine here tonight. Unless you just want to take her to your room why don't you just leave her in here so you don't wake her up trying to move her?"

"Are you sure she won't be in the way?" She asks.

"No, we would love to have her stay with us," John answered.

Patty said, "Ok." And she went to her room.

The next morning John and Sarah sat in the kitchen drinking coffee trying to decide what to make for breakfast. Patty came in and sat down with them. The three of them agreed on Oatmeal with hot chocolate for Abby, who had not got up yet. While Sarah was preparing the Oatmeal and John was making the hot chocolate, Abigail came into the room rubbing her eyes.

When Patty went to her to pick her up, she said all excited. "Mommy, Mommy!"

Patty answered, "What honey?"

Abby said, "Mommy, God loves you!"

Patty paused for a moment, handed Abigail to Sarah, burst out crying and ran to her room. When John and Sarah went after her to find what had just happened she would not talk to them.

When John tried to console her, she pushed him away and demanded, "Why did you tell her to say that?"

John stood there with a puzzled look.

Patty turned to Sarah and ask, "Mom did you tell her to say that?"

Sarah looked at John and they turned and replied, "Patty we did not tell Abby to say anything. We are just as surprised as you are. We were hoping you could tell us what is going on."

Patty put her hands over her face and began to cry again. John and Sarah went to her to try to comfort her when Abigail repeated, "Mommy God loves you!"

Patty turned to Sarah and John and asks, "Why is she saying that?"

John answered, "Honey what she is saying is true. God does love you, but we do not know why she is telling you about it. Have you talked to her about that?"

John knew something was brothering Patty and he suspected that it had something to do with what the Preacher preached on in the Sunday Sermon 'without forgiveness through Christ we were all going to Hell'.

John asks, "Patty did something happen in Church Sunday that has upset you? You have been very quiet all week."

Patty stood looking at John without saying a word. John reached out to take her hands and she began to tremble.

John asks, "Honey what is wrong?"

She began to sob and weep bitterly and said, "Daddy I am going to Hell! I am going to Hell! I am so scared!"

When John put his arms around her she was crying so hard she was trembling. John said, "Patty, honey you don't have to be afraid of that. Christ paid the price for all of our sins. All we have to do is accept his gift of love and forgiveness and we all will be saved. We will spend eternity with God in His Haven. We will not go to Hell."

"But Daddy I don't know how to do that!" She cried. "Last night I tried to pray and nothing happened. I ask God if he could love someone like me to tell me and nothing happened!"

John asks, "Patty, did you say you ask God to tell you if he loved you?"

She shook her head yes.

John said, "Oh honey don't you know what has just happened? God has answered your prayer. He has used your precious baby to tell you that he does love you."

"Daddy I am so scared. Help me please!" She cried.

As John held Patty in his arms, Sarah came to her and put her arms around Patty as well. Abigail for the first time ever was just watching without making a sound.

John asks, "Honey, speaking to Patty, would you like to accept Christ as your savior and be saved?"

She shook her head yes and ran to the bed where she knelt down. While she knelt and wept, John and Sarah knelt one on each side of her. Abby did not know what was happening, but she got on her little knees by the bed too.

John told Patty, "Repeat what I say. And he began to lead her in the sinner's prayer." While the three adults were praying, Abigail had put her little hand on top of John's hand that was on Patty's shoulder. All through the prayer, she was patting John's hand with her little fingers. When they finished praying, John asks Patty if she meant what she had prayed and if she believed God had heard her.

She answered, "Yes I do mean it and I know God heard. I am not scared anymore. What do I do now?"

"Well, honey it is kind of simple. Study the Bible and follow the instructions for life in the word of God and you will have the very best life you can have. When you are ready, we will tell the pastor and he will set a date for you to be baptized."

After they talked about baptism for a while Sarah suggested that everyone go back to the kitchen so they could continue with breakfast.

Patty asks. "Mom, Dad, I am not hungry. Would it be ok if I take a nap? I have not slept all week."

John pulled the blanket back on the bed and said, "Sleep as long as you need to."

Sarah grabbed Abigail who was trying to get in bed with Patty and told her, "You come with Grandpa and me and let your mommy rest."

Patty did study the Bible. Not only did she study the Bible with John and Sarah but, she read and studied on her own. She became excited about going to church and was always ready on Sunday morning before everyone else.

CHAPTER TWENTY-EIGHT

BOY MEETS GIRL

Everything went well for the next three weeks. But, Patty came home after church one Sunday very upset. When she was asked what the problem was she replied, "Dad what you have done to me in just cruel."

When John asked what she was talking about, she said, "You brought me up here, got me going to church with good people and now a good boy has asked me to go out with him."

John asks, "What is wrong with that?"

She answered, "What do you think he is going to do when he finds out that I am a Whore?"

John asks, "Honey, are you still selling your body?"

"Daddy you know I am not doing that anymore. But when I was in L.A. I did. What will he say when he finds that out?"

"Patty, are you talking about Gary?" John asks.

"Dad how did you know… Who told you it is …? I mean what makes you think it is Gary?" She answered.

"Patty, honey everyone sees how you look at him and how he looks at you. It is very obvious that there is a strong attraction between the two of you."

"Ok, just for the sake of discussion, let's say it is Gary. Now, what do I do? Just what do you think he will do when he learns about my past?" Patty asks.

John replied, "Honey, do not give up on Gary until you give him a chance. This is what I think you should do. Sunday is the annual picnic at church. If he shows an interest in you take him to the side where you two have some privacy and tell him about your past. One of two things will happen: either he will accept you for who you are now, which is good, or he will walk away from you. If he does walk away he is not worthy of your time and you need to know that now. Leave him alone. There will be someone else. I believe God has the right person for you and if you are patient He will bring him to you."

Patty spent the rest of the week thinking about what John had told her. Everyone was getting ready for Sunday and the picnic; Sarah and John were packing a lunch large enough to share with others while Abigail was trying to get into everything. John noticed that Patty had put on a really cute dress. He reminded her that the picnic would be outside and suggested that a pair of jeans would be more appropriate. She looked at what John and Sarah were wearing and quickly changed.

The service was short and sweet and it was time to eat. Patty was trying to fix her plate when she was bumped from behind. She tried to ignore it and continued to fix her plate but, she could not move without being bumped. When she turned to see what was bumping her Gary was standing so close to her that she could not move without bumping him.

She protested, "What do you think you are doing?"

He replied, with a boyish grin, "Trying to get your attention."

She grinned with approval and replied with a chuckle, "Ok, you nut, you have my attention. What do you want?"

Gary asks, "Can we eat together?"

Patty remembered what John had suggested and thought, "This is a good time to tell him." She tilted her head to the right and replied, "Ok."

After Patty and Gary got their plates full Patty led Gary to a table away from the crowd and sat down.

Gary asks, "Why are we so far away from everyone else?"

Patty replied, "I want to talk to you and I do not want everyone else to hear what I have to say." Patty talked to Gary for over thirty minutes. She told him about all the horrible things she had done when she lived in LA and what a horrible person she was before she got saved. She said, "I want you to know what you are getting into before this relationship goes any further."

Gary just sat staring at her with big sad eyes for what seems to be an eternity to Patty.

She demanded, "Don't you have anything to say?"

Without saying a word, Gary grabbed Patty and passionately kissed her.

When she caught her breath she pushed him away and demanded, "What do you think you are doing? I did not tell you could…I didn't give you permission…What do you think you are doing?"

"I have found my soul mate!" Gary exclaimed and he grabbed her hands.

Patty demanded, "Let go of me! What do you think you are doing?"

Gary pleaded, "Patty please let me explain. I have been an outcast every sense I have been in Alaska. I have a sorted past also. Please let me tell you about it. Please. I apologize for my actions but, when you told me about your past I knew you would understand the trouble I have been in. And maybe you would accept me for who I am now as I accept you. Will you listen to my story?"

Patty pulled her hands-free and stated, "Ok. As long as you keep your hands to yourself I will listen."

Gary began, "I grew up in Pittsburg, Pa. My dad was killed in an auto accident when I was four. My mother never got over the loss of my dad and she became a drunk. I grew up on the streets mean and tough. At least I thought I was tough. I was arrested twice before I was fourteen. When I was seventeen I was in the process of robbing an old woman when she walked in on me. I didn't know it but she had already called the cops when I attacked her. I had her on the floor beating on her when the cops came in, knocked me off her with a night stick, and arrested me. I sat in jail for three weeks until the trail. My grandmother came down from Alaska and pleaded with the Judge to let her take charge of me. After they talked for over an hour the judge signed papers giving my grandmother custody of me until I turned eighteen. The last thing I wanted was to move to Alaska and leave all my friends and my gang. But, the judge lets me know that if I did not go with her I would be tried as an adult and go to jail for assault and robbery.

The last thing I intended to do was stay in Alaska. I had decided to rob my grandmother to get enough money to get back to Pittsburg. When she caught me trying to do that and tried to stop me, I hit her with my fist. She fell against the fire place. She came at me with a steel poker from the fire place and hit me on the side of my head. When I came to John was there and I was on the floor in hand cuff and leg irons."

Patty asks, "Are you talking about John, my dad?"

"Yes, John. By the way is he your dad or step dad?"

Patty said, "He is not my birth dad but he is the only dad I have ever had. Go on with your story. What happened next?"

"Well, when I came to I heard grandmother tell John that she could not control me and she reminded John that he had agreed to help. John told her he would take care of the problem. He grabbed the hand cuffs that were behind my back and jerked me to my feet. He dragged me out to his truck and tossed me in the back of his truck like I was a bag of trash. When we got to his cabin he opened the tail gate and dragged me out onto the ground. When he turned to unlock the cage, I tried to run but a huge bear grabbed me by the shoulder and threw me to the ground. He put his paw on me and smashed my face into the dirt. It scared me so bad I wet myself. John told the bear to bring me to him and the bear grabbed me by the coat and dragged me back to him. John took me into his cabin and threw me in a box. He slammed the door and told me that I would stay in there until I got some manners. He kept me in that box for…Patty is holding her hand over her mouth and trying not to laugh, but she is about to burst with laughter. Gary asks, "What is so darn funny?"

Patty replies, "I can just see you in that box after about a week. I bet you were a site and I bet you smelled good too."

Gary said in disgust, "It was not funny. It was the most miserable two weeks I have ever spent. If you had to go through that you would not be laughing."

Patty reached out and took Gary's hands and told him, "Gary, John gave me an attitude adjustment also. When he brought me out of LA., he put me in the root cellar at the lodge. When he let me out I could not stand myself. You see, I do know what you went through. And, you are correct, it is not funny"

Gary just stared at her for a moment. Then he began to laugh and said, "You mean you were in that root cellar without being able to brush your teeth, comb your hair, or wash your face, and you didn't have toilet paper? I bet you were a...

Before he could finish Patty said laughingly. "Gary if you know what is good for you, you won't go there."

Patty and Gary spent the next hour and a half talk and laughing and just sharing their thoughts and dreams for the future. When Patty told Gary, she had not finished high school Gary told her he had not finished either. He told her how John had tutored him and helped him get his GED. After he got his GED, John helped him get into Collage and was giving him money for tuition.

Patty asks, "Are you talking about John my Dad?"

Gary answered, "Yes. Your Dad is the very best friend I have. I wish he was my Dad."

Patty just sat there not saying a word. The rest of the day the two of them talked and laughed and had a great time together. They played games at the picnic as partners. They entered the three-legged race and won it. By the end of the day, it was obvious to all that the two of them had a great time together.

When they all got back to the lodge and got everything unloaded from the things they had taken to the picnic they sat down at the table to rest. Sarah had made a small snack of milk and cookies and they sat around the table talking about how much they all enjoyed the picnic.

Patty turned toward John with a grin on her face and said, "Dad you are just awful. I never know what to expect from you and...well, Daddy, you are a wonderful person, but you are still just awful."

John was puzzled by what she said and he asked, "What did I do to cause you to say that?"

She responded, "Daddy you know Gary. You know all about him and his past and you did not tell me anything about him. You let me worry myself sick about what he would do when he found out about my past. You could have told me about him. I love you daddy but, you are just so awful." It was obvious that what she was saying was intended to be playful she was grinning joyfully.

Sarah on the other hand who had no idea what was going on asks, "What are the two of you talking about?"

Patty replied, "Momma, Daddy gave Gary an attitude adjustment like he did me. He put him in a box also."

Sarah more perplexed than ever asks, "John what on earth is she talking about?"

Now John who is laughing tries to regain his composure so he can answer Sarah's question. He replies to Sarah, "Before I met you Gary's Grandmother brought him up here from Pittsburg. I helped her straighten him out like I did Patty when she first got here."

Sarah just sat there with her jaw dropped. "John! you didn't put him in a horrible place like you did Patty, did you?"

John paused for a moment and answered, "Well, yes I did.

And before he could say anything else Sarah demanded, "Did you scare the crap out of him with that darn bear also?"

Now John and Patty were laughing so hard that John could not answer but, Patty said, "Momma he sure did! Gary told me that he was so scared that he wet himself."

Sarah just sat there shaking her head as though she was saying no. Then she said, "John you are awful. Patty is right you are awful."

John said, "Maybe so but, it worked. After I got his attention I was able to tutor him to get his GED. He is now in college ready to start his third year and he is doing well."

Patty asks, "Daddy, Gary said you are paying for his college. Is that right?"

John answered, "Yes honey, I agreed to pay for his college expenses as long as he maintains a B average or above."

Sarah asks, "Why are you doing that?"

John replied, "He is a good young man and I am helping him. It is as simple as that."

Patty told John and Sarah that Gary had asked her to go to college with him. She asks, "Momma, Daddy is there any way I can go to college? I guess that is a dumb question. I didn't even finish high school."

John told her, "Patty if you will study and work hard your mother and I will help you get your GED and by fall semester you can go to college with Gary."

CHAPTER TWENTY-NINE

A FRESH START FOR PATTY AND GARY

Patty studied and worked hard at it. John helped her and so did Sarah. Gary even came to the lodge and helped her study. She got her GED and that fall she started to college where Gary was attending. John and Sarah thought it best if Patty had a room in the dormitory at the school in case the weather prevented them from traveling between the lodge and the college. Patty would spend the week at school and John and Sarah would get her and bring her home for the weekend if weather permitted.

Abigail stayed with Sarah and John, of course, she insisted that she be allowed to go to college too. It took some explaining to her to convince her that she had to stay home and help Grandpa and Grandma. After several hours of coaxing, and bribing, Sarah and John convinced Abigail to stay at the lodge while Patty attended school. There was, however, a compromise that had to be made Abby was told she could not go to college because she did not have her GED. John had to agree to help her get it. It started out to be a game to keep her occupied but John and Sarah quickly seized the opportunity to turn the time into a home schooling event. It was amazing how fast Abby learned. The first year she learned the entire alphabet and was righting her name and short sentences before she was three years old.

John and Sarah took turns teaching her and they made it fun for her. John added fishing to her training and took her with him when he would go hunting. She even met Brutus and loved him. She gave him the nick name 'Bruty'. Sarah would protest every time Brutus came around but, Brutus was very tolerant of Abby and with John's supervision, Abby would ride Brutus in the yard. Sarah was so glad when Brutus went into hibernation for the winter. Sarah taught Abby to make cookies and to clean her room. They also did some small sewing projects together in addition to teaching her the Alphabet.

One morning when John came in the lodge after doing chores he heard Sarah laughing. It was so pleasant to hear her laugh that John hurried to where she was to find out what was so funny. Abby was standing on her hands and one foot trying to get her other foot into one of John's boots. John sat down on the love seat beside Sarah and the two of them laughed at Abby's little attics for another six minutes laughing continuously. When Abby finally got into John's boots and stood up, she could not walk because they were too heavy. After falling down several times, she gave up and sat on the floor in obvious disgust. John turned to Sarah and said, "It is so good to hear you laugh." And he kissed her.

Abigail asks, "Grandpa, what did you do to Grandma?"

John replied, "Kissed her."

Abby asks, "Why?"

John answered, "Because I love her."

Abby said, "I love Grandma too."

John said, "Why don't you give her a kiss?"

Without another word, Abigail scrambled out of John's boots and climbed into Sarah's lap and gave Sarah an open mouth kiss right on Sarah's lips baby slobbers and all. It was a kiss that only a Grandmother could love.

Sarah did not want John left out so she asks Abby, "Don't you love Grandpa too?"

Before John could react, Abby scrambled from Sarah's lap into John's lap and planted the same kind of kiss on him. The two of them laughed and wiped baby slobbers. They continued to kiss and love on Abigail until she got tired of it and escaped to the floor. John reminded Abby that she only had one hour to play before Home School started. While Abby was playing with her toys, John and Sarah sat there talking about Patty and Gary.

Sarah asks, "Do you think they will ever 'hook up'? I mean…"

Before Sarah could explain what she was asking, John replied, "I wouldn't be surprised if they haven't already done that. They are obviously in love you know."

"John!" Sarah said in disgust, "I meant to ask you if you think they will get married!"

John paused for a moment and with a mischievous grin on his face replied, "I believe they will. At least I hope and pray they do. They are made for each other. And, I believe they would have a great life together."

The rest of the winter was for the most part routine: Abigail attended home school, John and Sarah attended to the family needs, and Patty attended college. Patty and Gary were spending all of their spare time together. The bond between them had obviously grown serious. Two weeks before spring break Gary borrowed his Grandmother's truck and brought Patty home for the week end. While Gary sat outside in the truck, Patty came into the lodge and demanded an audience with Sarah and John.

Patty stated in a firm voice, "Gary and I have plans to get married and we want your approval. We will not take no for an answer!"

John and Sarah looked at each other for a moment. When John was sure he and Sarah were in agreement, He turned to Patty with a blank expression on his face and said, "Ok."

The silence in the room was profound. Patty stood staring at John and Sarah for a moment and then burst into tears. She ran to her room and fell across her bed where she continued to cry.

John turned to Sarah with the palms of his hands turned up and asks, "What did I do wrong? I said ok."

Sarah assessing the situation and understanding it as only a mother could, puts her arms around John and said, "Bid daddy, your daughter who loves you so much was so afraid you would not approve. She needs your reassurance. Why don't you go to her and tell her what you think?"

John looked at Sarah and said, "She is almost nineteen years old. She does not need my permission to get married."

Before John could say anything else, Sarah said, "John she needs your reassurance. And you know she will need your help. Go to her John."

John stepped out the back door where Gary was setting in the truck and motioned for him to come in the lodge. When Gary got in the lodge John told him to set down. John thought about grabbing Gary and Patty, dragging them down to, and throwing them in the root cellar to let them think about this marriage for a while. As he walked toward Patty's bedroom he decided that would be too much of an 'over kill'. So, he went into the bed room where Patty was still lying on the bed crying and ask her to come into the room where Gary was. When she got there, John instructed her to set beside Gary.

John looked at the two of them and said, "You two have my blessings on this venture under one condition: you both finish college."

Patty with her head down, still crying said, "Daddy we don't know how we can do that. We don't have any money for college."

John sat there for a moment. He leaned his head back in his chair and closed his eyes. Tears began to run down his cheeks. Sarah who was sitting beside him reached over and took John's hand. John leaned forward and said, "Patty, honey don't you know that your happiness and future means more to us than life itself? We will make it happen if you two will promise me that you will finish college."

Gary who had not said a word was beginning to tear up also, looked at John and shook his head in approval. Patty got out of her chair and ran to John and Sarah, who were now standing, and through her arms around both their necks. She began to hug and kiss both of them.

Patty, still crying, said, "Mom, Dad, you two are the very best and I love you so much."

Gary came over and joined in a group hug.

For the next two weeks, Gary and Patty were occupied with finals while John and Sarah were making plans for the wedding. Abigail, on the other hand, was a completely different story. She would come in the kitchen in the morning still so nearly asleep she would be rubbing her eyes and ask about school. After Sarah and John would end the home school session so they could work on the wedding, Abby would start her own school. She would take all her stuffed animals that Sarah and John had bought her and she would line them up for school. She would read to them for hours. Then she would shake her finger at them and sternly warn them about the importance of doing their homework. She would play with them for a while then school would start all over again. John and Sarah would get so tickled and amused at her that they were having trouble getting anything done with the wedding plans.

In spite of all the distractions from Abigail, the wedding was scheduled for June. All the plans were in place. There was to be an informal wedding at the lodge with family and close friends. The list included: Don and Jenny; Art from the FBI; Gary's grandmother; the local family that made the bearskin rug for John; the preacher, his wife who also played the organ and the choir from the church. Patty had picked out a beautiful ecru (off white) dress with matching shoes. She had met a young lady from church that she had become good friends with named Carolyn. Carolyn was to be the maid of honor. Gary would wear a black suit with a white shirt and a light pink carnation in his lapel. John was going to be very busy: not only did he have to give the bride away but he was the best man. And then there was Abigail. She wanted to be the Bride, the maid of honor, and of course, she wanted to be the flower girl. Abby (who was convinced to be the flower girl) was to be dressed in an off-white dress and matching shoes with a light blue sash over her right shoulder and around her waist. Sarah was in charge of the flowers, but John had to scold her for being too conservative. John had to keep reminding her that this was her only daughter and this was the only chance she had to get it right get the best and forget about the cost. The flowers cost over two thousand dollars and Sarah was horrified.

John told her, "Honey calm down. Patty is our only daughter so let's do it right. Let's make it a time to remember."

John was so pleased with the flowers, they were stunning. Sarah had done a fantastic job. There were Carnations, orchids, roses and an assortment of other arrangements (Many of which had to be flown in special) and there were lots of Alpine Forget Me Nots, the state flower. The bride's bouquet was an arrangement of white and pink rose buds.

All the arrangements were in place and all that was left was to have the wedding. And then it happened. The first Saturday in June was here. All of the guests had arrived at John and Sarah's lodge, and the wedding was on. The organ began to play 'here comes the bride' and the most beautiful young lady that ever lived took John's arm.

As they slowly walked down the aisle Abby stood up in her chair and told Sarah, "That is my mommy and she is getting me a daddy!"

All that heard her were amused at her antics, including Sarah, were trying to hold their composure when Sarah took her by the arm and told her, "Set down you little monkey before you fall and break your neck."

John, who heard her too was trying to be serious as he went through his part of giving Patty away. When he finished, He joined the men at the front of the marriage assembly where he was the best man. At the appropriate time, John handed a very nerve groom the ring.

When Gary had successfully placed the ring on Patty' shaking, trembling hand and they had both repeated the marriage vows after the pastor, the pastor said, "I now pronounce you man and wife, you may kiss the bride." He then turned to the crowd and said, "Ladies and gentlemen I give you Mister and Mistress Gary Heart."

John and Sarah had made arrangements for Patty and Gary to go to Hawaii for their honeymoon and there was a limousine out in the yard waiting to take them to the cruise ship. When they opened the gate to let the Limousine in they forgot to close the gate. When Patty turned her back to the girls waiting in the yard to ketch the bouquet, you guessed, it Brutus walked into the yard. Just as Patty tossed the bouquet there were blood-curdling screams and girls running for their lives. When Patty turned to see which girl caught the bouquet all the girls were gone. Brutus was setting in the yard holding the flowers and eating the rose buds. Sarah ran in the lodge screaming, Patty was leaning over the hand rail with her jaw dropped, Gary was trying to hide and John was hurrying to get Brutus out of the yard.

Just as John got to Brutus and started to lead him out of the yard, Patty called out to John, "Daddy wait! Daddy wait! Can we have our picture taken with Brutus?"

Gary protested, "Not me!"

The Camera man said, "I am not going near that bear!"

Sarah cracked the door just enough to plead with John, "John please make him go away!"

Patty asks again, "Please Daddy. Can we have our picture taken with Brutus?"

Brutus was not camera shy; John had taken hundreds of pictures of him. In fact, he was a great big 'ham' he loved having his picture taken. When John asks Brutus if he wanted his picture taken he shook his head up and down to signify yes.

John said, "Ok all of you get down here and let's get it done."

While the camera man was trying to protest, Patty grabbed Gary's arm and dragged him down the steps to where John and Brutus were. John told the camera man that he was not leaving until he took the picture. He pleaded with John to let him do it from the balcony. John agreed but told him the picture had better be good or he would not get paid. John had Brutus set facing the balcony and put Gary on the right and Patty on the left. The camera man took several shots. He got one shot as Brutus turned to Gary and licked his face. Gary was not pleased, but he knew better than to provoke Brutus.

John led his old friend out of the yard and gave him several 'bear treats' John had made especially for Brutus. When Brutus had gone back into the woods and the yard was secure, John helped the kids get ready to leave on their honeymoon.

Sarah helped also, but she was still upset over Brutus interrupting the wedding. When the kids and the guest were gone, John and Sarah sat down at the kitchen table where Sarah had poured them a cup of coffee. John was waiting for Sarah to say something about Brutus coming into the yard. He knew that it was her that had opened the gate and left it open. It was her fault that Brutus got in and ate the bouquet.

Finley, Sarah said in disgust, "Why did that darn bear have to spoil everything?"

John replied, "I do not know. Who left the gate open so he could get in?"

Sarah said, "Ok John! You know that I opened the gate to let the limousine in so I suppose that is your way of telling me that it is my fault."

John said, "Honey we don't have to blame anyone. It was a little awkward, but how many newlyweds can say that their wedding pictures included a picture with a live grizzly bear? You know that Patty loved it."

Sarah shook her head and said, "John you are incorrigible. I don't know what I am ever going to do with you."

While John and Sarah were talking, Abigail came into the room and wanted to know why she couldn't go on the honeymoon. John told her it was because it was her bed time. She protested that she was not sleepy and crawled into John's lap. She was asleep in five minutes. Sarah took her and put her to bed and she and John continued talking and unwinding from the day's activities.

CHAPTER THIRTY

A TIME OF REFLECTIONS

Patty and Gary had a wonderful time on their honeymoon and returned with all kinds of stories to tell. They spent the week end with John and Sarah at the lodge before returning to school. Summer classes would start in two weeks, but they had already signed up for classes. They wanted to take Abigail with them for the two weeks to give her a chance to get to know them in their new life. Monday morning, they loaded up in the new midsize SUV John and Sarah bought them for a wedding present and left for school. John and Sarah watched them drive out the gate and closed it behind them.

As they walked back into the lodge John commented, "I have heard of an 'empty nest syndrome', but I never had any idea what it felt like until now. It sure is quiet here without the little squirt. I sure miss her already."

Sarah who was tearing up replied, "I have lost my girls again."

John answered, "Honey Abigail will be back in two weeks. They can't take care of her while they are going to school. And, we have not lost a daughter; we have gained a son and a very good one at that."

Sarah replied, "You are right about that. Gary is a great person and I thank God for bringing him into Patty's life. They seem very happy together."

While they missed the kids, they made good use of their time without them. John talked Sarah into fishing with him and she loved it. He was even able to talk her into meeting Brutus. She stood on the balcony and scratched his ear while he stood up against the hand rail. It was a short meeting, but John was so pleased.

They had lots of time to talk and share with each other. One evening, while they were talking John, commented, "We have been married almost three years now. After thinking about all that has happened do you have any regrets?"

Sarah paused for a moment and answered, "Yes I do have regrets."

John over analyzing everything expects the worst. He was afraid that with all the threats against Sarah neutralized that she would not need or want him in her life. He paused for a long while before he got enough nerve to ask her, "Do you want to explain what you mean by that?"

She turned toward John and said, "Do you remember the night you rescued me from the snow storm? Remember when that bear head scared me and I jumped into your arms? I regret that I didn't know you like I do now. If I did I would have stayed in your arms. I regret that we lived together four mounts and I thought you didn't like girls. I thought you were one of them."

"What do you mean; one of them?" He asks.

"You know what I am talking about. I thought you were a homosexual." She replied. "They have got to be miserable people and I know God must really hate them."

John was quick to answer her, "No honey. God does not hate the homosexuals. His Son died on the cross for them just as he did for you and me. We have all sinned and come short of the glory of God and we all need a savior. God does not hate them. He does not accept their life style. This would be a good topic for a Bible study."

"Does the Bible have a lot to say about the homosexuals?" She asks."

"As a matter of fact, it does." And it is very plain how God feels about them. The first thing that must be known about Homosexuals is that God loves them. He does not love the life style they have chosen to live. James 1:14 15 says, 'But every man is tempted, when he is drawn away of his own lust, and enticed. Then when lust hath conceived, it bringeth forth sin: and sin, when it is finished, bringeth forth death.'". "I do not know what a Homosexual feels or thinks. It is obvious that they are born with a very strong temptation to live the Homosexual life style but, it is a sin that God does not accept. From the time in Leviticus God made it plain that the Homosexual life style was not acceptable. It was even punishable by death. Look at what the Bible says in Leviticus 18:22 'Thou shalt not lie with mankind, as with womankind: it [is] abomination.' In Leviticus 20:13 it says 'If a man also lie with mankind, as he lieth with a woman, both of them have committed an abomination: they shall surely be put to death; their blood [shall be] upon them.'"

"The word abomination occurs sixty-nine times from Genesis through Revelation. This word must be important. Look at what the Bible says about it in Revelation 21:8: 'but the fearful, and unbelieving, and the abominable and murderers, and whoremongers, and sorcerers, and idolaters, and all liars, shall have their part in the lake which burneth with fire and brimstone: which is the second death.'"

Sarah asks, "In that scripture, is the word abominable the same as the word abomination?"

John replied, "The word abominable refers to those engaged in an act that God calls an abomination. The homosexual life style is called an abomination in Leviticus 20:13."

Sarah stated, "I sure was miserable during the four months we spent in the cabin when I thought you did not like me because I was a girl. I felt totally rejected and worthless just because I thought you did not like girls."

John chuckled and said, "I hope you know that I do like girls especially one in particular."

Sarah ran to where John was sitting on the love seat and jumped into his lap, hugged and kissed him. She said, "Yes I know you love girls and I am so glad I am the 'one in particular'."

He grabbed her in the ribs and began to tickle her.

She protested loudly, "John! John! John! Quit! You know I can't stand that!" She paused and stated, "We need to get back to the Bible study."

John pulled her to him and passionately kissed her and asks, "Are you sure you want to quit this and go back to the Bible study?"

She took a deep breath and replied, "John you have me so confused I don't know if I am going or coming. Why couldn't you have done this to me the night you rescued me from the snow storm? That way I would not have suffered for four months thinking you did now like girls. Now can we get on with the study?"

John pulled her back into his arms and told her, "Honey you don't know how much I wanted to hold you in my arms that night. That was a very lonely time in my life and I desperately wanted someone to hold and love. There are no words that give me the tools I need to express to you how much you mean to me. You have given me my life back beautiful lady."

Sarah snuggled as close to him as she could and replied, "I know how you feel. Before you came into my life, I did not know what love or happiness was. I thought I had a good day if I wasn't cursed, yelled at, or beaten. And, then you came along and you are everything a girl could ever hope for. You are the kindest, most gentle, caring, human being I have ever known. Sitting here in your arms like this gives me a sense of peace and joy I have never known and I thank God for you every day. John, I am still learning how to love and I adore my teacher."

They sat there for a while just talking. Then Sarah picked up her Bible and said, "John I really like this Bible study we are doing. Can we continue? Don't the Homosexuals claim that God made them the way they are and therefore it is just another life style?"

John answered, "They do claim that they are made that way and that they can't help themselves but, so do the pedophiles, mass rapist, and mass murderers. They all say that they are made that way and they cannot help themselves. But, that is not true. Every since sin came into the world by Adam and Eve; we all have to deal with temptations. How we deal with the temptations is a choice we have to make. The Northern Colorado Gazette published an article where the pedophiles, in the area were demanding the rites that were being given to the Gays. The Gays in the area were the first and most vocal protesters. The book of First John 2:16 says this:

'for all that [is] in the world, the lust of the flesh, and the lust of the eyes, and the pride of life, is not of the Father but is of the world'."
"According to First John, they are a product of a sinful world they are not made that way by God.

The Old and the New Testament both condemn the homosexual life style. We just read the scriptures in Leviticus 18:22 and Leviticus 20:13. Romans 1:26 through 28 also condemns it. Revelation 21:8 says that the abominable will have their place in the lake of fire. In other words, those who live the homosexual life will go to Hell."

Sarah asks, "Is it possible that their temptation is so strong that they can't help what they do?"

John answered, "Not according to the Bible. Look at what first Corinthians 10:13 says: 'There hath no temptation taken you but such as is common to man: but God [is] faithful, who will not suffer you to be tempted above that ye are able; but will with the temptation also make a way to escape, that ye may be able to bear [it].'

The 'way out' that this scripture talks about is given in the gospel of John. John 1:12 says this: 'But as many as received him, to them gave he power to become the sons of God, [even] to them that believe on his name.'

"The expression 'sons of God' occurs eleven times in the Bible and every time it does it refers to either a direct creation of God—Angles--or someone that has been re-created or restored to a perfect condition. In Luke 17:11 through 19 ten Lepers cried out for Christ to heal them. Christ told all ten of them to go show themselves to the priests. On their way, they were cleansed. They still had the scars of their disease but they were now cleansed and the priests would allow them back into society. However, when one of the lepers saw he was cleansed he turned and worshiped Christ. He did not have to show himself to the priests because he was not just cleansed, he was made whole. Christ told him to go his way. His faith had made him whole.' He was re-created.

According to this scripture, the homosexual can be re-created and does not need to give in to the temptation.

Homosexuality is a plan of Satin and will be worse in the tribulation period then it was in Sodom and Gomorrah in the Book of Genesis chapter eighteen. In the book of Leviticus 20:13 it is called an abomination. In the book of Daniel chapter nine says because of the overspreading of abominations. Or, in other words, because of the protest of the Homosexuals he, the Anti Christ, (who is a Homosexual according to Daniel 11:37) will break his contract with Israel and stops their evening sacrifice in the temple and replace it with the old sun god worship of Bail.

There are many other scriptures that deal with the subject, but one of my favorite scriptures is in Revelations twenty-two verse fifteen. This scripture is talking about when God will completely restore his creation. It is called the new Jerusalem. It states: 'For without are dogs, and sorcerers, and whoremongers, and murderers, and idolaters, and whosoever loveth and maketh a lie.'

The word dogs always troubled me. Why would God not want dogs, man's best friend, in his New Jerusalem? So, I did an in-depth study on the matter. The Bible is translated from Hebrew and Greek (the old testament from Hebrew and the new testament from Greek). During the time the Bible was written, Homosexuals had over run the Greek society and the Christian Greeks called the Homosexuals dogs. That is why they are called dogs in this scripture. That is why Philippines 3:2 says; 'Beware of dogs, beware of evil workers, beware of the concision'. That is what the Greek Christians called them when the Bible was written."

Sarah asks, "John how do you know so much about the Bible?"

He replied, "I grew up reading the Bible. Leigh and I read to each other when we were just starting to read." John paused for a moment and said, "I am sorry, I didn't mean to bring up Leigh's name."

Sarah responded, "That is ok John. I don't mind if you talk about her. She was an important part of your life. In fact, I would like to ask you something about her."

John said, "Well go ahead and ask. What would you like to know?"

Sarah was quiet for a moment and John encouraged her to ask her question. When she looked at John it seemed as though she was trying to hold back tears when she asks, "Did you love her more than you love me?"

John reached out and took her in his arms and just held her for a moment without saying a word. When he spoke, he said, "It is strange that you would ask that question because I have thought a lot about the relationship I had with her and the one I have with you. I can't say that I loved her more than I love you. My life with Leigh was totally different than the one I have with you."

Sarah interrupted, "Didn't you love her?"

He replied, "Of course I loved her. But, I never had to fall in love with her. We were always together. Somewhere in my picture albums, I have a picture of me holding Leigh when she was just two hours old. I did not know what life was like without her until she died. I have never held another girl. I never ask another girl for a date. I did not want to be around another girl. Leigh was my life. From the time she died until I met you I did not have a life. I just went through the motions of life. The first time I saw you in the restraint you opened in Purgatory I was working on the FBI case and I was there to investigate you. I observed everyone that came in and went out of Purgatory in pursuance of my investigation of Silk Willy. While I sat there eating the club sandwich and drinking my coffee I found myself having strange feelings. I was looking at you, a strange woman, and thinking how beautiful you were. I had never done that before."

Sarah commented, "You can't tell me that you never looked at another woman while you were with Leigh. That is just not like a man. At least not like any I have ever known. Carl was always messing around with other women. As a matter of fact, it was not uncommon to go into my own bed room and find him in the bed with one of the dancers from the club. If I said anything he beat me."

John answered, "That will never happen with me. I hate that kind of foolishness. Marriage is sacred to me and I intend to always keep it that way."

"John." Sarah stated, "You have not answered my question. Did you love her more than you love me?"

He replied, "No I did not love her more than I love you. My life with her was different than it is with you. She was always with me and she was everything I wanted in a mate. I had to fall in love with you, but I love you two the same; with all my heart, body, and mind. You complete me just as she did. You have all the love there is in this old man. I hope that answers you question."

"Can we get back to our Bible study?" She asked. "If God loves the Homosexual how are we supposed to feel toward them?"

John replied, "First of all, we are to pray for them to be saved. We are not their judge so we cannot condemn them. However, we cannot condone or support their lifestyle in any way. To do so would be the same as agreeing to send them to Hell. As a Christen, we do not want anyone to go to Hell so we cannot, in any way, support their choice to live in their sin. Do you understand what I just said?"

Sarah replied, "You mean that if we encourage them or support them we are encouraging them and therefore condemning them to Hell?"

"Yes." He answered. "We are actually condoning their sin and that is the same as condemning them to spend eternity in Hell. As Christians, we cannot and should not do that. Do you have any more questions about the subject?"

"No, but it was a very interesting study. Now can I ask you some more about you and Leigh?"

"What would you like to know, my love?"

She asked, "When you were growing up did you always spend time with her or did you have male friends too?"

"No. I preferred to be with Leigh so I spent all of my time with her."

"Didn't you get picked on by the rest of the kids?" She asked.

"All of the time." He answered. "One day when I was eight I came home with a bloody nose and my shirt torn off. My Dad decided that I need to learn to defend myself. He put me in a self-defense class taught by a Krav Maga instructor. Krav Maga is a self-defense system developed for the military in Israel that consists of a wide combination of techniques sourced from boxing, savate, Mau Thai, Wing Chun, Judo, Jiu Jitsu wrestling and grappling along with realistic fight training. Krav Maga is known for its focus on real world situations and extremely efficient and brutal counter attacks.

I studied that martial art until I became an instructor. Then I taught it to the teens I worked with in Kentucky. I taught it to Gary the summer I worked with him. He is quite good at it."

Sarah commented, "John I thought you worked with troubled teens. Isn't that insane to teach troubled teens to be killers? You taught Gary! What if he gets mad and hurts Patty or Abigail!"

John laughed and said, "Honey the reason most teens are troubled is that they have no confidence in themselves. They feel like losers and they act badly to cover their sense of worthlessness. The 'martial arts' training is all about discipline and self-confidence. If a troubled teen can regain his or her self-confidence they also learn to respect themselves and others. That turns them into productive citizens, not killers. As for Gary hurting Patty or Abigail that will not ever happen. As a matter of fact, his training has made him a much better person. He now respects himself and he would give his life for Patty and Abigail because of his loves and respects for them.

And by the way, Abigail saw Gary and me working out and she wants to learn martial arts. Do you think that if I teach her it will turn her into a killer?"

She replied, "Oh John don't be silly. You are not going to teach her that." She paused and asked, "Are you?"

He answered, "Oh yes I am. And, I am going to teach Patty and you as well." John said, "You know that all of that martial arts training has turned me into an absolute killer and you must know how to defend yourself when I get mean."

She told him, "Oh John will you stop being so silly. You have never been mean to anyone or anybody. I don't think you know how."

John, in a playful mood told her, "You can't ever tell when I might have a bad spell and turn mean. You had better be ready I think I feel a bad mood coming on now." He lowered his head and turned it slightly to the right and begins to growl like an angry dog. He slowly got up out of his chair and started toward her with his hands turned in and distorted to look like claws growling as he went.

Sarah protested, "John will you stop that? You look so stupid."

He continues toward her still growing. When he got to where she was sitting on the couch she tried to jump up and run but he caught her and wrestled her down on the couch and began to tickle her and bite her on the neck growling all the time. She screamed, kicked and hollered at him to stop. They wrestled around until they landed on the floor with Sarah still screaming and squealing for John to stop. John turned her loose and just lay on the floor beside her. She was still screaming until she realized she was loose.

She turned toward John and hit on the shoulder with the first like it was a hammer and said, "John you are awful! That was... I was so ... John that was just... I don't like for you to do things like that. I was scared!"

John gently pulled her to him and softly touched noses with her and told her, "My precious, precious lady don't you know that I would rather die myself than to ever hurt you in any way?"

While they lay there, he took his index finger and gently pushed her hair back out of her eyes.

She lay there for a while then began to laugh softly and responded, "You horrible man. I never know what to expect from you. Sometimes you are just wearied! But there is one thing about it, there is never a dull moment living with you. And, I have to admit it: I would not change you for nothing."

While they lay on the floor facing each other, John asked her, "Beautiful lady have I told you lately how much I love you?"

Sarah grinned and asks, "Are you going to sing to me like you did that night on the cruise ship? By the way, why haven't you ever sung to my sense that night?"

John got up and took Sarah by the hand and helped her get up. He suggested that they make some soup and sandwiches and go sit at the table in front of the window and watch the lake 'critters while they ate the snack.

Sarah insisted, "John you are ignoring my question. Why haven't you ever sung to my sense that night on the ship?"

He replied, "Honey! After I sang to you that night, you cried for three days. I don't want to make you cry again. I did not think my singing was that bad, but it sure made you cry."

"John!" She exclaimed, "Your singing was not bad It was wonderful! You have got to understand. I was a new bride, standing on a stage in front of thousands of strangers and you were holding my hands and singing the most touching love song I had ever heard. John my emotions were shot! My knees were shaking, my heart was beating out of my chest and I could not get my breath. I thought I was going to pass out. All I could do was cry because it was so touching. And yes, I cried for three days because it was so touching. If I don't stop talking about it I am going to start crying again whether you sing or not."

John and Sarah spent most of the evening eating their tomato soup and grilled cheese sandwiches at the lake window table and reminiscing about everything they had done together from the time John rescued her from the snow storm until now. A flock of geese landing on the lake distracted Sarah while John got up and put a CD in their stereo player. When it began to play, John stood up and asks Sarah if she would dance with him. When she stood up to dance, John just took her hands and waited for the song to begin to play. It was the music to the song he had sung to her on the cruise ship. When he began to sing to her she gasped and just stood looking at him. Before he could finish the second verse, she was holding John's hands against her cheeks and crying her eyes out. Just as John finished the song, Patty, Gary, and Abigail came in.

Patty saw that Sarah was crying and ran to her and ask, "Mom! What is wrong?"

Sarah answered, "Honey, not a thing is wrong. Your daddy just sang me a love song that was so beautiful that all I could do was cry."

Patty stood there with a shocked look on her face. Then she said to Sarah, "Daddy sung you a love song that made you cry? It must have been a dandy. I did not know daddy could sing." She turned to John and said, "Daddy you 'old romantic'."

John chuckled and said, "I am glad to see you too honey." He gave her and Gary a hug and picked up Abigail.

The rest of the evening was spent listening to Abigail telling about her two weeks with her mom and new daddy. It was a time of sharing stories and laughter. It was a very special family night.

CHAPTER THIRTY-ONE

THE GROWING YEARS

For the next few years the members of the family spent time getting to know each other and learning to accept each other's quarks', and there was never a dull moment. Abigail was smarter than any child her age and John and Sarah encouraged her in her effort to learn. At the age of seventeen, she had graduated from college with two master's degrees. That did not satisfy her so she went back to college and became a doctor. The boys were intimidated by her so it was a while before she found a partner.

Patty and Garry added to the family a little boy they named John Mark. John after John and Mark after Garry's Grandfather. John and Sarah had their hands full. Not only did they have to take care of Abby, they had to take care of John Mark while Patty and Gary finished Veterinary College. Patty had John Mark just after she finished regular college and was ready to start Veterinary College. If anyone would listen to John and Sarah complaining about all the work that they had to do to take care of the two kids it did not take a genius to realize that Sarah and John were not complaining, they were bragging.

Patty and Gary finished Veterinary school and worked for a time for a local Veterinary Clinic.

John Mark was born in the spring when Abby turned six. She had to be watched constantly to keep her from getting him out of the crib. The little 'skunk' had learned how to drop the rails on the baby bed and Sarah caught her trying to drag him out of the bed into her little red wagon. She told Sarah she was going to take him outside to ride Brutus; Sarah was horrified! John had to go into the next room so they would not see him laugh.

John Mark grew up in spite of Abigail's attempts to give him a ride on old Brutus. After he finished high school, he joined the Navy and became a Navy Seal. The assignments he had as a Seal caused him to be withdrawn. After he got out of the Navy, he spent most of his time by himself. He found that camping alone seemed to give him peace from the memories of the engagements he was in as a Seal. As time went on he became more and more of a recluse. John insisted that he attend Church and he met a girl there. John Mark did not want any company but Katy would not give up on him. It took a lot of patience and persistence, Katy stayed with John Mark and they eventually married.

John encouraged Sarah to get involved in the work he was doing with young people and she did. She became a great help to John in his work. She reviewed applications of those that applied for scholarships and John was elated.

The growing years were a time of great joy for the most part. There were some bumps along the way, but the family grew closer and learned to depend on each other.

CHAPTER THIRTY-TWO

AND THEN THERE
WERE FROGS

John did his best to keep Abby out of trouble with Grandma.
Abby was always trying to get John Mark out of the house. John
tried to distract her by taking her with him as he went out to fish.
The browns were running upstream to spawn and He would gather
about three to four hundred pounds to put in his smoker; enough
to last for the rest of the year. He would do the same thing in the
fall with the salmon.

Early that spring as they were working their way up the edge
of the stream to John's nets they came to a small 'wadding pond'.
That pond was full of tadpoles. Abby wanted to know what kind of
fish that was. John told her that they were not fish they were frogs.

Abby protested, "Grandpa, they are not frogs! Frogs have legs.
These don't have legs."

John replied, "If you watch them they will grow legs and hop
out of that pond."

While John ran his nets and cleaned the fish, Abby watched the
tadpoles in the pond. They did not grow legs and she was mad at
grandpa. John had to explain to her that it would take some time for
them to grow legs. She wanted to know "how long it would take?"

John got the bright idea that if she had her own frog pond it
would keep her out of trouble that summer. So, he asks her, "Abby

174

would you like to have a frog pond at the house so you could keep up with the frogs and see them grow legs?"

She thought that was a great idea and that evening they went to town and John bought a pond liner that would hold close to a thousand gallons of water. John looked 'on line' and found out what to feed the tadpoles and purchased some at the local pet store.

After he got it set up, every time they went to the stream Abby would use her little net and catch as many tadpoles as she could and take them back to her pond. Things went well until the frogs started to grow legs and hop out of the pond they were everywhere! John began to catch them when Abby was not looking and take them back to the lake. He could not keep up! The Frog population was growing faster then he could catch them and get them back to the lake. It got to where it was hard to go into the back yard without stepping on a 'darn' frog. The frog pond idea was doomed the second that one of the frogs got into the house. To say that Sarah was not pleased was a gross understatement; she was hysterical!

That night when she and John got into bed, she rolled over facing John and got his attention by gently patting him on the chest. When John looked at her she asks him, "Honey." She paused and then asked, "Will you do something for me?"

He replied, "Of course I will if it is something that I can do. What do you want me to do?"

She said, "Will you please get rid of the frogs? They are driving me crazy."

He looked at her and began to laugh.

She said, "John, it is not funny. I opened the back door to check on Abby and one of them got in the house. I tried to get it out with the broom but it got away and was about to get into the bed room with the baby and I hit it with the broom and killed it."

John still laughing ask her, "What did you do with the dead frog?"

"I flushed it down the toilet. I did not want Abby to know I had killed one of her precious frogs."

He jokingly told her, "You know she will miss the dead frog. She has given them all names, you know. She was picking them up one by one and naming them Billy, Jack, Jerry … I interrupted her by asking her how she knew that they were all boys. She paused for a while, looking at the frog she had in her hand and called it Jenny. She put it down and started naming them again…"

"John! Will you stop it?" She protested. "There is no way Abigail can possibly miss one frog. There must be a thousand of them. John, will you please get rid of the frogs?"

John put his arms around Sarah and as he hugged her whispered in her ear, "Yes honey, I will get rid of the frogs." When he released her from the hug, he rose up on his elbow facing Sarah and said, "I will tell Abby that the frogs need to go back to the lake and make her help me catch them. To tell you the truth, I don't like them either. This is one of those projects that I let get out of hand. I think I have a little bit of an idea of how Pharaoh felt when Moses Prayed and God turned the frog loose on Egypt."

The next morning John took Abby to the back window and showed her all the frogs. He told her that all the frogs needed to be back in the lake.

She protested, "Grandpa, these are my frogs and I love them!

John reminded her that frogs need the lake to live and if she really loved them she would take them back to the lake before they all died.

The next day John made a cage for the frogs and he and Abby started catching them. Four hours and many trips to the lake on the 'four-wheeler' the frogs were all in the lake but not without incident. The releasing of frogs had attracted a lot of 'largemouth' Bass. One of them jumped out of the water and caught one of the frogs and swallowed it. Abby saw it and threw a fit!

"Grandpa!" She yelled. "That big fish ate one of my frogs! Do something, Grandpa." She cried again frantically as she used a stick to beat the water.

John thought, "Oh Lord! What am I going to do now?"

John took Abby in his arms and tried to explain to her that some of the frogs would get eaten by fish but most of them would be ok. That was not good enough. She wanted John to kill that mean old fish. He said, "Baby doll if I could catch that fish we would have it for dinner. But that is just the way life is. Frogs eat bugs and flies, fish eat frogs, and we eat fish. But we will take the rest of your frogs to a different part of the lake and turn them loose on the bank so the fish can't get them." That seemed to help but she was not happy about that 'bad' fish eating one of her frogs. When she and John got to the place where they were going to turn the rest of the frogs loose she made them go up the bank away from the lake. As soon as all the frogs were out of sight in the woods, John grabbed Abigail and headed back to the lodge. When they got to the lodge, parked the ATV and headed in the house Sarah met them and started to point to one of the frogs that had escaped the roundup. John stopped her by putting his finger on his lips. As he went by her he whispered, "I will take care of it. Take Abby in and wash the frog smell off of her."

It had been a long day and all that 'rounding up of frogs' had tired Abby out and it was not long before she was fast asleep.

CHAPTER THIRTY-THREE

JOHN AND SARAH SHARE THOUGHTS ABOUT HEAVEN

After John and Sarah put Abby to bed and checked on John Mark they sat down to a light snack and began to talk. John had been concerned about Sarah for several weeks. She had been very withdrawn and seldom spoke to John.

John asks Sarah, "Honey why did you hesitate to ask me to get rid of the frogs?"

Sarah did not answer for several minutes. She just stared at John for a while before she answered. Then she replied, "I didn't want to interfere with what you were doing with Abby like I did when you were trying to break Patty. You remember the way she treated us when she first got here because she hated me so much. I almost lost you because I interfered."

John stated, "Sarah, Honey that was not your fault. It was my fault because of the way I handled that situation."

Sarah completely confused asks "John what do you mean about how you handled the situation. What you did was kind of harsh but, if you hadn't done what you did, I don't think we could have saved her. She was so full of hate that no one could talk to her"

"The problem is not what I did; it is how I did it. I never involved you in the planning process. I totally ignored you and did it all on my own. And that is just not right. You are my partner in this thing we call life and you and I should always plan everything about our lives together. And never implement any plan until we both agree on it together." He answered.

"It is a good thing that you were in our lives at that time. I was so upset by the way she treated us especially me I didn't know what to do. All I could do was sit around and cry. I am not as smart as you, John. I don't know how to deal with that kind of problem. I never even went to high school" She stated.

"I wish you would not degrade yourself. Anyone who could evade the FBI and Carl's gang for five years has to be pretty smart. You may not have a college degree, but a degree is only a tool to be used by the holder. Without common sense, it is useless. I love you and believe in you. I want you involved in everything I do. Next week the kids will be out of school until the summer class start. I want them to take the babies so you can go with me to Kentucky. You know I still help needy kids with college and I need to go to one of my support groups and take care of a problem. Will you get involved?" He asks her.

"John, I don't know anything about things like that. I think what you are doing for the kids is wonderful, but if I got involved in it I would just mess everything up."

"Sarah, I would love for you to read the applications that come in from the kids so we could discuss their qualifications together. I really want your input. Will you give it a try?"

"I think you are making a mistake by getting me involved, but we will see."

The next week John and Sarah gave the kids to Patty and Gary and caught a flight to Southern Indiana. They rented a car and drove to the area in Kentucky close to where He used to live. He rented a motel room where they spent the night. The next day they drove to the town where John used to live. He took Sarah to the local restaurant for breakfast. Several of John's old acquaintances recognized him and came to their table to talk with John.

Most of them were friendly, but one older woman was not. Her remarks made Sarah angry. When she accused John of being a pedophile that molested young girls and ask Sarah if he was molesting her. Sarah had all she could take.

She jumped to her feet and screamed, "You stupid fat slob, this is the finest, loving, gentlest, caring, man, that has ever lived! He is not molesting me; He is my husband! You...you ..."

John had never seen Sarah so angry. He quickly jumped up between them. He was afraid Sarah would attack the woman physically. He stated calmly, "Honey, we need to go." He gently led her to the counter, where he paid the bill, and then to the car.

Sarah was still mad. She in an agitated voice said "John, why did you just sit there without defending yourself against that... that bit..."

John interrupted her before she could finish what she was going to say. He said "Sarah, honey that is Sadie Snodgrass. She has been a 'boil on the butt of society' ever since I have known her. She started out as a prostitute, became a madam and wound up in prison. There she studied journalism and came out of prison and became a columnist in the local paper. She has stood against everything that is decent in our community ever since. She wrote some very nasty articles about the work Leigh and I did with the kids in the area. She viciously, attacked Sharif Bill calling him 'The Gestapo' every time he arrested a 'call girl'. She viciously attacked the judge in her article several times when he overturned my conviction. Judge Carter got tired of her and filed an injunction against her. He threatened to throw her back in prison and that stopped her. She is just a miserable person and I do not want you to let her 'drag you down to her level'. The last thing you want to do is get into an argument with her, that is what she wants. She will tear you apart in her articles. The best way to deal with her is to remain calm in her presence and tell her that Jesus loves her she hates that. But, remember what the Bible says in Proverbs chapter fifteen, verse one: "A soft answer turneth away wrath: but grievous words stir up anger". She is a self-proclaimed atheist and she gets fighting mad when someone reminds her that Jesus died on the cross for people like her. Even thou it is the truth, she hates it."

Sarah still mad said, "Why doesn't someone tar and feather the old bit…"

"Sarah!" John exclaimed firmly. "Let's change the subject." I want to show you something."

"Ok." She said, "What do you want to show me?"

By that time, they were in the car and headed for the cemetery where Leigh was buried. He told her, "I want to show you Leigh's burial site and get your permission for an idea I have."

She asks, "John what on earth are you talking about?"

When they arrived at the grave site, John pointed at Leigh's grave and told Sarah, "There are several sites available here and I want to buy them and make this a family plot. I want to be buried next to Leigh and I want you buried next to me. To put it plainly, I want to be buried between the two most beautiful gals in the world.

Sarah just stood there with a blank stare on her face. She turned toward John, crossed her arms, cocked her head to the right, and asks, "Why are you bringing this up now is there something you are not telling me? Are you going to…to she was afraid to ask the question that was on her mind?"

He put his arms around her to reassure her, "No honey. I am not sick and I am not going to die yet. At least I don't think I am. It is just that we are here and I want to take care of it while we are here if you agree."

She responded, "I don't know what to say. I guess it will be ok if that is what you want to do. I mean I don't see anything wrong with it. You just caught me off guard talking about death and burning. I just don't know what to say."

"I am sorry Honey. I did not mean to put you on the spot. We don't have to make a decision now. Just think about it and we will talk about it later."

They drove for over an hour headed for the lake without Sarah saying a word. When they arrived at the wrangler's camp, John rented a cabin for him and Sarah. After he unloaded their things and closed the door to their cabin he took Sarah's hands and turned her toward him and asks, "Honey what is wrong? You have not said a word for over an hour and a half."

She looked at John and her bottom lip was quivering as thou she was about to start crying.

John sensing that something had upset her pulled her into his arms to console her. He asks her very apologetically, "Have I done something to upset you?"

She buried her face in his chest and began to sob.

John pleaded, "Honey what is wrong? Please tell me what I've done."

She patted him on the chest and said, "John you have not done anything wrong. I just got to thinking. When you die and go to heaven and you are re united with Leigh where does that leave me? I have no one. I don't know anyone in Heaven. I will be all alone. What will I do?"

John shocked by her question, paused for a moment and then asked, "What makes you think I am going to go to heaven before you do?"

She replied, "Well, you do have a twenty-year head start on me. It just seems reasonable that you will go before me. You have not answered my question. You will be with Leigh. What will happen to me?"

He answered, "What are you worried about. Don't you know that I am man enough for both of you gals?"

She replied, "John will be serious just once. I am concerned about this and I want an answer."

"Well, first of all, you assume that I will die before you. Only God knows that. I may out live you a hundred years. So, let's look at the reunion with me and Leigh. In the Bible, in Mark chapter twelve, Christ was questioned by the Sadducees about a woman who had seven husbands on earth. They ask Christ whose wife she would be in Heaven. He reminded them that there would be no marriages in heaven, but they would be like Angels. So, my dear, when Leigh and I are reunited it will be as very, very good friends not as husband and wife. And these two friends will be anxiously awaiting their mutual friend, you. And, the three of us will stroll all over Heaven together."

Sarah asks, "John, how do you know that Leigh will like me. She has never even met me. I am afraid she will not like me when she finds out that you and I were married. She will be jealous."

"First of all." He replied, "God will not allow jealousy in Heaven. Emotions like jealousy, hate, anger, hurt, fear and such will not be in Heaven. We are all going to be happy there. There will not be any of those feelings that take away our happiness. Honey, as much as I enjoy holding you close to me and feeling your beautiful body in my arms, God tells us that what we will share in Heaven will be so much better than that."

"John when we hold each other like this I feel complete joy and peace. How can it be any better in Heaven if I have to share you with Leigh? I don't know how that can be." She sobbed.

"Well honey, remember what it says in first Corinthians chapter two verse nine; 'Eye hath not seen, nor ear heard, neither have entered into the heart of man, the things which God hath prepared for them that love him'. That scripture tells me that he has something so great that we cannot even imagine it. So, you can stop worrying about what will happen to you. God loves you and he is going to take care of you in a way so wonderful that we cannot even imagine it. And, you, Leigh, and I will enjoy it to gather." John said in an effort to comfort her.

The rest of the evening they talked and read the Bible together and ended the evening praying together.

CHAPTER THIRTY-FOUR

HORSES AND THE SPARK PLUG

The next morning the two got up and as they were getting ready to go out to eat Sarah asks John what they were going to do that day.

John replied, "We are going to go out for breakfast and then we are going to go horseback riding."

Sarah was walking from the bed room toward the bath room when John said that and she stopped in her track, spun around and stated, "John! The closest I have ever come to riding a horse was when Grandma took me to the amusement park. She put me on a horse on the merry go round. It went up and down, up and down, around and around, round and around." She waved her hand up and down to show the motion of the merry go round horse and stated, "I squalled until Grandma took me off of that thing. And you want me to get on a big hairy critter that can bite me, kick me, throw me, and stomp me! Surely you are joking."

John laughed so hard he could not get his breath. As he slowly walked to where she was standing he took her hands and told her, "My precious, precious wife. Don't you know that I know that you have never ridden a horse? And, it grieves me that you think that I would do anything that would frighten you. This is what I have planned: We are going to go to the Red Barn for breakfast and afterward we will shop for wranglers clothes there in their store. We need boots, jeans, a shirt and a hat..."

Before he could finish what he was trying to tell her, she interrupted, "John! I have never had a pair of cowboy boots and I don't wear hats."

He replied, "Well let's start with a good western breakfast complete with 'cathead' biscuits, with 'sawmill' gravy and country ham or stake, which ever you prefer. Then we will go to their store and see about a wrangler's outfit for each of us. We must look the part while we are in the wrangler's camp. I think you will look so cute in a wrangler's outfit. Will you do it for me?"

She hesitated for a moment and then answered, "John I will try the wrangler's outfit, but I am not going to ride a horse."

John chuckled again and said, "Let us go eat. I will explain the rest of my plan as we go along."

They went to the building on the wrangler's ranch that looked like a big red barn. Inside there was a restaurant and a store that sold everything a wrangler needed to look the part.

When they sat down to eat Sarah whispered to John, "Do they serve pancakes here?"

John looked at her with a blank look and said, "No they don't serve pancakes, but they do serve flapjacks."

She asks, "What is a flapjack?"

He replied, "The same thing as a pancake except they are bigger, better and they are fried in coon grease."

She looked at him with a disgusted look and said, "Are you going to give me a straight answer or am I going to have to go to the store and get me a can of beans?"

John was having fun picking on her, but he knew it was time to quit before he made her mad. He turned and looked at her and said, "Yes honey they do sell pancakes here, but they are called flapjacks. They are quite good. If you would like flapjacks, call them that so they don't laugh at you and call you a 'green horn'."

Sarah and John had breakfast and were ready to get outfitted with wranglers clothing. John was preoccupied with the thoughts of how his beloved Sarah would look in wrangler's outfit, and did not hear Sarah when she asked what they were going to do after breakfast.

When she got his attention she asks, "John did you hear me? What are we going to do after we get our 'cowboy outfit'?"

After he came out of his 'daydream' he said, "Well, we are going to go to the stable where Ashley Beth Carter works...."

Before he could finish what he was going to tell Sarah, she interrupted him by demanding, "Why are we going to the stable? I told you I am afraid of horses."

He responded, "Honey have you forgotten the reason we came down here?"

"No, but why do we have to go to the horse place? What do the horses have to do with you checking out whether or not the man running your Scholarship program is stealing from you, I mean us?" She pleaded.

John stated, "I hope Ashley and her husband will be part of the solution to the problem. Ashley is one of the kids I helped. She lost her parents in a car wreck when she was twelve and I got her in a foster home. I sponsored her through high school and sent her to college. Ashley was a feisty little squirt and I gave her two nicknames alphabet soup and spark plug. Her initials were 'ABC from Ashley Beth Carr so I called her alphabet soup or I called her my little spark plug from her first and last initials AC which are a popular spark plug for automobiles. She hated both nicknames, but she hated 'sparkplug' the worst. I heard her tell one of her friends that when she got married his last name would change her's and I could not call her 'spark plug' anymore. But she married Henry Carter and her initials are still 'AC'. I can't wait to see her and call her 'my little spark plug'."

Sarah asks, "If the nickname pestered her why didn't you just call her by her name? Why did you have to pester her?"

He replied, "Well as I told you, she was a feisty little squirt and she was always starting something so she reminded me of a spark plug, it starts a car. Besides, the little squirt was always pestering someone else so I liked pestering her. She was a tuff little monkey and she 'gave as good as she got'. I have tracked her progress

186

and I am very pleased with her success. She has done well in her life. She graduated from college with top grades and is an accountant like her husband. She is running the horse stables for extra income to help her and her husband gets started in life. And, she likes horses."

"Well, if we must go to the horse place let's get on with it. I am looking forward to meeting your 'spark plug'. She sounds like a real character. How are she and her husband going to help the problem with our Scholarship program?"

"They are both accountants and I hope to hire them to take over the program." He replied.

Sarah thought that was a good idea and they walked out of the restaurant, turned left and headed toward the horse stables. John reached out and took Sarah's hand and the two of them walked hand in hand like two teenagers in love as they went on their way. As they walked toward their destination they came to a petting zoo. There were several baby animals on display for petting, baby pigs, goats, rabbits, chickens, and ducks. John asks Sarah if she wanted to stop and pet the 'critters'.

She turned to John with a sad 'puppy dog' look and pleaded, "Can we?"

John chuckled and took her inside. He reached down and picked up an adorable baby pygmy goat and handed it to Sarah. She sat on a bale of hay held it, rubbed it, and tried to rock it to sleep. Everything was fine until she tried to put it down. It was used to being spoiled and threw a fit when she tried to put it down. It jumped right back into her lap and 'flopped' down there. She thought it was so quiet that she just held it until it wanted down. Sarah spent over two hours petting everything from baby ducks, chickens, to baby rabbits.

John asks her. "How many of the 'critters do you want to take home with you?"

She replied, "They are all so cute, but I am afraid that they would turn out to be worse than the 'frog' problem so I think we had better leave them here."

She asks John where they were going after they left the 'petting zoo' and he reminded her of their plans to go to see Ashley at the horse pavilion. He never noticed how Sarah began to tense up at the suggestion. When they arrived at the pavilion, John began to seek out Ashley. When they arrived at the pavilion John leaned against the fence and watched the horses. He never noticed that Sarah stood back away from the fence. After about ten minutes a young lady came to where they were and asks them if they would like to rent some horses to ride. When John turned toward her she just stood there for a moment as if in shock.

She took a deep sigh and asks, "You don't know who I am, do you?"

John stood looking at her with his arms crossed as though in deep thought and then said, "You are my little spark plug!"

She responded, "I had hoped you had forgotten that, but I see you have not. What are you doing down here? The last thing I heard about you was that you were in Alaska. Have you moved back to Kentucky?"

John assured her that he had not and introduced her to Sarah. They talked for about an hour and a half between her renting horses and taking care of her work. The horses were everywhere and Sarah was terrified, but she never said a word. John invited Ashley and her husband, Henry to have dinner with him and Sarah the next evening. He told her that he wanted to talk to them about a job. They set a time and place and John and Sarah headed for their cabin.

When they arrived at the cabin and went inside John was trying to talk to Sarah, but she was not responding. When he turned toward her to get her attention she was standing holding her left arm at the elbow with her right hand and staring out the window. He walked over to where she was standing and he put his hand on her shoulder she was trembling. He gently turned her around facing him and she had tears streaming down her face.

John, in shock, asks her, "Honey, what is wrong?"

She answered, "John I told you I was afraid of horses and you made me go there anyway. You are always doing me that way. I told you I was afraid of horses and you made me go out there. I told you I was afraid of Brutus and you made me pet him anyway. John, I just can't take any more. I just can't!"

He just stood looking at her. He felt so horrible that he had been so insensitive about her feelings that he did not know what to do. After what seemed to be an eternity he said, "Sarah, honey I am so ashamed. I have failed you as a husband and a friend. As a husband, I promised to take care of you and I have failed to do that. I never meant to put you in any situation that you are uncomfortable in. And, I never meant to frighten you. I am so ashamed that I have been so insensitive to your feelings. I don't know what to do or say. I am so sorry."

She stepped towered John and pleaded. "Hold me. Please just hold me."

When he reached out and took her in his arms she buried her face in his chest and wept. John felt so bad. This was the most important thing in his life--she was his life and he had failed to take care of her needs. He felt so miserable he just did not know what to do. She would not do anything but weep. John picked her up and laid her on the bed and lay down beside her. She finally cried herself to sleep. He lay beside her with his arm around her the rest of the night.

The next morning, John got up and Sarah was already up, sitting in a rocker on the front porch of their cabin. John asks her if she wanted a cup of coffee but she declined. He told her that as soon as he shaved and got dressed he would take her to breakfast. She did not respond. John was concerned, but did not know what to do so he left her on the porch and went back in to get ready. While he was shaving, Sarah came into the bathroom where he was shaving.

She asks, "John what are we going to do today?"

"What would my lovely lady like to do today?" He answered.

She walked over to where John was shaving and said, "I want you to teach me to ride a horse."

John dropped his razor and took hold of her arms at the elbows and pulled her to him. He said, "Are you out of your mind? After what you went through yesterday and last night, you want me to teach you to ride a horse?"

She replied, "Yes I do. After you went to sleep last night I could not sleep so I was up most of the night thinking about you and me. I have known you for eleven years and have been married to you for ten of those eleven years. In all that time, I have never thought about what you have been through. You have spent all that time taking care of me and mine, but what about you. You lost Leigh. You lost all your friends and your life that you worked so hard for and the first winter in Alaska you were completely alone except for your critters. All you had was that wolf pup, which my ex-husband's gang killed, and Brutus to keep you company. And then I came along and deprived you of their company just because I was too afraid. John, I am so ashamed and I am tired of being afraid. I want to share your life. I want to be part of the things you love and enjoy them with you. I want to be your life's partner. Will you help me? John, I love you so very much."

John just stood looking at her. He slid his hands up the back of her arms and pulled her into his arms. When he began to hug her, she started to protest because of the soap John was saving with. John said, "Honey it is just soap and I am sure it will wash off. That is the most un selfish thing I have ever heard. I love you more right this minute than I have ever thought possible to love anyone. And, my answer is absolutely yes. But, I will not put you through what you went through yesterday. If I think it is getting too hard for you I will stop and take you out. Understood? You are trembling and we aren't even near a horse. Are you sure you want to do this?"

She said, "John I am terrified. I am counting on you to get me through my fear. I want to do this. Will you help me?"

John answered, "Yes, my beautiful lady, I will help you. Let's go have some breakfast and talk about it."

Sarah asks, "Can we go to the red Barn and have some of those 'flappy' thingies?"

John chuckled and replied, "Yes honey, we can have some of those 'flappy' 'thingies'. And by the way, they are called flapjacks. That is cowboy lingo for pancakes. While we are there we will talk a little about horse edict."

"What is horse edict? She asks.

As they sat eating, John began to explain to her how to approach a horse without startling the horse. He talked about how to be around a horse without startling the animal and causing it to react in anger or fear that might seem aggressive to the trainer or handler. He encouraged her to call the horse by name as she approached it. He told her to approach the animal from the front when possible and when approaching it to offer the back of her hand to let the horse smell it so the horse could identify her. He cautioned her about making sudden moves that would startle the horse. He talked to her about simple things that she could do that would gain the horses acceptances of her.

They had a good day, awkward but good. Sarah was terrified, but John was with her all the way. He walked with her to the horses and picked out an older, gentle horse named General. General accepted Sarah's scratching and rubbing and when she quit he would nudge her with his nose.

Sarah changed that day. She changed from the person that constantly need help and need to be rescued by someone that wanted to give back. And, there was a determination in her demeanor to do just that.

That night John and Sarah had dinner with the spark plug (Ashley) and her Husband Henry. After dinner, John explained to Henry and Ashley the problems he was having with his college assistance program and ask them if they would be interested in taking the program over and running it for him. After some questions and a lot of explaining, they told John they would like to check it out further. They left for the evening after making plans for tomorrow.

CHAPTER THIRTY-FIVE

THE COLLAGE ASSISTANCE PROGRAM GETS NEW MANAGERS

J ohn had contacted the state police and ask them to send the appropriate help to take care of the problem. John had tracked the money that the manager of the program had stolen by listing college students that did not exist and sending the money to an off shore account. The only student that actually existed was the manager's nephew, but he was not going to college with the money he was receiving he was buying a new sports car and being a playboy. The manager had misappropriated over three-quarters of a million dollars.

When the crew Sarah, John, Ashley, Henry and the officer from the State Police walked into the manager's office unannounced and John unplugged all the computers before he could delete any of the information on them the manager threw a fit. He screamed and cursed at John demanding that he get out of his office before he called the police! The man had never met John and did not know who he was, he had taken over the program from his wife's grandfather and had never met John.

John introduced himself and Captain Jack with the State Police as the cuffs were being put on him and the charges were being explained to him. He was arrested along with his secretary who was involved in the scam with him. While the charges were being explained to them and they were being given their rights, Ashley and Henry were going over the computers looking for records of the money that the manager and his secretary had stolen.

Ashley and Henry were every bit as good as John had hoped that they would be. In less than thirty minutes they found nineteen factious students that had been paid over six hundred thousand dollars.

Ashley and Henry were examining the computers and the books in spite of the objections of the manager and the secretary. When they protested the intrusion without a search warrant, John was quick to remind them that he owned the place and the business.

While words were being exchanged between John and the manager, the manager's Nephew Billy Bob stormed in and demanded the where bouts of his uncle. When he stormed into his uncle's office demanding his college money at the top of his voice, he was greeted by Captain Jack who met him with a pair of hand cuffs.

Captain Jack called a tow truck to impound the boys' sports car and halled the manager, his nephew, and his secretary off to jail.

After the police left the office with the arrestees, John, Sarah, Ashley, and Henry sat down and made plans for Ashley and Henry to take over the program. Henry and Ashley accepted the salaries that John offered them. John also offered to support them for a year until they could to get their accounting business going. Part of the agreement included the use of the building for the new business for Ashley and Henry. John outfitted the place with all the equipment they needed to run a successful accounting business and take care of the collage assistances program for John.

After two days of talking, and planning everything was in place and all were in agreement. Ashley and Henry would give notices to their employers and take over the program in two weeks and start their own business.

John had accomplished what he had come to Kentucky to do and was ready to go home, but Sarah had other ideas.

CHAPTER THIRTY-SIX

SARAH GETS INVOLVED AFTER MORE HORSES

When John got to the cabin he started to pack for the trip back to Alaska. Sarah was making no effort to pack and John was curious about her attitude so he asked her what was wrong.

Sarah with a sheepish grin asks, "John, honey, can we stay down here another week?"

John was caught off guard by her request and paused for a moment before he answered her. He then asks, "Why do you want to stay? Is there something we have not done that you want to do or see?"

She walked over to John and put her arms around his neck and leaned into him and stated, "Honey you have not finished teaching me to ride a horse. I still want to learn and you promised me you would teach me."

"But honey, you are still afraid of horses." He protested. "You shake and tremble all the time we are at the horse barn." John had put his hands around her waist and gently pulled her to him and asks, "Are you sure you want to go through with the riding lessons?"

She answered, "Yes John, I want to be able to go into the barn, get General, put a bridle and saddle on him and get on him by myself. And, then I want to go riding on the trail with you on your horse. Yes, I am scared out of my wits, and I am counting on you to help me get over that. Now can we stay until we do that?"

John took a deep sigh and replied, "Yes honey, we can stay as long as you want to."

Sarah and John called the kids and told them that they were going to stay another week. Sarah and John continued the riding lessons until Sarah was comfortable with horses. By the middle of the week, she could saddle old General and get him ready to ride without help from anyone. She and John road ever trail at the Wranglers camp before they went back to Alaska.

The night before they were going to go back to Alaska, Sarah asks John, "Honey can we pray together tonight?"

John said, "Sure, we always do."

She said, "No John. I don't mean go to bed and pray while we fall to sleep. I mean can we kneel down beside the bed and pray together?"

John paused for a moment and turn toward her taking both her hands. He answered, "I would love to do that." He kissed the backs of her hands and said, "You are so special to me."

After they got ready for bed, Sarah took John by the hand and led him to the bed room and knelt down beside the bed. She put her elbows on the bed and clasps her hands together to pray. John knelt beside her, but he his arm around her waist.

Sarah protested, "John I thank you for hugging me, but this can wait. I want us to pray together now."

John responded, "Honey, I am praying. After what you have been through the past two weeks and what you have accomplished all I can do is just thank God for letting me share your life. I am so proud of you. I love you so very much."

She turned toward him and put her arms around his neck and they prayed together as they knelt. They prayed for each other, for their kids and thanked God for all the blessings He had given them. It was a wonderful conclusion to their trip.

After they got back home in Alaska, Sarah insisted that John teaches her to use the computer. John was surprised because she had never shown any interest in the computer, but John was glad to teach her. They spent many hours working on the computer together. Sarah learned fast and became very good at it. She was particularly interested in the request from Ashley and Henry for college assistance.

Just before the fall semester started they were sent four requests for collage assistances. Sarah studied all four, but she was particularly interested in one young girl. The girl did not meet John's standards she had a child out of wedlock and she had several tattoos. When she took the girl's application to John, He looked at it and threw in the trash. "This girl is not a good candidate for college. She has screwed her life up too bad for us to help her." John stated.

Sarah was angered by John's actions and without saying a word, she turned around and went into the TV room and sat down.

John knew he had upset Sarah and stopped what he was doing and just sat there thinking about it. He slowly reached over and took the application out of the trash and began to take another look at it. As he sat there reading the application his thoughts convicted him. He realized that Patty the only daughter he ever had, had a child before she was married. Had he been as judgmental with her he would have lost his daughter, son in law, granddaughter, grandson, and his precious wife. He would have screwed up his whole life. All he could think of was that he had to make this right. After thinking about it for a while, he got up and slowly walked into the room where Sarah was setting.

He said, "Sarah, honey I have done it again haven't I?"

Sarah, without ever looking toward John says, sarcastically, "Done what?"

John just stood looking at her for a moment and stated in a soft, humble voice, "I have to ask you, almost force you, to get involved in what I am doing and then when you try I won't listen. Honey, I am so sorry for the way I acted. I just realized that if I had been so judgmental with Patty, I would not have my beautiful daughter, my son in law, and my two precious grandchildren and most likely I would not have you. If you can forgive my stupidity, I would like to talk to you about this application."

She slowly turns toward John and said, "John I just think she deserves a chance."

John replies, "Ok we have four applications. What do you think of us going down to Kentucky and personally interviewing these candidates?"

She agreed and she and John made plans to go back to Kentucky to conduct interviews with the four candidates for college assistance.

The first candidate was a young man with a heart wrenching back ground: His parents had been killed in an automobile accident when he was fourteen. He had to go to work to feed himself and his kid brother. Two years later his kid brother died of Leukemia. Chad (the young man's name) continued to work his way through school. He now wanted to go to college and wanted help.

John and Sarah had thoroughly checked his background. He was well liked in the community and his church. He was not an A student but he was a hard worker.

John and Sarah were sure that working his way through school had affected his grades so they approved his request on the condition: he had to maintain at least a B average.

The second applicant was a young girl who had earned straight A's from the time she was in the fourth grade. She was from a very poor family that could not afford to send her to school. She earned a scholarship, but still need help. Her pastor asked John to help her and John and Sarah agreed.

The third candidate was Billy Bob's cousin. He was trying to do the same thing that Billy Bob had done, and he was quickly rejected.

The forth candidate was Katy, the girl Sarah was interested in. She came in the room wearing a skirt and long sleeve blouse. It was obvious that she was trying to cover up her tattoos. She was a quiet, polite, soft spoken child, but John began to grill her as though she was under an FBI interrogation. She took everything John ask her and never showed any sign of anger.

John reminded her that candidates must be of good moral character and could not have tattoos or body piercings. He then asks her why she should be exempt from these rules. She sat there for a while and slowly got up. She gathered her papers she had brought in with her and headed for the door. She turned toward John and Sarah with tears in her eyes and stated, "God forgave me for my sins and I hoped you might. She turned and slowly continued toward the door.

John was quick to head her off before she could get out the door. He stated apologetically, "Katy, please wait. Your answer has struck a nerve. You are correct. What God has cleansed no one has the right to judge and I am totally wrong to judge you. Now can we talk about helping you?"

She looked at John and Sarah ,who was now standing beside John, with tears streaming down her cheeks and said, "Mr. Henson it was a bad idea to ask for help to go to nursing school. I haven't even finished high school. I won't take up any more of your time."

As she tried to leave, Sarah took her hand and asks her to stay and talk to them. She stopped and Sarah began to tell her that she and John could help her get her GED and get her into nursing school if she was truly interested.

The three of them talked for over three hours making plans for Katy to go to school. John and Sarah made plans for Katy to move in with an older lady who took in foster children. John had worked with Betty before and she was good with young children, and would be perfect for Katy. Betty could babysit Katy's baby while Katy was working on her school work. Katy had to do her share of the chores around the home, but John and Sarah paid all of Katy's expenses at the home and for school. It was a good plain and everyone was happy. Sarah watched Katy's progress and was very pleased with how hard Katy worked.

Sarah and John spent a week in Kentucky with Ashley and Henry they even went horseback riding at the ranch together.

CHAPTER THIRTY-SEVEN

THE GROWING YEARS OF THE FAMILY

Over the next twenty-five years the family went through quite a metamorphose: John, Sarah, Ashley, and Henry helped over a hundred-young people through school; Patty and Gary established a successful game sanctuary; Abigail met a young man she could not intimate; and John mark found a very dedicated, loving friend. Although the trials of life were many, the family grew stronger and they owed it all to their trust in an almighty, Loving God.

It didn't take long before John and Sarah had invested almost twenty-five million dollars into the college assistance program and they were concerned about the cost. They were committed to helping as many young people as they could, and never reviewed an applicant without praying about it, but the cost was becoming a great concern. One day when they were praying about what to do, they got a call from Ashley and Henry. Ashley and Henry wanted to know if it would be alright to start fundraisers to support the program. Sarah and John knew their prayers had been answered they quickly agreed. Ashley and Henry were so successful that within a time period of five years the program was self-sufficient.

John and Sarah were so thankful for the dedication and effort that Ashley and Henry put forth that they eventually turned the program over to them completely. John and Sarah stayed involved as advisors at the request of Ashley and Henry, but for the most part, Ashley and Henry ran the program. However, when Ashley and Henry's twins were old enough to go to college, John and Sarah insisted that the program pays their way.

Ashley and Henry's accounting business was quite successful and Sarah and John helped them: They gave them the building where they set up their business and eventually purchased the wranglers camp for them which they used for extra income and also in their efforts in fund raisers.

Patty and Gary came across a mother badger that had been hit by a car. The badger died, but not before she gave birth to two female pups. Patty and Gary took the two to their home and raised them on bottles. They were cute, but as they grew they become so destructive that Patty and Gary could not keep them in the house. They moved them outside into a cage which the pups promptly destroyed.

After the mining company had exhausted the gold out of the mine John bought the land back for Patty and Gary to use for their Veterinarian practice. They had established cages for the animals they treated so they took the Badger pups to the cages. The little rascals hated the cages so bad that they 'pouted' like two spoiled kids that could not get their way they just lay on the floor; they refused to eat, drink or do anything but lay on the floor. Patty couldn't stand that so she let them out they trashed everything in sight. Gary and John built them houses outside the gates that they could get in to get out of the weather and take their food, but could not get in the house and that worked well.

The food that John and Gary put out for the Badgers soon attracted other critters. This gave John and Gary an idea; why not try to attract other critters and began an exhibition for the public. John and Gary put out food plots for a verity of critters and soon attracted coons, skunks, snow lepers, moose, deer, caribou, and even bears. It worked so well that John and Gary built a cage that the public could drive into and park. Then could get out of their cars inside the safety of the compound and view the wild life while they ate. Every kind of critter known to exist in Alaska came to the compound.

The venture was quite successful. And, of course, Sarah and Patty had to add their input; there had to be a petting zoo. Patty and Gary maintained their Veterinarian practice which included taking in wounded wild animals. And, many of the babies would wind up in the petting zoo. When the babies got too big and or too mean for the petting zoo they were released back into the wild. The venture was a very profitable addition to Patty's and Gary's Veterinarian practice.

Abigail traveled to Guatemala to volunteer her services as a Pediatric Surgeon during the great earthquake disaster that occurred. When she arrived at the center of the disaster she found complete chaos. There was so much pain and suffering: injured people were laid around like sticks of wood, no hospital, and very little medical help. One young man was trying to administer first aid. Abby immediately tried to tell the young man what to do--he ignored her. After the third time, he ignored her she proceeds to tell him of her training as a Pediatric Surgeon. He stopped just long enough to tell her if she wanted to help she need to go around the pile of rubble to where there was a make shift hospital set up in a tent. He suggested that she might be of help there, but to leave him alone. He informed her that he was a paramedic and he knew how to administer first aid. Abby's arrogance did not impress him at all; after he instructed Abby to go to the make shift hospital, he went back to what he was doing; administering first aid and directing the helpers as to where to take the injured.

Abby did go to the hospital and was quickly put to work. After twenty-one hours of continuous, exhausting work, Abigail was completely exhausted. She was trying to put a make shift splint on the broken leg that she had set for a child. She was so exhausted that she was about to collapse. When she staggered and nearly collapsed she felt someone catch her. She turned around to see the young man she had seen when she came to the site. He told her she would not be any good to anyone if she did not get some rest. She tried to protest, but he took her by the arm and led her to a part of the tent where there were cots set up for people to rest. She collapsed and slept six hours before she was awakened and put back to work.

For the next week, she repaired broken bodies--both adults and children. The horror of it all took its toll on her. By the end of the week, she was so exhausted that she collapsed on the operating room floor. Mayhew Ortega, the young man she met the first day at the site came to her rescue; he picked her up, took her to one of the cots, and was going to lay her down when she woke up.

She asks him not to leave. She asks, "Can I talk with you for a moment?"

They talked for the thirty minutes they took for their break. They spent all their break time together after that and became very good friends. They talked about everything, their past, their education: Abby was shocked to find out that Mathew the American name he took was a Lawyer (of Mexican ancestor), but American born and educated. He had worked his way through Law school as a Paramedic.

One day while they were taking a break Abby told Matt, the nick name she gave him, her concern about all the orphan children that the earth quake had left in the area. They decided to start an orphanage. Abby was sure that Grandpa could help so she found a working phone and gave John a call. John and Sarah stopped what they were doing and made their way to the Earth quake area.

While John and Matthew commandeered two used tents, one for the boys and one for the girls and some used army cots, Sarah and Abigail gathered up the orphaned children and put them in the tents. It did not take long to gather together thirty-nine children. The job was enormous: They had to be fed, they needed clothing, and their medical needs were overwhelming. With Matthew's help, John found a local earth moving contractor and made arrangements for him to build a landing strip for a small cargo plane. John knew a contractor from New Mexico that had an old cargo plane and made arrangement for him to fly supplies in for the kids.

The first load of supplies that John had flown in went well. The children had clothing, blankets, food and medical supplies for their needs. However, the next time he tried to fly in supplies they were confiscated by the local authorities. While John and Matthew were trying to work with the local authorities to get the supplies to the children they noticed their goods and supplies were being sold on the streets.

John and Matt had no luck with the local authorities. Every time they had supplies frown in the local authorities were there to confiscate them as soon as they were unloaded. They never helped with unloading, but they were quick to take them as soon as they were unloaded. The only way John and Matthew could get supplies to the kids was to buy them back from the authorities. There were no supplies local to be had and John was tired of having to pay for them twice. Even after he paid the local authorities he did not always get all his supplies back.

After three weeks of trying to deal with the local authorities with no luck, John and Matthew decided that something had to be done. John made arrangements with his friend from New Mexico for the largest cargo plane he had--an old military C130. When the plane landed and the helpers were unloading the boxes on one side of the plane Sarah, Abagail and their helpers were loading all the children into the plane from the other side. Away from the view of the authorities. John, Sarah, Abigail, and Matthew slipped into the plane from the side where the kids were loaded and the plane took off. By the time the locals came to the unloaded boxes to check their 'ill gotten gain' and found out that John had unloaded empty boxes to stall them, the plane had cleared the mountain range and was out of their control.

John and Matthew had made arguments to purchase an old school building in the town in New Mexico where John had rented the cargo plane. Sarah and Abigail went ahead to prepare the building for the kids. Matthew had taken care of all the legal paperwork to get the kids into the U.S.

When the plane landed all the kids were tired and fussy, but Abby and Sarah had prepared them a good meal and warm beds in the old classrooms so all ended well. The kids were off to a good start in their new home. Needless to say, but Abigail and Matthew got married and ran the orphanage together with John and Sarah's help.

CHAPTER THIRTY-EIGHT

AN OLD FRIEND DEPARTS

After John and Sarah got the orphanage set up so Abby and Matthew could run it on their own they left to go back to their home in Alaska. They arrived back at the lodge late in the evening and it was empty. John Mark was out on a hunting trip. John and Sarah took their showers and got into their night clothes and met in the kitchen to prepare their favorite snack tomato soup, grilled cheese, and a large dill pickle.

After they ate their snack they went into the living room where John found a good, nature move on the movie channel and they sat down to watch it together on the love seat. About half way through the movie, Sarah fell asleep. John quietly got up and went to the bed room and turned down the covers on the bed. He then went back into the living room and very gently picked Sarah up and took her into the bed room and put her on the bed and covered her up. The moon was filtering through the window blinds and shining on her. John sat watching her sleep reminiscing over how much she had grown in their marriage. She was not just physically beautiful, but she had become so loving and caring for others especially for John and his work with young people. She gave herself completely to loving and helping John and he was so pleased. As he sat and reminisced, he was consumed by how much he loved and appreciated her. He very softly kneeled down beside her side of the bed and started to thank God for his wonderful help mate.

The movement of the bed woke Sarah and she asks, "Honey what you are doing?"

He replied, "I was thanking God for my wonderful help mate."

She slipped out of the bed and knelt beside him and said, "Patty is right. You are such a romantic and I love you so very much. Let's pray together."

The next morning, they went into the kitchen and were starting breakfast when John saw Brutus outside the gate. He opened the gate. A few minutes later he noticed that Brutus did not come into the yard. He stepped out on the back porch and called Brutus, but he just sat there shaking his head. John sensed something was wrong so he took some treats he had made for Brutus and went out to greet his old friend. Brutus would not take the treats and John knew something was wrong. Brutus walked off a few steps and stopped. He turned toward John and groaned. John walked to him and he would move a few more steps away and turn and look at John and groan again. John said to him, "Do you want me to follow you?"

He shook his head up and down indicating yes. John went to the lodge and got his shoulder holster and his four fifty-four Casuel pistol. He came out to where Brutus was and Brutus started walking toward the mountains. Brutus seemed to be staggering as he walked and this concerned John. John walked as close to Brutus as he could, resting his hand on Brutus's front shoulder when he could. Brutus would walk for a while and set down. Then he would walk a little farther and set down again. They had walked about half a mile when a young male bear came into their path. This angered Brutus and he stood on his hind legs and growled. The young bear ran into the brush and did not return. However, the exertion tired Brutus and he sat down for a long while to rest.

After about a mile and a half, they came to the base of a large hill. There Brutus walked around the hill until he found a small opening into a cave. John stopped when Brutus went into the cave. Brutus came out and sat down and shook his head up and down and groaned. John knew that Brutus wanted him to follow him into the cave. He was not sure of what to expect in the cave so he entered cautiously. The cave was only about fifty feet into the hill and the walls were solid rock. It was dark in the cave so John made a torch of brush, but Brutus did not like it so John left it at the opening of the cave. It gave just enough light that John could see that Brutus had gone to the back of the cave and hunkered down.

When John got near him he rolled over on his back like he did when he was a cub. John sat down beside his old friend and began to scratch his tummy. This seemed to comfort Brutus so John kept doing it while he thought about what to do next. When John would try to quit, Brutus would throw his head to the side and groan.

After about thirty minutes Brutus took a deep breath and stiffened up. He seemed to hold his breath, but he then let his breath out and went limp and quit breathing. John immediately jumped up to check his old friend. He was not breathing and John could not wake him. John was devastated his old friend had not come to the cave to hibernate he had come to the cave to die. John was so lost. He did not know what to do. He just sat beside his old friend for over an hour.

When the torch started to go out he got up and got out of the cave and stood looking at the cave thinking about what to do next. After a while, he decided to make Brutus's final resting place secure so other animals could not get to him. He headed for the lodge to get his truck. He was going to go to town to get a track hoe with a grab finger on it so he he could pick up boulders to fill in the opening to the cave to seal it.

When he got to the lodge and started to get into his truck, Sarah came running out to the truck. She stopped John because she sensed something was wrong.

She asked him, "what is wrong John?"

He did not know what to say so he just looked at her and said nothing.

She could tell by the look on his face that something was terribly wrong so she grabbed his arm through the truck window and pleaded, "Honey what is wrong?"

John dropped his head for a moment and looked at her with tears running down his face, "Brutus is dead. I have got to bury him. I am going to town to rent a small track hoe."

She said, "Honey let me get a coat and I will go with you."

He really did not want company, but he did not want to hurt Sarah so he waited for her to go in the house and get her coat. All the way to and from the equipment rental yard Sarah talked and ask what seemed to John like a million questions. He did not want to hurt her feelings, but he just did not feel like talking. As they were driving up the road to the lodge Sarah dropped her head and began to weep softly.

With her head down she said, "Honey I have let you down again and I am so, so sorry."

He turned toward her and ask, "What are you talking about?"

She responded, "Brutus meant so much to you and I could never get over my fear of him. Now I will never get the chance. I feel like I have let you down and I am so sorry."

He replied, "Honey if you had known him as a baby, it would have been easier. But, he scared you the very first time you saw him and that kind of fear is hard to overcome. I don't hold that against you so stop worrying about it."

When they got to the lodge, John drove into the yard and started to unload the track hoe. Sarah asks to go with him. John told her to get the all train utility vehicle and follow him. When they arrived at the cave she wanted to go into the cave and see Brutus. John got a light and went into the cave to be sure that it was safe before he would let her get out of the vehicle. When John was sure it was safe he came back and got her. She was trembling as bad as if Brutus were alive.

He stopped her at the entrance of the cave and ask her, "Are you sure you want to do this?"

Her answer was, "Yes."

When they reached Brutus's limp, dead body, Sarah broke down and cried so hard that John had to catch her to keep her from falling. She just kept apologizing to John for not getting to know Brutus.

207

John just did not know what to do. He just held her in his arms as she sobbed and sobbed.

After what seemed to be an eternity, John softly said, "Honey I need to take you to the utility vehicle where you can stay out of the cold. I need to get to work closing the opening to the cave before it gets dark."

John then proceeded to place the surrounding large stones in the opening of the cave until he had completely closed the cave opening. When he finished closing the cave opening with boulders, he used the track hoe to dig dirt and pack it over the complete opening. When he was satisfied that his old friend's grave was secure he turned his attention to Sarah who was still sobbing. He locked the track hoe and got into the utility vehicle with her and headed for the lodge.

On the way to the lodge, John tried to comfort Sarah by telling her. "Honey old Brutus was a great friend and he was a comfort to me when I was alone, but Sarah, honey, you mean a million times more to me than Brutus ever did or ever could. You are my life. And, I am the one that needs to apologize to you for not making that abundantly clear to you all the time." He very gently reached over and took her hand and pleaded, "Please don't cry anymore. It breaks my heart to see you hurting like this. Nothing, nothing, nothing means as much to me as you do. You are my life."

When they got back to the lodge, Patty and Gary had arrived. Sarah had called them and told them about Brutus. Patty suggested that they could have Brutus stuffed and displayed in their zoo. That was offensive to John and he quickly said no. He let them know that his old friend would rest in peace where he was. He did, however, accept their offer to place a grave stone at the cave where John had buried him. Patty took the picture of her, Gary, and Brutus that had been taken at their wedding and had it engraved in the tombstone with all the appropriate information. Four days later with John Mark's help, it was placed in the cave for a marker for John's old friend.

CHAPTER THIRTY-NINE

THE GOLDEN YEARS?

John and Sarah traveled a lot over the next ten years: they would spend time with Abigail and Matthew in New Mexico at the orphanage; they traveled to the wrangler's camp to work with Ashley and Henry; they spent time with Patty and Gary; they even found time to go on a second honeymoon.

The work was hard and very tiring, but Sarah and John had a passion for the needs of children. At their age, the traveling and work with the children took its toll on them. John was in his eighties and Sarah was now in her sixties, neither of them were spring chickens anymore.

At John's age, he was struggling to keep up with the exhausting schedule they set for themselves and he did not notice that Sarah was having health issues. One evening after they had made their rounds to New Mexico, the wrangler's camp and the zoo they came home to the lodge late. When John had fixed Sarah and his dinner, he noted that Sarah did not eat. In his concern for her, he asked her what the problem was. As she was explaining that she did not feel well he noted that she had lost weight and this concerned him. He began to take note that she looked pale and she had dark circles around her eyes--she did not look good at all. The more he talked with her and the more he looked at her the more he was concerned.

He told her that tomorrow he was taking her to the doctor. She tried to protest, but he said she was going and that was that.

The next morning, they went to their family doctor. He took one look at Sarah, ran some blood test, and sent her directly to an Oncologist for further test. The tests were not good. The Oncologist diagnosed Sarah with stage four Pancreatic Cancer.

John and Sarah were speechless. Finley, John spoke up and ask the doctor what their options were and where they could get the best treatment. The oncologist suggested a treatment plan but told them that the outlook was not good very few people survived this type of Cancer.

John who was trying to hold back tears with a broken voice ask, "How long does she have?"

The doctor began to explain to them what to expect. He told them that the type of cancer she had was fast acting and that Sarah only had a few months. He tried to assure them that he would do his very best for her, and if they wanted a second opinion he would be glad to send them to another doctor.

John turned toward Sarah as if to ask her opinion, but she just shook her head no.

John turned to the doctor and wanted to know when he would start her treatment.

The doctor set the next morning to start her treatment.

John put his arm around Sarah who was now sobbing uncontrollably and told the doctor, "Whatever you do, do not let my wife suffer."

The doctor assured John that he would not allow Sarah to suffer if he had anything to do with it.

Sarah and John left for the lodge. John tried to be strong for Sarah's sake, but he was not able to do a very good job; the thought of losing his best friend was devastating and he broke. They arrived at the lodge, but it was no longer the happy home they had shared. It was a time of great sorrow so they cried, they prayed, and they cried some more. Out of complete exhaustion, they fell asleep on the love seat

The next morning John tried to fix breakfast, but Sarah did not want anything to eat she wanted to talk to John.

She said, "John I want to talk about the treatment for cancer. If the doctor cannot cure the cancer I do not want to take the chemo-therapy treatment."

John quickly responded, "Honey do you realize what you are saying?"

"Yes John, I do. I do not want to go through the Chemotherapy just to extend my life for a few months. I have seen people on Chemo and it is not fun. If I could get a few goods months it would be one thing, but if it means I have to suffer the Chemo just for a few months I don't want it."

"Sarah, honey you know I cherish every second I get to spend with you…"

She interrupted him, "John I know you do and I appreciate all you have done for me and I love you so dearly. But, John please don't ask me to suffer Chemo just for a few more days on this earth. I don't think either of us would enjoy it."

John just stood at the counter where he was fixing breakfast with his head down staring at the floor. When he finally looked at Sarah with tears in his eyes he said, "Honey you know I don't want you to suffer. It would be selfish of me to ask you to go through Chemo just to keep you around just for me. If that is what you want, you know I will support your decision." He gently took her in his arms and held her as he wept. After what seemed to John an eternity he said, "Let's wait and see what the doctor tells us tomorrow and we will take it from there."

She agreed and the rest of the day was nearly normal. The next day they went to the doctor and had a long talk about Sarah's condition, but the results were as Sarah had suspected the Chemo would not cure the cancer at best it would only give her maybe six more months. She told the doctor she was not going to take the Chemo. She told the doctor of her experience with her Grandmother and how much her Grandmother suffered. He could not change her mind. He told her that without the Chemo, she might have six months. She asked him to help her to be as pain-free as possible and let the cancer take its course. The doctor prescribed Morphine patches and instructed her and John in the proper uses of them, and she and John left for the lodge.

On the way back to the lodge she said, "John I want to go see the kids."

John started to ask her if she felt like taking that long trip...

She interrupted him. "John, I want to do it now while I can."

He asked her, "Honey do you want me to call the kids and tell them about your condition?" She said, "No, I will tell them when I get there. Can we go now today?"

John replied, "Let's go pack and I will make the arrangements."

By the afternoon, they were on their way to see Abigail and Matthew.

The trip was hard on Sarah and that night John had to help her apply her first Morphine Patch. It made her 'goofy' so John took it off and cut it in half. Abigail knew that Sarah was not herself and wanted to know what was wrong. John and Sarah sat down and explained the situation to both Abby and Matthew. Abby, being a doctor herself, was not satisfied and the next morning got on the phone to Sarah's Cancer doctor to get all the details. After a long talk with Sarah's doctor, Abby did not know what to do. She did not want to give up her Grandmother, but she knew that Sarah was right; the Chemo would be miserable and would not cure the cancer. It would most likely destroy what little time Sarah had left. All they could do was make the best of the time they had left.

John and Sarah stayed with Abby and Matthew for two and a half weeks. It was no surprise to John that Sarah wanted to go see Ashley. Sarah and Ashley had grown very close over the years. Ashley called Sarah 'momma Sarah (she also had a nick name for John--Papa John). Sarah and Ashley worked very closely on the Scholarship program and Sarah came to love Ashley like she was her own daughter. The two of them spent three weeks with Ashley and Henry and even went on a short horseback ride.

From there they traveled to see Patty and Gary. Patty and Gary went to see Sarah's Doctor to get more information. After they came out of the doctor's office, Patty broke down so bad that Gary had to help her into the car.

When she got back to where Sarah and John were, she ran to Sarah and cried, "Mama, mama I can't do this. I can't give you up. I just can't. There must be something we can do. Have you got a second opinion?"

John replied, "Yes honey, we have been to three doctors and the results are the same."

"Well, daddy do something. You can't just let mama die. Pray or something."

"Honey, we are praying. We do not always know why God does what he does, but he always answers our prayers. And His answers are perfect for the situation not always the way we expect him to answer, but the answers are always perfect."

At that moment, John was reminded of one of his prayers; He had prayed that God would allow him to live long enough to always be there to take care of Sarah. His thoughts were interrupted by something that Patty said and he went back to talking to her.

John and Sarah spent two weeks with Patty and Gary before Sarah got very tired and wanted to go home and rest. The six months that the doctor suggested that Sarah would have did not seem to be a reality. She was going down faster than expected. Just three months after she was diagnosed Sarah had become so weak that John had to help her dress and undress. She was not eating and was losing weight. When the pain got so bad that the morphine patches were not working John had to admit her into the hospital so the pain could be dealt with properly. He rented a room near the hospital so he could bath and change clothes. He stayed at the hospital the rest of the time.

After two weeks in the hospital, all the kids were called in. The doctors had Sarah on such high doses of morphine that she slept most of the time. One morning before daylight Sarah woke up and began to call for John.

John jumped up out of the recliner and took her hand and ask, "Honey what is wrong?"

She said in a very weak voice, "Hold me."

John very gently picked her up and sat down in the recliner with her. He asked her, "Are you hurting? Do you want me to call the nurses?"

She replied, "No, I just want to talk…"

John stopped her and said, "Honey, don't exert yourself. You need to reserve your strength." In a voice that was barely above a whisper, she said, "Please, John I need to talk to you."

He replied, "Honey I am listening."

She began, "John Leigh came to visit me last night." She struggled to get her breath and then said, "She is so nice. She told me all about Heaven and said she would show me around and introduce me to everyone. She is so nice and I am not afraid to die anymore."

John stuttered, "Are you talking about…about… my Leigh?"

Sarah replied, "Yes, our Leigh." Sarah chuckled and said, "By the way, she said to tell you that you just think you are man enough for both of us gals. Just wait until we get you to Heaven, we are going to run you ragged."

John just sat there holding his precious Sarah. He did not know what to say. Sarah just lay in his arms and grinned. She knew she had got the best of John and he was speechless. It pleased John that she was grinning so he grinned too, and he bent over and kissed her.

Sarah closed her eyes and struggled to breathe. With her eyes closed, she said, "John I love you so very much, but I have got to go. Leigh is here to take me home and I have to go with her." With that, she took a deep, jerky breath and slowly let it out. She went limp in John's arms.

The kids had come in and heard most of what Sarah said and knew she was gone. They all stood silently weeping. John just held his precious Sarah with tears streaming down his face and prayed, "Father, God I know that she is absent from the body and present with you, but Father I miss her so very much."

When all the monitors that were hook to Sarah 'flat lined' the nurses rushed into the room. They suggested that John should put Sarah back into the bed. He very gently picked her up and laid her on the bed, but he would not leave until he had fixed her bed like she was asleep. He very carefully unhooked all the wires and tubes that were hooked to Sarah. The last thing he did was pick up her right hand and softly kiss the back of it. As he laid it down he said, "Baby doll I love you and I will see you soon."

While the crowd was quiet, Patty spoke up and ask John, "Daddy what did Momma mean when she said Leigh was waiting for her? Wasn't Leigh your first wife?"

John replied, "Yes honey, Leigh was my first wife. Your mother and I had long discussions about her going to Heaven. She was afraid to go to Heaven because She said she did not know anyone there. I don't know if she had a dream or if God sent her an Angel to comfort her. I do know that God will send help when you need it. I had a dream or saw a vision after Leigh died and I had just gotten out of prison. What I saw in that dream or vision, which ever it was, is the reason I came to Alaska. I told you all about that."

"Yes, daddy you did," Patty replied. "Momma was not scared of death when she passed. I thank God for that."

All the arrangements were in place: the funeral was held at their church, after which the body was flown to Kentucky where John had made arrangements to bury Sarah beside Leigh. He left enough room for John to be buried between them.

John had not told anyone in Kentucky except close friends and family so there was no one at the grave site except family and close friends it was over quickly and everyone went home.

CHAPTER THIRTY-FIVE

JOHN IS HOME SICK

Everyone was back to their normal routine and John was alone in the cabin with just his thoughts. The reality of all that had taken place had set in and he was so very lonely. That evening he did not go to bed, he just sat down in the recliner. Before he fell asleep from shear exhausting, he prayed, "Father God, I know Sarah is with you and is in a better place than this old world, but Lord I miss her so much."

While he slept, he had a vision or dream, he could not tell which. A man in white apparel stood at John's feet. The man said, "John Henson you have fought a good fight. You have run a good race. Your work on earth is done. Get your house in order." With that, he disappeared.

John instantly sat up in the recliner. The room was dark and he was still alone. He just sat there thinking about the dream/vision. He began thinking about his affairs--were they in order or did he have arrangement to take care of? He went into the kitchen and opened the safe under the cabinet where he kept his papers. He took out his will and began to read it. He and Sarah had a huge fortune that he intended to leave to their kids so they could continue their ministries (over two hundred million dollars): Patty and Gary would get fifty million; Abigail and Matthew would get Fifty million; John Mark and Katie would get Fifty million and the lodge

(John and Sarah had already bought property for the other kids); and Ashley and Henry would get fifty million. Any monies that were left over after the will was executed was to go to their church. All of John's and Sarah's personal belongings were to be divided up between the four couples in the will. John had made Matthew executor of the will since he was a lawyer.

The next morning John got up late, around nine AM with no clear plans for the day. He made a pot of coffee and sat down to drink a cup. After an hour went by, He decided to take a trip out to Brutus's grave. He got dressed, loaded his forty-four-magnum pistol and got into his ATV and drove out to the grave. After about an hour of just sitting and looking at the grave, a male bear came into the clearing between John and the grave. The ATV was totality enclosed so John was not worried about the bear unless it got aggressive. The bear did not get aggressive, it was just curious about John and the ATV he was in. It came over and sniffed the ATV from top to bottom. When John was satisfied that the bear was not a threat he 'cracked' the window to let the bear sniff his fingers. The bear sniffed John's fingers and then licked them. John was satisfied that the bear was not going to get aggressive so he looked around in the ATV and found some dried Jerky. He offered some to the bear and he took it. After all the of Jerky was gone, John started the ATV and headed for the lodge. The bear watched John for a while then went back into the woods and out of sight.

When John got back to the lodge he warmed a can of soup and sat down to look at his picture albums. The albums held so many wonderful memories. They went back to when Leigh was born and John was just a small child.

Two pictures he had taken were of two churches across the road from each other. They had been built by two brothers. The two brothers had gotten into a heated argument over their interpretation of the Bible and each built their own church. They spent all their lives trying to steal each other's 'flock'. John could not help wondering if either of them made it to Heaven.

John was satisfied that his affairs were all in order so he went to bed. The next day he invited all the kids to come up for the weekend so he could talk to them. The kids arrived in couples: Patty and Gary came in, then John Mark and Katy; after that Ashley and Henry and last Abigail and Matthew arrived. They were all home with all their children. John told them he wanted them all to attend church with him and then he wanted to have an early Thanksgiving dinner together.

John had made arrangements with some of the local women to cook the dinner so the family could visit and just spend time together. It was a wonderful time of sharing and reminiscing.

After dinner that night John got up from the table and walked behind each of the kids and one at a time laid his hands on each of them and prayed for God to bless and guide each of them. An hour later he said good night and went to bed.

The next morning as everyone began to gather in the kitchen John was not with them. After ten AM, Patty was worried and went into his bed room to check on him. When she came into the kitchen, Abby noticed that her mother had been crying.

She asked, "Momma what is wrong?" and ran to Patty.

Patty replied, "Honey, sometime in the night daddy went home to be with momma."

Abby with a startled look stated, "You mean grandpa is … is dead? What happened momma? grandpa seemed ok yesterday."

"No honey your grandpa has been sick for some time. He was so sick that he did not notice that momma, your grandma was sick. When he found out that momma was sick, he felt so guilty that he would not let her do anything he did all the cooking and cleaning and taking care of her himself. I tried to help, but he would not let me.

He said, "This is my job and please don't take it away from me. It is the least I can do for your mother."

All the extra work made his situation worse. Even when he had walking Pneumonia He would not let anyone help, and he went 'downhill' really fast after momma got sick."

Everyone rushed into John's bedroom to see for them self. John lay there as though in a deep, restful sleep. Matthew took charge of seeing to it that all of the of the arrangements John had previously made were carried out: the mortuary came and got John's body and the funeral was held in their church. After the local funeral, the body was flown to Kentucky.

The local mortuary in Kentucky was run by Willy Jackson (the son of Bill the ex Sheriff and John's friend). When he got the notices that John's body was coming to Kentucky for burial he put it in the local paper and on the local news. He wanted everyone to know that John Henson was coming home to his final resting place. The interest was so great that he asked Matthew for permission to hold a service in the local High school auditorium so everyone could pay their respects. After Matthew discussed it with the rest of the family and they all agreed, he told Mr. Jackson it would be all right.

Eighteen hundred people filled the gym and waited outside to pay their respects to John for what he and his two wives had done for them.

One middle aged woman stood up and said, "My name is Sheila…" Before she could tell them her last name, someone in the crowd recognized Her as Sheila Smith and started to boo her.

Within seconds the entire crowd was booing her and demanding that she leave. She just stood in front of the microphone with her head down.

After what seemed an eternity, she spoke into the 'mic', "This day is not about me, it is about John Henson and I will have my say. If it takes all day and night I will tell my story about how John forgave me. All of you claim to be his friend, but how many of you were at Leigh's funeral? Not a one of you were there. I know because I was watching from the hill. I was too ashamed to go to the funeral, but I watched from the hill and none of you were there." The crowd got quite and Shelia continued with her story. "Furthermore, none of you attended His second wife Sarah's Funeral either. I was at that Funeral."

She began to tell the crowd how she and her mother had destroyed John and Leigh's life and their reputation. She said "If anyone had a right to hate anyone, John had the right to hate my mother and me. But, that was not Mr. Henson. He did not hate us. As a matter of fact, He actually reached out to both of us. When mother was dying in jail with Aids, Mr. Henson called her five times. Two days before momma died, Mr. Henson called and prayed with her over the phone; He led her to Christ that day. He got me into a great foster home and paid my way through Nursing school. It is because of Mr. Henson that I have dedicated my life to helping children. I now work for His granddaughter Abigail and her husband Matthew in their orphanage in New Mexico."

She stood in front of the microphone with her head down staring at the floor for nearly a minute. When she raised her head, tears were streaming down her face. She said, "I told you all that this day was not about me. It is a wonderful human being who spent his life helping others. This day is about Mr. John Henson. Thank you so much for listing to my story."

As Sheila slowly made her way to the exit one woman stood up and began to applaud her. Before she could exit the building, all the crowd was standing and applauding her. It just made her cry worse. She felt so guilty over what she had done to John and Leigh.

The gathering took so long that the burial had to be postponed until the next day. John was finally laid to rest between his two beautiful Ladies as he had planned.

A fitting conclusion to this story would be John, Leigh, and Sarah, in their Heavenly clothing standing together in the clouds waving to everyone. However, thank God, that possession is reserved for Christ. "Mark 13:26 And then shall they see the Son of man coming in the clouds with great power and glory."

By D. Anthony

CPSIA information can be obtained
at www.ICGtesting.com
Printed in the USA
BVHW010816230421
605713BV00023B/384